Praise for

# The Counterfeit Detective

"Detective stories contain a dream of justice" wrote Dorothy Sayers, herself the author of many. This new novel, clear and concise as a detective's client report, tells us a story about one such fictional detective, based on the activities of a real one. Author Paradise ensures a broader audience can know the value of the efforts of such professional investigators who by their vigilance and at personal risk, maintain that dream in a crucial but not well known part of the American economy as described so well in these pages."

**Steven M. Getzoff**
Author and Administrator of Trademark Management Services
Reed Smith LLP
New York, NY

"Paradise weaves fact with fiction, as his richly drawn character, Theo Jones, Private Investigator, takes the reader on a deadly journey into the dark underworld of trademark crime. *Counterfeit Detective* is a non-stop page turner."

**Catherine Taylor**
Author of *Essence of Lilacs* and *No Rest for the Wicked.*

*The Counterfeit Detective*
by Paul R. Paradise

© Copyright 2015 Paul R. Paradise

ISBN   978-1-63393-086-5

This is a work of fiction. The characters are both actual and fictitious. With the exception of verified historical events and persons, all incidents, descriptions, dialogue and opinions expressed are the products of the author's imagination and are not to be construed as real.

Published by

**◪ köehlerbooks**™

210 60th Street
Virginia Beach, VA 23451
212-574-7939
www.koehlerbooks.com

# The Counterfeit Detective ™

## Paul R. Paradise

VIRGINIA BEACH
CAPE CHARLES

*For Dorka*

# Preface

I FASHIONED THEO JONES the protagonist PI after real life private investigator David Woods. However, Theo Jones the character is my own invention, a failed actor who is engaged in a self-styled "War against the Counterfeits." Trademark counterfeiting, also called product counterfeiting, accounts for up to 10 percent of world commerce and has become a problem that threatens the world economy. Imagine if consumers had to worry if the cosmetics, medicine, food and other products used or consumed are fake.

In crafting Jones, I took inspiration from Andy Warhol, a commercial artist who moved to New York City in the hope of a career as an artist. Although successful as a commercial artist, he failed to find a place in the art establishment until he turned his artistic talents to the Pop Art Movement and created his most famous work *Thirty-two Campbell's Soup Cans.*

Pop Art was conceived as anti-art, a revolt against fine art by using the commercial art found in advertising as well as images from mass media. Warhol saw art in the Campbell's Soup trademark and the packaging, referred to as the trade dress in the industry. His vision was consistent with Pop Art's anti-art theme, because the purpose of a Campbell's Soup trademark is to sell soup. Until Pop Art was introduced, fine art had nothing to do with selling consumer products. Many art critics derided Pop Art and called it "fake." The initial showing of the *Thirty-two Campbell's Soup Cans* fared poorly; over time it was recognized as a masterpiece.

Theo Jones, the failed actor, pursues counterfeit trademarks (trademark counterfeiting), and his personal dilemma, his longing to continue as an artist and to be true to himself, reflects Warhol's quest to become an artist. Jones is reborn during the course of the story and rediscovers his passion for his craft as a result and, like Warhol, fulfills his dream of becoming an artist.

# Chapter One

I KNOW THE SHOCK of learning you're going to die. First, there's disbelief and denial, followed by anger, and then an eventual acceptance of your fate. I was in the acceptance phase that morning as I boarded the Brooklyn-bound subway for a rendezvous with John Hwa, my best informant. I would have looked forward to receiving a tip about the underground market in designer knockoffs—but I was contemplating a premonition my wife, Linda, had last night.

I had arrived at the detective agency filled with dread because her premonition was about death. *My death*! Coming on the eve of the one-year anniversary of my brother George's death was more than enough to rattle me. After a sleepless night, I thought about cancelling my meeting with Hwa. If I had, I would have saved myself a major headache.

He was supposed to meet me in front of a tenement building on Greene Avenue in Bed-Stuy, also called Little Harlem. I took the C subway to Nostrand Avenue, exited and started walking. To reach the rendezvous point, I had to pass through a block of rundown and abandoned brownstone row houses. The stench of decaying food and stale urine coming from inside an abandoned building on the corner led me to believe squatters had taken refuge. To those watching through boarded-up windows, I looked like just another middle-aged junkie in raggedy jeans and cowboy boots searching to buy crack. I wasn't carrying a gun. I rarely carry one.

I was a block away when I heard a woman shriek. I quickened my pace, as I looked up and then down the street. Nothing. I turned the corner, and across the street I saw a man on the sidewalk and two others in jeans and hoodies fleeing. I rushed to where Hwa lay flat out on the pavement. He had been stabbed. A switchblade was deep into his chest. I recognized his girlfriend, Jenny Ling, kneeling next to him and cradling his head. I squatted next to her.

"What happened?" I had met her last week and knew her English was poor.

"Them . . . them!" She pointed to two men on the run, now blocks away.

"Are those the attackers?" I asked.

"Yes, *aieeo, aieeo.*" She shook her head in anguish.

I watched them get inside a blue Chevrolet Camaro. I never saw their faces because of the hoodies. The driver started the engine and drove away in a flash.

"Easy, John." Hwa was in pain and gasping for breath. "Take it slow. Who were those men?"

"Don't know." Pain shot across his face, as he tried to sit up.

"Whoa, man, lie back." I placed a hand on his shoulder to steady him. His eyes were glassy and blood seeped through his shirt. I snatched the cell phone from the holster on my belt and dialed 9-1-1.

While I identified the location and the victim, Jenny gritted her teeth and reached for the knife handle.

"Don't touch him," I said. "He'll bleed to death if you pull it out."

I had taken first aid and knew only a surgeon could safely remove it. The danger came from the depth of the puncture and whether vital organs had been hit.

She withdrew her hand and stammered, "Try—try to help."

"Let me handle this." Hwa was wearing a blue shirt. The knife's black handle bobbed up and down with each breath. I unbuttoned his shirt and lifted up the right front panel about two inches to view the knife blade; it was in deep, but fortunately there was little bleeding.

Jenny gasped and started sobbing, tears streaming down her cheeks. I realized she shouldn't have seen the exposed knife. I let go of the shirt, put an arm around her shoulder. I could feel her trembling. "Help is on the way . . . Please don't cry."

A crowd formed around us. "Everyone move back," I said. "The police are coming."

When she had settled down, I told her Hwa's head should be resting on the ground. Using my hands for support, I lowered it with great care from her lap.

I took off my jacket, doubled it, and gently pressed against the sides of the knife.

His eyelids started to flutter. I feared he was going into shock. "John . . . John! Don't do this. Stay with us."

"Hurts . . . like hell," he muttered.

Hearing him speak was a relief. His condition appeared stable for now. *Thank God*

I could do nothing else for him. I felt helpless as I waited for the ambulance. *What's taking so long?*

© ©

I couldn't help wondering if the stabbing was connected to Linda's premonition, which coincided with the anniversary of my brother's death in the 9/11 terrorist attack. George, who was forty-eight, shared the sad fate of generations of men in the Jones family who had died young and violently. I rarely discussed the family history with Linda—until his death. After that, a barrier formed between us as she urged me to change careers and get out of the dangerous private eye profession.

Until last night.

© ©

"It was terrible—" Her shrill voice hit like ice water.

I turned and found her face hovering over me like an apparition. Even in the bedroom's darkness, I could see alarm mirrored in her eyes.

I bolted upright, looked past her, afraid a stranger was there. Nothing moving. "Linda, what is it? What's the matter?"

"I had a dream," she whispered. "It was a dream about death. Your death."

*My death? What was this about my death?*

She trembled as I took her in my arms and felt her warmth against mine. I waited before reaching over and switching on the lamp by the bedside.

"Better now?" I asked.

She blinked, looked around. Somehow she managed a smile, her smooth lips making a bow shape. She ran a hand through her hair.

"Well . . . tell me," I said. "What's this about a dream?"

I hardly had to coax her. "Oh god," she said. "Yes. It was a-a-a . . . a ghoul! I don't know how else to describe it. With a voice from hell."

"A voice from hell? Tell me how it sounded."

"I'm not sure . . ." She paused, turned her head away. I urged her to continue.

She took a slow, deep breath. From inside her petite frame came a bellow:

*Theo is going to die*

*A horrible death awaits*

"The ghoul's face was hidden behind a cape or garment. I tried pulling away the gray shrouds. That's when I woke up."

"Baby, sounds like a part I auditioned for." I tried to sound amused, but my heart raced. The voice sounded hideous.

"Don't laugh. I think it's related to your brother's death."

"You think my brother's death was the trigger?"

"Tomorrow's the one-year anniversary . . . Didn't you tell me the men in your family have died violently before age fifty?"

"Yes . . . I'm three years younger than George, the same age as my father when he died."

She paled with despair. "Theo, I couldn't live if anything happens to you."

"Don't even think like this." I reached over and hugged her. "It's only a dream."

She nestled in my arms. I found the closeness reassuring.

"Theo, didn't John F. Kennedy have a premonition about being assassinated in Dallas. Martin Luther King also had a premonition and knew he would never see the Promised Land."

"It was a dream," I reminded her.

"A dream?" she said, exasperated. "Didn't President Abraham Lincoln have dreams about being assassinated?"

"Let's forget it and get back to sleep."

We shared a silent moment before I turned the lamp off. After a spell, I felt her body relax and knew she was asleep. Not me. I could hear my clock ticking . . . louder and louder.

© ©

I had been so focused on Hwa I didn't realize the crowd swelled to about thirty bystanders. I was surrounded by a wall of people. The distant wail of a police siren, joined by another. The screech of tires.

"Who's Theo Jones?" I heard an officer yell.

"Down here."

The officer pushed through the crowd. He was tall and had already removed the hand-held radio from his duty belt to call Dispatch. "Do you know this man?"

"Yes, his name's John Hwa."

"Did you see who stabbed him?"

"I saw two men running away. Didn't see their faces. They got into a blue Chevy Camaro and drove away."

The officer knelt next to me and looked Hwa over. "Is that your jacket?"

"Yes," I said.

The officer switched on his radio. "Officer Baine responding on the 9-1-1 . . . Victim's an Asian male, late twenties. Name's John Hwa. Stabbed, looks bad . . . Roger that. Standing by. Out."

Baine replaced the hand-held. He removed latex gloves from his pants pocket, donned them, and lifted the jacket to inspect the wound. He asked Hwa if he was in pain. Hwa nodded, his breath coming in short gasps.

"Just relax." Baine removed the gloves. "An ambulance is on the way." Another officer emerged and covered Hwa with a blanket. My blood-stained jacket still staunched the bleeding.

An unmarked police car, strobes flashing, sped down the avenue and parked hard and tight against the curb. A tall man in a gray business suit stepped out. He looked like a former prizefighter, a tough Irish face, worn at the cheeks.

He walked over to us. "Hello, Rick," he said. "Central radioed me. What've we got?"

"Stab victim, name's John Hwa. Ambulance on the way." Baine pointed to me and said, "He called in the 9-1-1 and knows Hwa. Name's Theo Jones."

The detective nodded and motioned for me to stand. "I'm Detective Chris Harney."

"You with the 81st Precinct?" I asked.

Harney's eyes arched. "That's right. How did you know?"

"I'm a private eye. I've worked with police from many NYPD precincts, but not the 81st."

Harney's face soured as he looked me over, eyes lingering, obviously suspicious. I have mixed relations with the police. At any time I might find myself as either ally or obstructer, as friend or foe. Right now, Harney perceived me as a foe. My torn jeans and otherwise down-and-out appearance no doubt contributed.

"How do you know Hwa? Does he work for you?"

"Yes. He's an informant of mine."

"Sounds like we need to talk."

"Sure, I'll cooperate."

"Not here, tell me about it at the station." Harney turned and looked at the car parked behind his. "Is that your car?"

"No, I arrived on the subway."

"Fine, I'll have an officer drive you." He looked Jenny over. She was kneeling beside Hwa. "Do you know her?"

I nodded. "Her name's Jenny Ling, Hwa's girlfriend."

"What's she doing here?"

Harney's glance must have spooked her. She stood up and started running, brushing through the surrounding onlookers.

"Stop her," Harney said. Baine and another officer chased after her. She started wailing as they secured her, each officer holding an arm. Bystanders moved aside and gawked as she was escorted back to Harney.

"Sorry . . . sorry, stay now." She looked bewildered, arms held tightly by the two officers.

"What's the matter?" Harney asked. "Why did you try to run?"

"Sorry . . . sorry." She looked about nervously.

After a warning, Harney told the officers to release her and keep watch. Head bowed, she knelt beside Hwa.

The officers cleared a path for the emergency medical services ambulance. Three EMTs jumped out. Two of them opened up a gurney; the other knelt down and lifted up the blanket to inspect the wound. "Are you in pain?" he asked. "Do you know who did this?"

Hwa mumbled, said he was feeling sleepy.

"No, don't go to sleep." The technician looked to be in his early twenties but moved and talked as if he had been doing this for years. He patted Hwa's shoulder. "Relax, we'll take care of you."

Careful of the knife in Hwa's chest, the two technicians positioned the gurney and loaded him onto it. In one motion, they lifted and moved him inside the ambulance.

"I ride with John," Jenny said and tried to board the ambulance.

"No, I want to question you," Harney said. "We'll take you to the hospital afterwards."

I suspected Harney was suspicious and didn't want her trying to flee again. He ordered Baine and the other officer to seat her inside a patrol car. She refused, insisting on riding in the ambulance. I knew the officers would use force unless I intervened.

"Jenny, please," I said. "We have to go with the police. They want to catch the guys who did this."

I gently took her by the hand to the patrol car, helped her inside and then slid in next to her. The ride to the stationhouse was a blur. Baine turned on the strobes to clear traffic. The officers separated us inside the stationhouse; I went to an interview room, a claustrophobic room painted dull gray, with a metal table and three chairs.

I retrieved my cell phone, but before I had a chance to call the office, Harney and another detective arrived. They sat across from me and started firing away.

"You have no idea why Hwa wanted to see you?" Harney asked.

"None. I expected him to give me a tipoff."

"About what?"

"Knockoffs. He didn't mention a particular brand."

"What about Jenny Ling? Why did she run?"

"No idea," I said.

More questions. Harney and the other detective appeared to be annoyed, probably because I had little information. After more questions, Harney said I could leave.

"What about Jenny?" I asked.

"She stays," Harney said.

"What's going to happen to her?"

"That's my business. I'll be in touch." He ordered an officer to find me a jacket from the lost-and-found while I filled out a police statement.

I left the station house and headed for the subway. I wondered if Jenny had run because she feared the police. I knew little about her; she was almost a stranger. She was with Hwa when I met him for a payoff on Canal Street in Chinatown, a notorious location for knockoffs

©©

I usually found Hwa at the intersection of Canal and Centre Street. I had walked past open-air markets where the salty smell of bass, scallops, pork, and duck lured shoppers while street peddlers lined shoulder-to-shoulder on the sidewalk selling trinkets, vegetables—and of course, knockoffs: Polo by Ralph Lauren T-shirts, Calvin Klein jeans, Louis Vuittan handbags, Rolex watches. Most of the peddlers were Asians; however, interspersed were the so-called Senegalese street peddlers from West African countries. They arrived in the United States on visas, made fast money selling knockoffs, and then headed home.

Hwa looked respectable in clean denim jeans and a knockoff New York Knicks sweatshirt. He must have visited a barber because his hair was neatly combed and his Fu Manchu goatee and mustache had been trimmed. Then I realized he was not alone. A woman was by his side. A young, slender girl, much shorter than him.

There were eyes everywhere. I pretended to be a potential customer and picked up a Rolex watch, a Submariner, which usually sells for about five grand. It was one of a dozen knockoff Rolexes resting in a tattered brown briefcase, one salvaged from the garbage and laying flat atop a folding metal tray. If there was trouble, Hwa could pack up and flee in an instant.

"Hey, this Rolex looks great. How much?"

"For you, thirty dollars," he said and winked.

I bartered with him, trying to talk down his price. Part of my spiel was to ask about other knockoffs for sale. This was his opportunity to give me a tip. "Naw, can't help you today," he said.

I purchased the watch and handed him five rolled up Ben Franklins for his last tip.

After he had pocketed the money, I asked to be introduced.

"This is Jenny. She's my girl."

She smiled meekly. "Pleased meet you."

I shook hands with this shy Asian waif, whose English was unexpectedly broken. I spoke with her the next day when I telephoned and asked for Hwa. She said he had left.

We never spoke again until the day Hwa was stabbed. I realized if he died, Jenny would be the only person who knew what his tip was about.

# Chapter Two

I WAS WORN OUT and wanted to return to the office. I called Stella Barker before boarding the Manhattan-bound subway. She was the first private investigator I hired, now the office manager and lead investigator.

"Stella, John Hwa's been stabbed," I said.

"My God! What happened?"

I told her how I'd found him on the sidewalk with a switchblade in his chest and with his girlfriend, Jenny Ling, by his side. She wanted to discuss it further, but I asked her to wait until I returned to the office.

I exited the subway at the Prince Street Station. I hadn't had lunch and was hungry but didn't want to stop. I continued six blocks to 236 Thompson Street. The Chameleon Detective Agency rents two suites on the second floor. One is my personal office, shared with Stella; the other is for my staff and referred to as "the boiler room."

A block from the office, my beeper sounded. My office staff has my cell phone number with instructions not to call unless it's urgent. I change cell phones every three months to ensure clients and law officers beep me instead of calling, because I can't risk a call when I'm working undercover.

The caller was Sergeant Manny Ortiz, supervisor of the NYPD's trademark infringement unit, sometimes called the "T-shirt squad," because it's seized so many knockoff T-shirts. We were working on a Roving John Doe seizure order and targeting vendors at the Roosevelt Flea Market. I decided to return his call when I got to the office.

I entered the building, took the elevator, and walked down the corridor. I opened the door and entered the office. There were two desks inside for myself and Stella. The back half of the room resembled a flea market; boxes of knockoffs, stacked one atop the other, tagged by client and file number and waiting to be shipped to off-site storage. Most of the knockoffs were seized on the street—Rolex watches and pirate music CDs from artists like Madonna, Fleetwood Mac; also purses, sweatshirts, jeans—all bearing the familiar trademarks of our clients: Polo by Ralph Lauren, Calvin Klein, Louis Vuitton, and others. The agency rents space in eleven off-site storage companies for larger counterfeits like aircraft propellers, automobile transmissions, fake pharmaceuticals, and computer monitors.

Stella's dark eyes flashed against her ebony complexion. "Theo, I'm glad you're back. Sorry to hear about Hwa. What happened to his girlfriend?"

"Hwa was taken to the hospital. Jenny's in police custody. Not sure what will happen to her."

Stella nodded and told me I missed a call from Sergeant Ortiz. "He said it's important."

"He beeped me," I said. "Let me call him, and then we'll talk."

I sat down at my desk and used the telephone. Manny picked up on the second ring.

"We got troubles, Shakespeare," he said, using my nickname.

"You know, Manny, hello would be nice once in a while," I said.

"Hel-l-lo, are you happy now? I spoke to Detective Chris Harney."

"He called you?" I hadn't mentioned Manny's name to the detective.

"He called because you told him Hwa was into knockoffs. Hwa's dead. He died in the hospital."

"Dear God." For a moment I was silent. Hwa and I might

not have been blood brothers or even friends, but the news of his death hit hard.

"I need to talk to you about the murder," Manny said.

"We're talking now," I said.

"No good. We have to meet."

"Will this be official?"

"Unofficial for now."

"Is this about the killers? I didn't see their faces."

"No, I want to talk to you about Hwa's girlfriend, Jenny Ling."

"How is she?"

"That's why we need to meet."

"I have an appointment in Midtown at ten tomorrow. Maybe we can have lunch."

"Perfect. Let's meet at McLoone's. I'll know more about Jenny by then. Bring a list of the cases you worked with Hwa."

With Hwa dead, not only was Jenny's life in danger—so was mine. If the killers murdered Hwa in retaliation for a tip, they would be coming after me next. No wonder Manny wanted a list of Hwa's cases. At last I had found a connection to the premonition. I felt spooked because a memorial service for George would be tonight.

I hung up and looked over at Stella. "Sounds serious," she said.

"Manny got a call from Harney, the Brooklyn detective. Hwa's dead."

She shook her head in sadness. "How terrible. Maybe he snitched once too many."

"I hope not. I'm the one who turned him."

I didn't like thinking I was responsible for Hwa's death. But this was my job. Hwa's last tip led to the arrest of John Haines. The shipment we seized from Haines—three hundred drums of what was supposed to be hi-tech fertilizer destined for Kenya— was actually three hundred drums of chalk. The Monsanto label and packaging looked genuine. The crop in Kenya would have been ruined, and Haines would have netted two million dollars. Hwa's tip saved lives, but he couldn't save his own.

Hwa was the latest casualty in what I call "The Counterfeit War." Nearly every consumer product in the marketplace has been counterfeited, from auto and airplane parts, birth control pills to baby food. That fake Coach or Louis Vuitton bag you bought on the street last week for twenty bucks may not seem worth all the law enforcement fuss, but the underground counterfeit trade is big business. The loss in tax revenue to the city alone is in the billions. Trust me, it's worth the fuss. Though not a war in the conventional sense, there were casualties. I didn't know whether Hwa was a player or bystander in the events that led to his murder, but I intended to find out.

"Do a computer search," I said. "Manny wants a list of cases John tipped us."

"Honey, it's going to be a long list." The printer sprang to life and page after page fell into the tray.

"Thanks," I said, pulling the sheets out of the tray. I put them into a manila folder.

We discussed the murder.

"If Hwa was killed for a tipoff, the killers might come after me," I said.

Her eyes widened in concern. "What are you going to do?"

"Nothing until I meet Sergeant Ortiz tomorrow," I said. "Please don't mention this to the other investigators until then."

"What about Hwa's tip?" she asked.

"That's where Jenny comes in. Hopefully, she knows something."

Before I left the office, Stella gave me a warm hug. "Sorry about your brother."

"Thanks." I said. She knew about the memorial service, but I hadn't dared to mention Linda's premonition, just as I had never told Stella about the family history of early death.

I discarded the jacket the police gave me, put on a spare kept in the closet, and headed home. The anniversary day, with my best informant dead and killers after me, wasn't over yet.

# Chapter Three

AFTER LEAVING THE OFFICE, I walked to the Ninth Street PATH station. PATH is the subway that travels underneath the Hudson River and connects Hoboken to Manhattan.

I was convinced Hwa's killers were in pursuit. Although I'd received numerous death threats over the years, I'd never been targeted by murderers. I knew it could happen. With a family history like mine, I expected it. That's why I moved to Hoboken, New Jersey. I had received the first letter death threat when Linda was pregnant with Josh, who is now seven. Three months later, I bought a brownstone on Garden Street.

I had always felt secure in this small town, with its many family-owned stores lining Washington Street and its location a heartbeat away from The Big City. But as The Counterfeit War escalated, so too had the danger. When I started out twenty years ago, the counterfeiters were street peddlers like Hwa. Now armed criminals and interstate networks dominated the underground market.

© ©

Exiting the PATH, I walked to Third and Washington Street, quickening my pace as I headed home. With killers possibly after me, I was worried about my family.

"I'm home," I announced. No answer. I heard a noise coming from the kitchen and presumed it was from Linda preparing dinner. I had invited the Bells and my mother, Lucille, for dinner and a short memorial service. The Bells are Linda's parents and live in Riverdale, a neighborhood in the Bronx. Mom visits them once a month.

I headed toward the kitchen, but not without stopping first in the living room to see if Josh was here. The daily newspaper was resting atop the television and the sofa beckoned, but no Josh. I placed my briefcase on the Chippendale-style secretary, a present from Linda for my office work and set against the bay windows.

She had placed Swiss Rose linen on the dining table and was standing at the stove. I knew she was preparing spaghetti because the sweet smell of simmering tomato sauce wafted through from the kitchen.

I met Linda in acting school during a production of Chekov's *The Seagull*. She played Irina and I played the brother, Pjotr. I was taken in by the fragile beauty mirrored in her eyes and voice during rehearsals. We dated three months before living together. Her appreciation for fine art opened up a new world for me. Unable to find steady work, she became a teacher and opened the world of art to her students. When Josh started school, she resumed as a substitute.

I walked to the stove and held her gently. I had never involved her in my work and didn't dare to mention Hwa's murder.

"Fair maiden, how now do I beseech thee?" I spoke in a deep baritone, trying to mimic a Shakespearean character.

Ladle in hand, she turned, replied in falsetto, "Oh, Caliban, horrible beast, thou art the epitome of artfulness."

"Oh fair maiden, thou doest your humble servant well." Impulsively, I hugged her tighter, savoring a closeness I feared might come to an end.

She giggled. "Hey, what's this for?"

"I missed you," I whispered into her ear. "How are you feeling?"

"You mean after last night?"

"Yes." I hugged her again.

"I'm feeling better."

"Good, what's for dinner?"

"Spaghetti and tomato sauce. Want a taste?" She dipped the

ladle into the pot and lifted it to my lips. I took a sip, savoring the tangy garlic and tomato. "It's great."

"Aren't you going to change?" She eyed my bedraggled work attire.

"Of course," I said and left the kitchen.

I decided to sneak up on Josh. I ascended the stairs on tiptoe. On the second floor landing, I walked quietly past the master bedroom to his room. The door was slightly ajar. Watching the budding artist filled me with pride. I saw myself in him, seated behind a table, back to me, and concentrating with drawing pen in hand on an exercise in a sketch pad.

A creaking floorboard gave me away. He turned and smiled. "Dad! You're home."

I greeted him, using my best Irish brogue. "How're ye, laddie?"

"Oh, stop kidding." he laughed. "See this giraffe. I'm painting him purple, like the Purple Cow on television."

"My, my, tis a fine color for a giraffe, that it is."

"You sound so funny when you talk like that."

I asked him if anything exciting happened in school. He pouted and told me about his friend Mike DaRoma. "Mike said he can do everything better than me."

"I thought he was your friend," I said, dropping my accent.

"He is . . . well, he was."

Josh said Mike yelled at him during recess. They were playing catch. Mike kept dropping the ball. Josh kept telling him to keep his hands in front of his body; no good, Mike wouldn't listen and got mad.

"Sometimes, it doesn't pay to be helpful," I said.

He resumed drawing. I watched him, amazed at how quickly he was growing up. He was innocent and had not made a connection between George's death and the death of many generations of men in the Jones family. I dreaded having to tell him, while realizing that he might find out sooner than expected.

I went into the master bedroom, which was nearly as large as our studio apartment when we were struggling actors in Greenwich Village. I remembered how happy Linda was after selecting the oak bureau and king-size futon bed. Hard to believe our lifestyle might end after so much effort.

I donned a pair of corduroy slacks, a button-down blue

shirt and loafers and went downstairs for a beer. I opened the refrigerator, snatched a can of Budweiser, and cracked the lid.

"Theo, I've told you not to drink from the can." She set the ladle down. She opened the cupboard and removed a glass mug. "Here, use this."

"Thanks." I filled the mug.

"I've got good news," she said. "The principal wants to hire me full-time. I'd be teaching fine art and English, same course load I was carrying in the New York public schools."

"That's good, isn't it?" I asked. She looked troubled.

"You know I've never liked you in the investigation business."

"Oh boy, here we go again." I feigned a chuckle. With killers after me, I wondered if she was right.

"I'm serious this time. The principal wants to hire me full-time."

"You mean you'd like to be the main breadwinner?"

"I could support us." Her voice trailed away.

"You want me to sell the business, don't you?"

"I want what's best for both of us."

I set down the mug and walked over. She turned her back to me. I moved closer, put my arms around her and hugged. "Maybe I'll consider selling the business in a few years," I whispered.

"Will you?" she asked.

"I promise, but give me time."

She turned to face me, eyelids fluttering, kissed me lightly on the lips. I held her closer, luxuriating in the warmth of her breath against my neck.

I cheered her by nibbling on her ear. She laughed playfully, pushed me away. "Caliban, loathsome beast."

I released her, returned to the table and finished my beer.

My mother, Lucille, arrived with the Bells. Her gray hair looked flashy in a fresh coiffure. "Where's my grandson?" she said and hugged me. "I have something for him."

"Theo, good to see you." Jack looked comfortable in dark slacks and a white button-down shirt. Mattie was by his side. She was a petite woman. In her hand was a freshly baked French bread.

"You shouldn't have," I said. "Linda cooked a feast."

Josh wanted to start on the chocolates Grandma gave him.

They were tempting rounds, ovals, and squares.

"Josh, no sweets until after we eat," Linda said.

We retired to the kitchen and sat. Jack said a short prayer of thanks and then started passing around the salad, spaghetti with meatballs, and sauce.

"Delicious, Linda," Mattie said.

We ate and chatted about family and Josh's school. I loved how the Bells doted on JJ. Afterwards, we retired to the living room. The Bells and Mom sat on the sofa. Josh sat with me on the stuffed chair. Linda lit a candle and turned down the lights.

My mother had never discussed the family tradition of early, violent death. It occurred to me, as she talked about dad's death and her love for George, that maybe she never knew about it. I began to feel spooked, as if I was attending my own memorial service, and when she cried, I hugged her gently, and tried not to think of the misery she would feel if I perished.

Linda said a prayer in George's memory. Josh, innocent of the larger tragedy, was quiet throughout. Everyone held hands, while I eulogized about his life. I knew it would be difficult, and I began by talking about growing up with George, playing football, best man at my wedding. I paused as tears welled up. The Bells said their remembrances. Only Josh was silent. He never got to know Uncle George, but the tragedy and loss felt by everyone was reflected when he took my hand. I prayed for him, because he might be fatherless.

The Bells left with Mom at nine. Linda took Josh upstairs and returned to wash the dishes. She joined me in the living room, and we snuggled in silence.

"Do you really want me to get out of this business?" I asked.

That got her attention. She looked at me, as if trying to discern what had caused the change.

"Theo, I want what's best."

I wanted to unload and tell her about Hwa's murder—but I couldn't. I didn't dare expose her to the danger I was facing.

"I know you do," I said. "Give me time."

"Sure, Theo. I'm sorry I mentioned this in the kitchen. I should have known better than to pressure you before a memorial service."

"Don't worry; you did the right thing."

# Chapter Four

*MY DEATH?*

I prayed her premonition was the work of her subconscious. Otherwise, I had to accept the family tradition would claim another. *Me.*

I was distraught enough to consider staying home the next day. I muddled through breakfast and left the house. I melded into the morning hordes of rush hour. I boarded the PATH, and as I travelled under the Hudson River for Manhattan, I pondered the unknowable.

*Can death be predicted?*

I know Shakespeare's answer. His plays reflect the popular belief in fate and the supernatural. My favorite character is MacBeth, whose fate that he would be killed by a man not borne of woman, as predicted by the three witches, came true. He was killed by McDuff, born by Caesarian section.

I felt like MacBeth, caught in a whirlwind of escalating danger and headed for a tragic end. Linda was right: I should get out of this dangerous profession. However, even with my own safety to consider, I felt compelled to continue my work. Only a handful of investigators specialized in *trademark cases*, as they're called in the business, and I was saving lives, victims of an avalanche of fake consumer products that included electrical wiring, contact lenses, cancer drugs, and cosmetics.

I arrived at the office and busied myself reviewing e-mails. Stella had settled down after yesterday's excitement. Murder was rare in our line of work. For the most part, people who died from counterfeit products were unintended victims. Receiving a death threat paled to actually being targeted by killers.

"Be careful," Stella said as I prepared to leave.

"I'll be fine." I took the manila envelope and left.

I thought about Hwa on the subway trip uptown. Before he died, Hwa helped stop an epidemic of deadly fakes. Scum like Haines counterfeiting fertilizer; Sam Jiang selling GM automobile brake pads made of compressed wood chips; and Mitch Ho, who nearly succeeded in selling fake cancer drugs.

I remembered Jiang spat in Hwa's face when the police handcuffed him. "You set me up. I trusted you."

Hwa had worked with the police on this one. "Fake brake pads—it's murder," an outraged GM executive said at a press conference, adding that the defective brakes, packaged to look genuine, right down to the GM trademark, would have failed after ten thousand miles.

Maybe Hwa died because he did a good deed. If so, he died a hero and not a low-life street peddler selling knockoff watches.

From Grand Central, I took the shuttle to Times Square. I walked up the cement steps to the street level and was dwarfed by the pulsing, blinking, subliminal neon and LED light show of familiar and famous brands lining Broadway. People might think it strange that I noticed the brand names overhead, from the yellow Sanyo to the stately red Coca-Cola. Maybe it goes with years of trademark cases.

I walked across Broadway to 4 Times Square. After passing security, I took the elevator to the law office of Klein & Klein on the twenty-fourth floor for an appointment to meet the new corporate counsel for IG International Ltd., the music and apparel empire for the rap superstar International Gangster, and a big client of mine. The company had recently been purchased by Premier Financial Equities, which was building its portfolio of notable brand names.

The meeting was arranged by Brian Zeckindorff, a powerhouse entertainment lawyer and partner. Klein & Klein's reception area looked like a spread in *Architectural Digest*: hardwood floors with plush chairs positioned around a tinted glass lounge table. I greeted Mary, the receptionist. She waved me through. "You know where his office is. Follow the sound of his voice." It was an underhanded joke in the law firm. Zeckindorff was an old school litigator who considered it good business to loudly curse out his office staff. The other partners had warned him to tone it down.

I walked down the corridor. Sure enough, I could hear his voice from a distance.

"You goddamnned son-of-a-bitch! I have a client in my office, and I want that file. I want it NOW!"

I turned the corner and spotted him shaking a fist at Cisco, the paralegal, who cowered. Zeckindorff resembled a crude caricature of a devil. He favored dark suits and was menacingly tall, with a well-trimmed black goatee. His demeanor changed as I approached.

"Ba-a-a-a-by!" he cooed. He addressed anyone who was important as "ba-a-a-a-by." Anyone else, he ignored. It simplified doing business.

He gave me a toothy smile, hugged me, and escorted me into his carefully arranged power office, with a landscape view of the Times Tower directly across the street. This is the place to be on New Year's Eve, when the ball drops down from the top of the Tower to usher in the New Year.

I had been in the office many times over the years. His desk was spotless. The fresh scent inside came from an imported tincture of pine that his secretary, Annie, sprayed each morning. Behind the desk was a long table with a personal computer and printer; underneath were case files, lined back-to-back. His law library, housed in a bookcase behind his desk, resembled a movie marquee of big names with *Prosser on Torts, Nimmer on Copyright*, and other names in the legal field.

Sitting behind a cherry wood table in the center of the office by the window was the new corporate attorney—and he looked like a powerhouse, from his finely chiseled features and razor haircut to his custom tailored blue pin-stripe suit and paisley tie. I would have guessed he took his law degree from Yale and owned a condo on the Upper East Side.

"Theo, this is Robert Caldwell, the new corporate counsel for IG International," Zeckindorff said.

Caldwell looked me square in the eyes and then stood. "Pleased to meet you." He had a firm handshake. I sat down opposite him. Zeckindorff took the remaining chair.

Caldwell cleared his throat. "I'm glad we scheduled this because I got a call an hour ago from a detective named Chris Harney. He's investigating the murder of John Hwa."

"John Hwa?" I had been expecting to discuss a counterfeiting investigation at Drake's department store. "Why did the detective call you?"

"Do you know this guy, Hwa?"

"I was supposed to meet him yesterday. He's an informant who supplied tips on many knockoff brands—but never the IG trademark." I told them about the knife attack.

"The police questioned his girlfriend." Caldwell frowned. "She's a seamstress at the Asian Seas sweatshop. It's producing knockoff IG sweaters."

I was investigating knockoff IG sweaters selling in Drake's department store, so that appeared to be a connection.

"I'm already involved in a murder investigation after a week on the job," Caldwell said, practically spitting the words at Zeckindorff, as if this was his fault.

Although Zeckindorff didn't know Hwa, Caldwell continued to chastise him, even after I reminded him I was the one who knew Hwa.

"Look, ba-a-aby—" Zeckindorff schmoozed.

"Don't baby me," Caldwell said. "You were hired to handle a small investigation of knockoffs at a department store. Now someone's been murdered."

"Relax, ba-a-a-by, we're on top of it." Zeckindorff turned to me. "Right, Theo?"

"Absolutely," I said. "I'm meeting Sergeant Ortiz to discuss the murder. The knockoffs may have nothing to do with the murder."

Caldwell glared at us. "I have more bad news. The detective said the FBI may get involved."

"The FBI?" The usually unflappable Zeckindorff was surprised. So was I.

"Harney's friends with an ASAC named Tom Richardson. He's in charge of a task force based in the Newark field office that's investigating the World Trade Center attack. Richardson wants to know about any trademark counterfeiting in the tri-state area, especially if any of the defendants are from the Middle East. I told him you've identified Musa Ahmad and his company, Raiments, as the manufacturer of the knockoffs at Drake's. Asian Seas could be involved with Ahmad."

The task force sounded familiar.

"The FBI must have reconvened the 1993 task force that investigated the blind Sheik Omar Abdel Rahman," I said. "The Sheikh had a base in Jersey City and funded his organization from the sale of knockoff T-shirts."

Caldwell nodded. "After I mentioned Musa Ahmad, Harney said he'd arrange for me to meet with the ASAC. I'll want both of you with me."

Cisco came into the office. He was carrying a case file. "I found the file."

With a huff, Zeckindorff took it and dismissed him. He opened the flap, removed several reports, and handed them to Caldwell. I spotted the one on Chameleon Detective Agency letterhead covering the undercover site visit to the department store.

"Remember this?" Zeckindorff reached inside the folder and took out a knockoff black IG cashmere sweater. I picked it up and ran my fingers over the fabric. The sweater, one of three I purchased undercover, looked and felt like expensive imported Turkish Cashmere. The knockoffs were believed to have been imported from Pakistan; instead of goat wool, the sweaters were made from acrylic fiber.

The stylized IG letters on the neck label and over the left breast completed the ruse. Whoever manufactured the sweaters were pros at "stealing the brand."

Caldwell paused as he read my investigators report about how I bribed an employee who identified Musa Ahmad and Raiments and then assigned Stan Good, one of my investigators, to cold call the company for additional information. The Drake's investigation began after a customer complained to the corporate office after the dye had washed out from a sweater purchased at Drake's department store. The customer was told to send it in for a refund. An inspection by Quality Control determined it was counterfeit. Zeckindorff assigned me to canvass the department store.

"We don't have much on Raiments or Ahmad," Caldwell said, as he leafed through the report. "What will Stan come up with?"

"I'll let you know," I said.

"We need to sink our hooks into Saul Drake for information," Zeckinforff said.

Caldwell directed his steely gaze at Zeckindorff. "Harney wanted to arrest Saul Drake for selling knockoff sweaters, but I asked him to wait because we have enough evidence to file a civil seizure order. He agreed and is sending me an IG sweater from Asian Seas. We're going to match it with the ones Theo purchased."

Caldwell handed back the reports. "Brian, I want you to file the department store seizure order ASAP."

"I'll file it this afternoon," Zeckindorff said, "and meet with the judge in chambers."

"Good, we'll meet with the FBI before executing it. IG International has a growing counterfeiting problem. My boss thinks the answer is to establish an in-house unit," Caldwell said.

"Where would I fit?" Zeckindorff asked.

"You'd be handling licensing and other IP matters and reporting to me. But counterfeiting investigations will eventually be handled internally by the corporate office."

"So you won't need Theo's help?"

"I want him to continue for now," Caldwell said. "Barry Farnsworth, chief counsel for Premier Financial Equities, will make the decision about the anti-counterfeiting unit. He'll go ape-shit after I tell him about the murder and the FBI."

Caldwell stood, gave me a power handshake, and was escorted out of the office by Zeckindorff. I could hear the two talking outside the door.

While I sat there, I pondered the turn the Drake's investigation had taken. I didn't mention Hwa's killers might be after me. I rarely discussed my safety with clients, even with the FBI getting involved because of a possible terrorist connection.

The FBI's 1993 investigation didn't go far. After arresting the blind Sheik, seized documents fingered a secondhand store in the Greensville section of Jersey City. The counterfeiters renting the store were from the Middle East and selling counterfeit Calvin Klein T-shirts. They used fake names but had already vacated the store and fled the United States.

The FBI task force contacted Jim Creedy, a name partner with Creedy McShaw, a boutique law firm that handled intellectual property matters for Calvin Klein. The FBI learned I had executed a seizure of knockoff Calvin Klein T-shirts sold by Fahlid Fazar's fashion boutique on Central Avenue in Jersey City. Creedy gave the FBI a case file on Fahlid, who was small time and, as it turned out, had no link to the terrorists.

The FBI's involvement in 1993 marked a turn in the war, which was beginning to escalate.

When I started out in 1981, the counterfeiters were mostly street peddlers, but gradually, more and more trademark cases, like a small investigation involving a department store selling knockoffs, led to a larger sinister operation; or a routine meeting with an informant turned deadly. That's why I called this a war. The enemy was the invisible underground economy for counterfeits that had taken Hwa's life—and might take mine as well.

# Chapter Five

ZECKINDORFF RETURNED AND SAT down. "Whew, that guy is something," he said. "Caldwell bitched about the cost of anti-counterfeiting operations."

"I can understand his concern."

"Hey, screw him." His voice rose. "This is a business, and we both need the fees. I had to do a major sales job earlier to allow you to continue undercover."

"I appreciate the effort. Is Caldwell serious about the anti-counterfeiting unit?"

"You bet. Now what's this about another investigator at Drake's?"

I had mentioned meeting Bull Fogarty by phone the other day. "He was my boss when I started out at the Madison Detective Agency."

"Are you sure he spotted you?"

"Positive. I bumped into him as I was leaving the department store. I found out he's working undercover for National Wholesale."

"Christ! How many knockoff brands is Drake's selling?" Zeckindorff shook his head. "I've heard of this investigator and spoke to him last month. He sent me some IG knockoff polo shirts he purchased at the Roosevelt Flea Market. He wanted me to fund an investigation. But I refused."

"Things must be going downhill if Bull is working on spec," I said. "An investigator can get into big trouble."

"I'll remember that if he calls again. Don't worry about Bull or National Wholesale." He drummed his fingers on the table. "Call me after you meet the cop. Give me something to settle Caldwell down."

"What about the FBI?"

"You heard Caldwell. The detective is arranging a meeting."

He escorted me to the reception area and gave me a hug. He turned and walked away, and disappeared from view. Before the elevator arrived, I could hear his booming voice, cursing out the paralegal.

©©

*Expect the unexpected!*

This was the first thing Bull Fogarty taught me when I started with the Madison Detective Agency. Bull was an ex-cop and a great PI until something caught up with him and he took to drink. He was the last person I had expected to meet when I left the department store, but when I passed through the revolving door, there he was.

"Wha—what the hell!" he sputtered. "What are you doing here?"

He looked gaunt, eyes sunken. He'd lost weight, hardly a surprise for a heavy drinker, but he looked respectable in a tan suit and blue tie. "Easy, big guy." I tried to smile. "Just doing some shopping."

I suspected he was investigating Drake's for a different client than IG, which was mine. I had been engaged in a long-running battle for business ever since I broke away from the Madison Detective Agency to start my own.

"I suppose you have your Christmas shopping in that portfolio." He eyed my salesman's portfolio, a match to the one he was carrying.

"It's not Christmas, and I don't know what you're talking about," I shot back as I walked away from the unruly drunk.

I had to act fast. Bull likely had a sales meeting scheduled with Saul Drake and could find an opportunity to ferret my cover. I pulled out my cell phone and called Brenda Pills, Drake's personal assistant whom I had met earlier.

"Hello, its Frank Winston," I said, using my cover name.

"Yes, Mr. Winston."

"Sorry to bother you. I need your help. Does Mr. Drake have a meeting scheduled with another salesman? A big guy, older, maybe late fifties. Sound familiar?"

"Why do you ask?"

"Because I bumped into him on the selling floor. The guy's a jerk, a real backstabbing pisser I used to work for years ago. For the life of me, I can't remember his name or what company he's with these days. Could you help me?"

She paused before answering, "He's with National Wholesale."

"Never heard of it. What's his name?"

"Nick Carter, an account rep."

"Sure, Nick Carter. How could I forget?"

I knew most of Bull's cover names, but not this one. National Wholesale was unfamiliar as well, likely a startup.

"I need another favor, Brenda."

Another pause. "What is it?"

"I told Nick I'm retired. I don't want him to know what outfit I'm with these days. So, if Nick questions you, ignore him. Could you do that? I'll send you a bouquet of flowers. Is it a deal?"

Another pause, longer than the others.

"All right, but don't send me flowers."

"Fine. Thanks for your help."

Meeting Bull was like a sweet and sour dish, savory and bitter. I admired him when I started in 1981. Together we developed investigative tactics to combat the counterfeiting epidemic that was taking off.

At one time, he was a great investigator who could out-talk a used car dealer and out-think a sewer rat. Yet something happened, and he started to slide into drink. I wish I could have helped him. He was a casualty of another war, a personal battle that dragged him ever downwards. In the end I had to save myself and try to go it alone.

After I broke away, a rivalry developed that became dark and ugly as clients from the Madison switched agencies. I heard stories about Bull that were sad and painful. He had disintegrated and was nothing like the person I once knew.

There was a spark of decency left in him. I received a card from him after my brother, George, died. I never knew how he found out but was grateful that he had thought of me.

# Chapter Six

ONE OF MY FIRST acting jobs was as a waiter at McLoone's Tavern, located on 50th Street and 8th Avenue. At one time, it was a favorite watering hole for cops, particularly if they were Irish, because the bartenders invariably had first names like Liam or Paddy and were newly arrived from the old country.

The owner liked to hire actors who could mimic an Irish brogue. Being part-Irish, I enjoyed greeting customers and had a repertoire of phrases, everything from: *how're ye today* and *top of the mornin'* to *me Irish eyes are a smilin'* and *would ye like a wee bit of ale with supper*?

I enjoyed working here because of the décor, a replica of a 1900 Irish ale house with paintings of quail hunting and another of fog rolling in off the bogs adorning the walls and, of course, the enticing smell of corn beef and cabbage from the kitchen. The bar had the lustrous shine of genuine Irish oak and the earthy scent of carrageen moss, and the tap had dark imported ale from Killarney that tasted tart and sweet. The tips were great on St. Patrick's Day, when the crowd waiting to get inside stretched around the corner.

I met many police officers and got my nickname of "Shakespeare" from a cop buddy when I became an investigator.

I walked inside and spotted Manny seated at a booth. He's a second generation street-smart Puerto Rican who was in uniform. I didn't need an introduction to the man sitting with him, Chris Harney.

Manny spotted me and waved. I walked over, saw he was drinking a Guinness from the bottle; Harney, a bottle of Murphy's.

"Hello, Shakespeare, I think you know Detective Chris Harney," Manny said.

I tried not to act surprised as I sat next to Manny and shook hands with the detective. "Do you know a corporate attorney named Robert Caldwell?" I asked.

"Never mind how I know him," Harney said. "How do you know him?"

Just like a cop, I thought to myself. They all want to ask the questions, not answer them. "I just met him," I said. "IG International is a client. I've handled several knockoff investigations for the rapper."

"Manny told me Hwa was the informant you used for a Monsanto fertilizer bust. Fake shit; now that's cute."

"Caldwell was upset over the FBI," I said.

"That's his problem." Harney shrugged. "If this investigation escalates, the FBI task force is going to take over."

I was about to hand Manny the manila envelope, when the waiter, a freckle-faced young man in dark trousers and a starched white shirt, came to the booth.

"Top of the morning. What's yer pleasure?"

"I fancy a Beamish, laddie," I replied in my best Irish brogue.

"Erin Go Braugh! A man after me own heart!"

"Used to work 'ere in me younger days. Are you'n actor?"

"That I am, fine sir. I'm studyin' at the Actor's Studio."

"Begorrah! Studied at the Tisch Performin' Arts. Did some acting, mostly forgettable like my acting career."

"Pleased to meet ya, I'm Tom McGurney."

"An Irishman, how quaint." I introduced myself and the others.

"Manny said you used to be an actor," Harney said. "I'm taking acting lessons."

I was not surprised. Many cops moonlight as extras or work as technical advisers for television and movies. "I used to be an *aspiring* actor—and I use that term loosely. I did more aspiring than acting. Where are you studying?"

"The Columbus School of Acting. A couple cop buddies and I go on weekends to study voice, improvisation. Scene and monologue work. My hero is Manhattan North Detective Mike Sheehan."

"The one who cracked the preppy murder case involving Robert Chambers?"

"The same. Manny knows Sheehan."

Manny raised his bottle. "Cheers."

"Here's looking at you, kid," I said in return.

I knew stardom was a dream ticket for many cops. Crack a big case, get into movies, and move on to something better. It was a fantasy that belied the unglamorous life.

After the waiter took my order, I handed Manny the manila envelope. He opened it, looked over the list of cases, and then handed it to Harney, who fingered through the pages. "This is a haul."

"Two years' worth," I said. "Hwa had connections."

"Caldwell mentioned executing a seizure at Drake's department store," Harney said. "Any idea when it's going down?"

"Likely sometime next week."

"Who's Musa Ahmad? Where does he fit?"

I told him about my undercover assignment and how I wrote up an order with the owner, Saul Drake, and then got friendly with an account manager who gave me Ahmad's name, after I slipped him some cash.

"The manager wasn't suspicious?" Harney asked.

"Not in this business," I said. "Nothing is as fleeting as fashion. Apparel firms send in undercover personnel to find out what's on the racks at the big department stores. Bribing an employee for sales information happens all the time."

Harney asked if Ahmad could be connected to Hwa's murder. I shrugged and said we'd know more after the seizure at Drake's was executed.

Harney nodded and took a hit of beer. "How well do you know the girlfriend?"

"I told you at the station. I met her once and talked to her on the phone. I didn't know she worked in a sweatshop."

"When did you meet her?"

"About a week ago. She was with John on Canal Street. That's the last time I saw him alive . . . Now maybe you can answer some questions."

He nodded. "Depends on the questions."

"What will happen when we meet with the FBI?"

Harney shrugged. "You'll find out . . . Next question."

"Do you know why Hwa was killed?"

He didn't answer right away, instead took a hit from his beer. "We may have an MO. This wasn't a professional hit; only the lowest street trash uses a knife." He took another belt from his beer. "The girlfriend hardly had time to see the killers but believes they're part of a gang that broke up a strike at the Asian Seas sweatshop."

"I didn't know about the strike," I said.

Now it was Manny's turn. "Hwa's girlfriend worked as a seamstress. She called our hotline, a few words in broken English about the sweatshop producing IG knockoffs. Are you familiar with Asian Seas? It's on Tillary Street near the BQE."

"I don't think so." The agency had raided many sweatshops because of knockoffs, but I had never heard of this one.

Manny continued. "Before I had a chance to investigate, Chris called me. That's when I learned she had organized a strike. Four goons wearing hoodies to hide their faces broke up the strike. Jenny believes two of them attacked the next day."

"Hwa's attackers wore hoodies," I said.

Harney nodded. "That's in your police statement. The owner shut down the business and disappeared. Jenny doesn't know his name. Everyone called him *Uncle*. John Doe arrest warrants have been issued for him and the attackers."

Harney took another hit of beer. "She hated the Uncle, a sadistic bastard who slapped and yelled at the seamstresses. She wanted to hurt him by hurting his business. That's why she left a tip about the knockoffs."

"She must have told Hwa about the knockoffs," I said. "That's why he wanted to meet."

Harney nodded. "All of the employees have fled. The business records have been shredded, so Jenny's our only link. So far, she's given us names and claims not to know any addresses."

"Wow! So everyone's a fugitive," I said. "What happened to the IG knockoffs?"

"The sweatshop bins are full. Don't worry, the place has been padlocked."

"How many bins are there?"

Harney paused. "My guess is about twenty, maybe more."

I paused and did some calculations. Both men were surprised when I told them the retail value of the sweaters in the bins was about a half-million dollars.

"That much!" Manny whistled.

"Twenty bins, that's over three thousand sweaters, and at one hundred and fifty bucks a sweater, that comes out to a half-million."

"Someone's waiting on a big order," Harney said.

"Yeah, but who?" I asked.

"I asked Jenny, but she doesn't know any clients," Harney said. "Turns out she's been in the country less than a year and is an illegal alien. The other sweatshop workers are probably illegal, too. That would explain why they've disappeared."

Manny corrected him. "I believe the legal term is undocumented."

"Excuse me for being politically incorrect," Harney continued. "Under questioning, she admitted to being paid in cash. She's in trouble for evading taxes, not to mention being involved in a murder. But deporting her would shut down the investigation. The INS is getting involved. Maybe she'll wind up in an immigration detention center."

"Where's Jenny now?"

"In Hwa's apartment. A plainclothes detective from the 111th Precinct is watching the building."

I was beginning to believe Hwa's death was in revenge for Jenny's organizing the strike—not for his tip-offs. However, I had to speak to Jenny to be sure. She might have withheld information to protect herself.

"Look, Chris, can I talk to Jenny?"

Harney pursed his lips. "Why do you want to talk to her?"

"She trusts me. I'll take one of my investigators along. She's Chinese and used to work in a sweatshop."

"You mean Kimberley Chung?" Manny's eyes widened.

"Wow, she's hot!"

"Easy, big boy. Kimberley's my ace for dealing with Asians and speaks five Chinese dialects. Maybe the two of us can get information the police can't."

"I don't want private eyes involved," Harney said. "What's Kimberley's background? Was she ever an illegal—excuse me—undocumented alien?"

"No. Kimberley was born here. She was orphaned at age ten and grew up in foster homes. When she was seventeen, she started working in sweatshops. That's how I met her. Give us a chance with Jenny."

Harney was adamant and shook his head. "No, I don't want PIs interfering when we're investigating a murder."

"Listen, Chris, clients and cops come to me because they need my expertise with IP."

"IP? What's that?"

"Intellectual property. People are dying from knockoff car and aircraft parts, fake pharmaceuticals—you name it. Asian Seas was producing knockoff IG sweaters. You've got to let me in on this."

"Murder is murder as far as I'm concerned. Besides, I have Manny when it comes to knockoffs."

"Give Theo a chance," Manny said. "I learned a great deal from him."

Harney became sullen. "I'm sure you're good, Theo. But the IG knockoffs may have nothing to do with Hwa's murder."

McGurney arrived with my Beamish, and after he left, I put it flat to Harney.

"Look, Hwa was my informant. If you want my cooperation with the cases on that list, let me talk to Jenny."

Harney remained silent, as he looked over the list. "Sorry, Shakespeare, I don't make deals with PIs."

Harney polished off his beer. "Can I take the manila envelope?"

"Be my guest," Manny said. "Fax me a copy later."

After a goodbye handshake, Harney reached for his wallet and removed a ten-dollar bill and handed it to Manny for his beer. After he had departed, I needled Manny. "Was bringing the detective your idea or his?"

He smiled. "I was trying to do you a favor."

"No shit. Couldn't you warn me? That list of Hwa's tips was for you." I took a hit of Beamish. It was stronger than a domestic and burned going down.

"Yeah, and I would have eventually given it to Harney. How well do you know Jenny Ling?"

"Like I told Harney, I met her once and talked with her on the phone."

I realized that the sweatshop conditions must have been horrendous for undocumented aliens to stage a labor strike that could draw the attention of the INS. Perhaps they were fearful for their lives. That could explain why Jenny's boyfriend was murdered.

"What do you know about the strike at Asian Seas?" I asked.

"Nothing much." He raised the beer bottle, took a haul. His eyes narrowed. "Say, why are you getting involved in Hwa's murder? You hardly knew him."

Nice and direct. That's what I liked about him. "I'm the guy who turned him. I owe him one. Besides, he put bad guys away and saved lives."

"Snitches are the bottom rung in the criminal world. I'm wondering if Chris was right. Maybe you should forget about Hwa, let the police handle it."

"Look Manny, someone *died*. Remember 'protect and serve.' Maybe Hwa was a smalltime hood. But he deserved something better than dying in the gutter."

"You're a piece of work."

"Funny you should say that—it's a line from *Hamlet*. Want me to recite it?"

Manny laughed. "I should have known. Sure, go ahead."

In my best baritone:

*What a piece of work is a man! How noble in reason! How infinite in faculties!*

*In form and moving how express and admirable! In action how like an Angel!*

*In apprehension how like a god! The beauty of the world! The paragon of animals!*

"Bravo!" Manny cheered. He lifted his beer bottle in salute.

# Chapter Seven

WE PAID OUR BILLS and left a nice tip for McGurney. It was a warm September day outside. "Keep in touch," Manny said. After shaking hands, he walked away.

I retrieved my cell phone, speed-dialed the office. "Stella, its Theo. Is Kimberley in the office?"

"Yes, everyone's here."

"Good, I need her for a special assignment. The Drake's investigation is heating up. The FBI might get involved."

"The FBI!" She had questions galore. I told her to head for Laguna's coffee shop to discuss it further over an espresso.

Laguna's was located at St. Luke's Place in the West Village. Linda enjoyed this spot, especially in late autumn when the Ginkgo tree leaves start to yellow. When we first saw it, we were awed by the 1920s Italianate brownstone and red brick townhouses. I could easily imagine the poet Marianne Moore walking up the steps of No. 14, or Theodore Dreiser peeking out from the window of No. 15 while working on his masterpiece *An American Tragedy*. The neighborhood was beyond our financial means, but not our dreams.

I often had lunch with Stella at Laguna's. After a ride on a downtown subway, I walked over and found her seated and sipping an espresso.

"Been waiting long?" I sat down opposite her.

"Not long. I told the other investigators about the FBI. What's up?"

"Remember the 1993 FBI task force, the one formed after the terrorist attack?"

"Of course I remember. We were involved with that snake Fahlid who was selling knockoff Calvins. The FBI thought he was a terrorist."

"The same task force reconvened after the 9/11 WTC attack."

Stella sat silent for a moment, then her eyes widened. "My God. Musa Ahmad!"

"That's right. The task force is interested in anyone selling knockoffs in the tri-state area, especially if they're from the Middle East."

I ordered an espresso and relaxed. "The detective who questioned me yesterday is a friend of an ASAC named Tom Richardson, who wants to discuss Ahmad. Zeckindorff and I are going with Caldwell."

"Will the FBI take over?" Stella asked.

"It's possible."

The espresso was served. I took a sip. It was bitter and strong. I told her about my meeting with Manny and the detective. Her eyes bulged when I told her a half-million dollars of IG inventory was sitting on the sweatshop floor.

"Lordy! Someone's waiting for a big order."

"That's right, and it could be connected to the murder. I've got to talk to Jenny Ling. That's why I need Kimberley. Any word from Stan?"

"He cold-called Ahmad as I was leaving," She sipped her coffee.

"Anything exciting?"

"You'll have to ask him. What about Bull Fogarty?"

"Zeckindorff said not to worry. But I want you to investigate his cover. Give me some background on National Wholesale."

©©

Stella and I finished up, paid the bill, and took a cab to the office. She called Stan, a tall, lanky black guy who was in the boiler room and working on the Drake's investigation with me. He arrived, carrying a notebook and pen, and pulled up a chair. Stella moved her seat closer to complete a semicircle. She'd already told him about the FBI's interest in Ahmad.

"This thing's heating up," he said. "The FBI!"

"Let's not get carried away," I said. "What have you got for me?"

He read from his notes. "I cold-called and talked business with Ahmad. He's sending sample IG cashmere sweaters."

"Great, how did you arrange that?"

"Gift of the gab. Ahmad says he does work for the 'Gangsta.' His partners are two brothers, Orlando and Pete Smith, and used to hang with the rapper. The brothers have both done time."

"What were they put away for?" I asked.

"Orlando did six months for grand theft auto. Pete did two years for armed robbery."

"Real sweethearts," she said.

I asked Stan what he used for a cover. My investigators use various aliases.

"Luther Pine, sales manager for Fashion X. Ahmad speaks with an accent. I told him Fashion X plans to open a branch office in Philadelphia. I told him Fashion X wants to use local contacts to handle manufacturing and distribution for the New York-New Jersey area."

"Nice. What did Ahmad say?"

"He was blown away when I told him Fashion X is hoping to do two to four million dollars in business a year."

"Yeah, probably saw dollar signs in his sleep. What does Raiments handle?"

"Musa said the company imports fabrics from around the world, particularly Pakistan and India. He handles bulk for many New York fashion companies and ships fabric to outfits in Texas and Mexico that do garment work for brands like Polo by Ralph Lauren, Izod, Steve Madden, and Amalgamated Apparel. Oh, yes, Ahmad also subcontracts small orders."

"Subcontracts?" I was hardly surprised. "Probably uses sweatshops locally. Did he mention any companies?"

"I asked for references of companies he's done business with. But he was evasive."

"Hardly a surprise, if he's involved with knockoffs," she said.

"Any connection to Drake's department store?" I asked.

"None so far." He flipped a page and said, "I researched the company. It's listed in the phone book, has a web site, and is located in Whittier, New Jersey. I ordered a Dun & Bradstreet report."

I walked to my desk and leafed through my Rolodex for Hwa's home number. I wrote it down on a notepad and left with Stan for the boiler room.

I greeted Kimberley Chung, who was seated at a desk in the first cubicle. She looked hotter than a prairie fire in July, dressed in skin-tight leather pants and a baby blue turtleneck sweater. Her pageboy hairdo and charm made her nearly irresistible to the counterfeiters, who were usually men.

"You look ready for action." I let out a low wolf whistle. She looked great in leather apparel, something of a personal brand.

"Thanks," she said demurely. "What's this about the FBI?"

I told her about the task force. "Get hold of Jenny Ling. She's John Hwa's girlfriend." I gave her the number. "Call and see if you can arrange a meeting."

"What should I say?"

"She should remember me. Tell her I'm working with the police. It's urgent."

I knew Jenny's English was poor and hoped Kimberley could find a common dialect. While she dialed the number, I greeted Angel, who occupied the cubicle behind her. He was twenty and wearing jeans and an extra-large sweatshirt.

Angel had been with the Agency for three months handling routine desk assignments. He was a former student of Linda's. I admired his enthusiasm and hoped to take him into the field.

"Will I get involved in the FBI investigation?" He'd heard me talking to Kimberley.

"Not this time around," I said.

Kimberley, who was on the phone, waved me over. "Theo, I've got Jenny on the line."

She handed me the phone. "Jenny, this is Theo Jones. Remember me? John introduced us."

"Yes, remember," she said.

"We're working with Detective Harney and Sergeant Ortiz.

I'm sorry to hear Hwa died."

"Thanks. Very terrible."

"We'd like to help."

"Yes, Kimberley explain."

"Can we meet? It's urgent."

"Yes, when?"

"In thirty minutes."

# Chapter Eight

I LEARNED ABOUT SWEATSHOP life from Kimberley, who started out doing low-paying piecework. She hoped for *sho yu guy* work—soy chicken for sewing that was easy to do. *Jin tau gwat* was difficult piecework that looked like savory meat, but turned sour and was difficult to digest. I met her while executing a seizure at a shop. She provided tips on the underground market until I offered her a job. She went to night school after joining the agency.

"Did Jenny say anything about Asian Seas?" I asked as we left for the subway.

"She mentioned the sweatshop. Her English is poor. She's from Fujian Province. Fortunately she speaks Mandarin. She's grieving and fears for her life."

"Do you think she knows Chen-Kuo?" I asked.

"It's possible," Kimberley said. "I'm sure Chen-Kuo has heard about the strike and the murder by now."

Kimberley had introduced me to Hur Chen-Kuo, founder of the Asian Staff and Workers Association, or ASWA. Chen-Kuo was a legend. His name, literally translated, means "savior of the country." He initiated the sweatshop labor movement in New

York City that broadened to include Asian restaurant workers. His initiative aligned with a national front for better wages for low-income workers.

I learned from Kimberley, and later from Chen-Kuo himself, how posters with pictures of his face were placed in the windows of restaurants in Chinatown warning workers about the "labor devil." He told me the ASWA had endured bomb and death threats, lockouts, lawsuits, intimidation, and beatings over the years.

We took the subway to Flushing, Queens, a largely Asian neighborhood nearly equal in population to Manhattan's Chinatown. As we walked, we enjoyed a private conversation about this store or that street location where we'd seized counterfeit merchandise.

"Flushing is nearly as big a war zone as Canal Street," I said.

Kimberley frowned. "Theo, I know the situation is bad—but you keep referring to it as a war. Is it that bad?" She looked at me with dark luminescent eyes that could melt a man's insides.

"I believe it is. Knockoffs are for sale on city street corners around the world. The problem is big enough to be called a war."

"I think you're exaggerating," Kimberley sniffed. "The problem is certainly escalating; maybe it's getting out of control. But a war?"

"Then it's a war for people's minds. People see nothing wrong with buying fakes, although the crime threatens the legitimate economy."

We walked by young and elderly Asians. Traditional Chinese *sizhu* music could be heard from inside the numerous tea cafes. The usual beverage was a sweet, milky tea, served hot or cold, known as "bubble tea" or *boba nai cha*, to go with dumplings, rice cakes, and other snacks. We continued until we came to the tenement building. I spotted a blue Malibu across the street with an Asian man seated behind the wheel.

"That's got to be the plainclothes detective," I said.

"Is he expecting us?" Kimberley asked.

"Hell, no—he's keeping watch on anyone who enters and leaves the building."

"That means he'll write up a description of us and the time we entered the building," Kimberley said.

"That's right—hopefully that will be it. Unless someone's stalking Jenny and makes a move on her today."

"In which case, the cops will be looking for us," Kimberley said.

I had never been inside Hwa's apartment. We went inside the building and walked up the stairs to the second floor. I rang the buzzer. Jenny Ling partly opened the door and peered at us with suspicion.

"*Ni hao*," Kimberley said. "We spoke on the phone. You remember Theo."

She scowled, "No speak now; come another time."

"*Dao mei*," Kimberley said. "We want to assist. You must trust us."

"Go away." She shook her head but didn't close the door.

I remained quiet while Kimberley assuaged her in Mandarin; finally, she relented and forced a smile. "Must be careful," she apologized.

We entered a studio apartment that was small even by New York standards. She was wearing jeans and a sweatshirt with the polo player symbol on the chest. Conspicuous brand-labeled products were everywhere.

Jenny ushered us into the kitchen for tea. We took seats at a teak table. After boiling water, she served jasmine tea. I savored its tartness and looked around. On the sofa were three Louis Vuitton handbags with the distinctive interlocking LVs and Japanese floral symbols, several pairs of Gucci sunglasses, and three boxes of Channel perfume. Four boxes of Calvin Klein underwear were stacked on the coffee table. Two Burberry knapsacks nestled on the floor.

This was expensive merchandise for a seamstress's salary.

"Jenny, is any of this counterfeit?" I asked.

"No, no counterfeit," Jenny said. The corners of her mouth turned downwards. "In China everything counterfeit . . . in America find *dào dì*."

Jenny spoke to Kimberley in Mandarin. She turned to me and translated. "Jenny purchases genuine apparel and ships them abroad to friends for a small commission."

I understood why the Chinese would want genuine brands. The underground market had stamped out the legitimate market.

"I heard about John's death from Sergeant Ortiz," I said. "Please accept our condolences."

"*Sheh-sheh*," she said. "Are you police?"

"No, we're investigators. I worked with John, remember?"

"Not police?" She remembered meeting me but knew little else. I realized Hwa never told her he was an informant.

Kimberley told her IG International was a client. Jenny looked confused, until I reminded her about the trademark infringement unit's hot line and Manny.

"Fake! Yes, that what Lucy say," Jenny said. "She seamstress like me. Tell me all fake, call hotline."

"What's Lucy's last name?" Kimberley asked.

"Lucy Zhu . . . Police ask where she live. Not know. Maybe someplace in Brooklyn, near C subway stop."

"Did you ever see any counterfeit sweaters?" I asked.

"No, no see." She explained that she never handled sweaters, which involved sewing labels. I asked why she had called Sergeant Ortiz. She explained, somewhat suspiciously, that she did so because Lucy asked her to, even told her to say IG knockoffs. Rather than continue to question her about the fake sweaters or Lucy Zhu, I asked who ordered the IG knockoffs.

She vaguely recalled a man who came to the shop. "Yes . . . yes. He come. Maybe he order."

"What did he look like?" I asked.

"Small man. From India or Pakistan maybe," Jenny said.

"Do you know his name or what company he's with? Is his name Musa Ahmad?"

"No, not sure."

"Did you mention the man to the police?" I asked.

"No . . . Afraid of police."

Next, I asked Jenny who organized the strike. She hesitated. Finally, she said it was Lucy, who talked about fair wages and being paid by the hour instead of by the piece.

I had learned from Chen-Kuo that paying by the piece was an illegal practice dating back to the 1800's, when shops subcontracted work and their profit was proportionate to the work "sweated" out of a worker, hence the origin of the term. It was pioneers like him and other organizations that had begun to fight for better labor conditions.

Jenny had never heard of minimum wages or the other "rights" Lucy talked about. Nonetheless, she sided with Lucy, who shared a common hatred for the Uncle—or big boss.

"He slap me many times," she said.

Kimberley reached over and took her hand. "The police are looking for the Uncle. Don't be afraid."

"Police ask me," Jenny said nervously. "Not sure. Everyone afraid. Very afraid."

"What happened to your co-workers?" I asked.

"Moved, gone underground."

That made sense. The murder was meant to intimidate the workers. I decided not to ask if they were undocumented.

"Do you think the men who attacked you will return?" I asked.

Jenny nodded. "Afraid, I walk outside. Look behind all time . . . move soon."

According to Jenny, no one knew the name of the owner of Asian Seas, who was addressed as Uncle. Kimberley, however, had picked up something, a non-verbal queue in her body language and use of the Chinese word for uncle. The term she used was something akin to the mob's godfather.

"*Dao mei,*" Kimberley said. "Is Uncle a *shetou?*"

I had heard of the *shetou.* Kimberley suspected that the Uncle, as he was called, was a *shetou,* or snakehead, an organization that helped mainland Chinese to illegally enter the United States—for a price.

Taken by surprise, Jenny became agitated and stuttered, "No *shetou*—no." She looked at us fearfully now. "No tell . . . no tell police."

"Nothing's going to happen to you," I reassured her.

"Please . . . no tell."

Kimberley took her hand and said something in Mandarin that settled her. I promised her we would not say anything to the authorities about the snakehead. She smiled weakly, and while we sipped tea, she told Kimberley in Mandarin how she came to the United States.

©©

*I was born in a village in Fujian province. My father's name was Wei, and he owned a boat and was a fisherman. Dad sailed the waters near the Penghu Islands in the Taiwan Strait for mackerel that my mother, Mui, would sell at market in a nearby town.*

*Mom was born in the village and had long flowing hair. When I was born, Dad wanted to abandon me because he wanted a son, but she refused. Dad beat her and tried to take me away, but eventually resigned to having a daughter.*

*When I was young, drift net fishing was banned because of the damage caused to marine life. This was a death sentence for Dad, who continued to fish illegally. His catches were poor, not like before, because he had to be careful to avoid getting caught. To survive, Mom went to work as a seamstress in a garment factory to help support the family when I was seven. Eventually, I joined her and learned the trade. The owner came to the factory once a month. He wore a business suit and tie and talked with Ur, the foreman.*

*Times were changing. The Tiananmen Square protest had opened a dream to a life in America. This was appealing to the Fujianese. They are known as "the overseas Chinese" and for centuries have settled abroad while continuing to do business with the mainland.*

*Young men in the village talked about leaving for America. It was exciting! Freedom was on everyone's mind. Freedom! Freedom from poverty. Freedom to live and to learn. Getting an education was important in a village without a school. I saw for myself that the men were leaving for America and heard stories about the shetou, the clandestine network.*

*When I was sixteen, I met Jiang Hwa and fell in love. Jiang's father, Ko-lin, had used a shetou to enter the United States years ago and was sending home money earned from driving a cab. Shortly after Tiannamen, President Bush signed an order that allowed illegal Asian immigrants who had entered the United States before 1982 to become permanent residents. Overjoyed, Ko-lin became a naturalized citizen and brought over his wife Lijuan and Jiang, who took the name John when he applied for citizenship. He obtained a C-8 immigration card that would allow him to be legally employed.*

*John returned to assist a cousin, Wen-ching, to come to America and used a* shetou *named Gwego. Gwego helped Wen-ching and many others travel to America for a new life. Wen-ching eventually settled in Boston's Chinatown, and through the local snakehead found a job as a tutor to pay off his debt.*

*Hwa wrote letters to me and after a year asked me to join him as his wife. My parents wept at the idea that they might never see me again.*

*I made an appointment to meet Gwego and rode my bicycle to the town where he lived. He was a short compact man who rarely smiled. He was all business.*

*"You do as I say," he warned. "Get in big trouble. Go to jail."*

*He told me I would be travelling through several countries and arriving in Canada with three others. A Caucasian named Tim would escort us at night through the woods and into a neighboring town in Michigan. Everyone would depart for destinations in America.*

*"Everyone destroy passport," Gwego said. "Harder to deport if caught."*

*The price was nearly two hundred thousand Yuan, or about thirty thousand U.S. dollars. No one could hope to raise this kind of money. Everyone had to have connections or* guanxi, *Gwego said. Everything could be arranged through the network known as the snakehead. It was a form of indentured servitude that had existed since the Middle Ages and was now reborn with a new name,* shetou.

*I travelled by plane to the Philippines and then to South America before heading to Canada with the other people. As directed, we crossed the border from Canada. From there, I travelled to New York City to be with John. He cried tears of happiness. I moved into the studio apartment he had obtained through* guanxi, *through connections. We planned to marry so I could obtain U.S. citizenship.*

*I had never been to a big city before. I was amazed at the bustling people and the cars. In the village, a car was rare. Everyone used a bicycle. Arrangements had been made for me to work in a sweatshop. John told me not to get too friendly or ask questions.*

*"Work hard," he told me. "Must pay off debt."*

*My debt amounted to some twenty thousand dollars. I worked behind a sewing machine for fourteen hours a day. I was paid two hundred dollars a week for six days' work with the understanding that sixty was for repayment to the snakehead. I later learned the Uncle was withholding ten dollars for himself, but I didn't care. Two hundred dollars! This was three months' wages in China. It was Lucy Zhu—not me—who talked about being cheated. The Uncle knew Lucy was a troublemaker and slapped her, but that made her resolute.*

*"This America," Lucy told everyone. "They have minimum wage laws to protect workers."*

© ©

Jenny finished her story and started speaking in English.

"Why I listen to her?" Jenny said Lucy convinced her to call Sergeant Ortiz on the hot line. Mentioning IG knockoffs was an act of rebellion unthinkable in her native country, where the Tiananmen Square protest was crushed by the army.

Now I understood why the Uncle had disappeared and destroyed his business records. Even if he had nothing to do with Hwa's murder, smuggling aliens and human trafficking were serious crimes. The police would have a difficult search, since he worked for a group that moved people clandestinely.

Kimberley warned her about what happened to people who did not pay the snakeheads.

"Maybe bad . . . but John gone." Jenny said the *shetou* were more honorable than the killers, who were Caucasians and had no connection to the snakehead.

"How will you pay the snakehead?" I asked.

"I find way," she said softly. "My dream come to America. I stay."

As gently as I could, I asked about the strike.

"After Uncle kicked Su Mei, everyone leave. She pregnant seamstress, fall to floor. She hurt but able to walk and take cab home. Everyone want to leave, but Lucy said now time for strike! Others follow Lucy. Use cardboard box tops, make signs."

She said within two hours of setting up a picket line, they were attacked by five men wearing hoodies that partially covered their faces. Jenny believed the leader was the same man who killed her husband. She described the assassin as over six feet tall, solidly built, with a scar on his left cheek.

The next day, Jenny went with Hwa. She never asked where they were going or why. She heard a noise and turned. She briefly saw the man's face—enough to see the same scar. He was with another man; both were wearing hoodies that partially hid their faces. The leader slammed into John and then quickly moved away. He slumped to the ground, a knife in his chest.

"Use knife . . . not see. Very fast! Tried to scream. Other man hit me, fall to ground."

Jenny started to sob. Kimberley reached over and hugged her and said something in Chinese that calmed her.

"Do you know Hur Chen-Kuo?" I asked.

"Who?" she replied numbly. "Who he?"

"He started the Asian Staff and Worker's Association," I said.

"Not know . . . not know," she tried to sound composed, but a hint of desperation flashed in her eyes.

"We're friends of Chen-Kuo's," I said. "Please trust us."

"Not know . . . you leave now." She rose from her seat. She glared at us and pointed to the door.

"Please trust us," Kimberley said.

"Please go." Jenny said loudly. "Must go."

As Kimberley and I were leaving, I put a business card on the table and asked Jenny to call. She followed us and closed the door when we were in the hallway.

# Chapter Nine

"WHAT WAS THAT ALL about?" I asked.

"I have no idea," Kimberley said.

"We need information. Contact Chen-Kuo; find out what he knows about the strike and the murder."

"I'll call him when we get back."

We retraced our route to the subway and headed back to Manhattan. Although I had heard of the *shetou*, I knew little about them.

"It's an underground network, much like Jenny described," Kimberley said. "The *shetou* are portrayed as ruthless criminals in the Western media, but no Chinese would do business if the snakeheads were that cruel. However, the Uncle, as Jenny calls him, is probably a little snakehead, a *jianghu*."

"*Jianghu*? Did I pronounce it right?"

"Not bad. The word means small-time opportunist."

"Does she know his real name?"

"I'm not sure."

"What about Hwa's murder?" I asked. "Could the *shetou* have arranged it? Maybe Hwa got in trouble with them."

"Not likely. With Jenny working to pay off a debt, the *shetou* would have tried to settle things peacefully."

Everything was making sense now. "Why didn't you ask questions about the Uncle? Try to get a name."

"Theo, come on . . . she's grieving. You saw how excited she is."

I had to agree. "You're right. But even if the Uncle's a snakehead, would he have had Hwa murdered?"

"Doubtful. Look at the result. His business is ruined, and the police want to arrest him."

That left the foreign man who was likely Musa Ahmad. Would knockoffs have been enough of a motive to commit murder? Kimberley assured me it was.

"Apparel companies don't want to be embarrassed by publicity from unfair labor practices," she reminded me. "I'll bet the man she described was a big client of Asian Seas. If the newspapers and television reporters did a story about the sweatshop strike, his company would be out of business."

"That would explain why the strike was broken up so quickly," I said. "Before the press picked it up."

"Exactly. Remember how I met Chen-Kuo?"

I nodded and recalled how she was working behind a sewing machine for fourteen hours a day in the Oriental Stitch sweatshop, a hell hole that used cameras to monitor them and allowed a two-minute bathroom break. The supervisor was a disgusting leech who yelled at everyone.

Chen-Kuo organized the workers and arranged a strike that was covered by the newspapers. Vosage Fashions was a big client doing business indirectly through the Fabric Source, an Asian apparel manufacturer that subcontracted with the Oriental Stitch. When the CEO learned about the strike, he dropped Fabric Source as a vendor. Other fashion companies dropped the Fabric Source, which went out of business a day after the sweatshop was padlocked by the police for labor violations.

"So the strike became a threat," I said. "I find it hard to believe anyone would get desperate enough to kill."

"It wouldn't be the first time . . ." Her voice trailed away. "Who cares about a seamstress working in a sweatshop, especially if she's illegal?"

"I believe the correct term is undocumented."

"Undocumented. Illegal. Whatever."

We exited the subway and returned to the office. Stella was seated at her desk and working on the computer. Kimberley moved a chair in close to complete a semi-circle.

Stella was as fascinated as she was perplexed. "Who are these snakeheads? The *she-two*?"

"That's *shetou*," Kimberley corrected her. "I don't know much about them. Smuggling undocumented aliens is big money, and most of the business comes from Fujian province."

"How much does it cost?" Stella asked.

"Jenny Ling said thirty thousand bucks," I said.

"Wow! That's expensive."

"Especially in China," Kimberley added. "People use a down payment and then an installment plan to pay off the debt."

"That poor woman," Stella said. "What's going to happen to her?"

"The INS is familiar with the *shetou* and will eventually find out about her connection," I said.

"What about Jenny's friend, Lucy?" Stella asked.

"Another question mark." I turned to Kimberley. "Maybe Chen-Kuo has the answer."

"I'll see if I can get hold of him," Kimberley said. I told her to sit at my desk and use the phone. While she dialed, I told Stella Musa Ahmad might be the foreigner Jenny identified.

"Do you think Ahmad had Hwa killed?" she asked.

"It's a possibility."

"Theo, I've got Chen-Kuo on the line," Kimberley said. "He wants to talk to you."

I walked over and took the phone. "Hello, Chen-Kuo."

"Hello, brother."

"Kimberley told you about the strike?"

"Yes. And the murder. This pains me so much."

"I understand." I could practically feel the echo inside Chen-Kuo, who had endured countless labor strikes and strike breakers. "Jenny became upset when we mentioned your name."

"Yes, Kimberley told me."

"Do you know Jenny Ling?"

Chen-Kuo sighed. "I cannot discuss this matter over the phone. Can we meet?"

"We're planning a peddler's sweep on Canal Street. We could drop by in the afternoon."

"Good, I look forward to seeing you, brother."

I hung up the phone. Chen-Kuo was like an all-seeing oracle when it came to labor disputes involving Asians. But how much did he know?

I was getting ready to leave for the day when Sergeant Ortiz called.

"Hi, Manny."

"We got trouble, Shakespeare."

"Who's got trouble, me or you?"

"Both of us. We found the owner of Asian Seas. He's dead."

Now that was a surprise. "Manny, that's number two."

"Tell me about it. The Uncle was stabbed to death, same as John Hwa. Now I got detectives from two boroughs breathing down my ass."

"Look, Manny, I'd like to help, but I'm busy and can't leave the office right now."

I wanted to put off answering questions about Jenny and Asian Seas. For Jenny's sake, I had promised to keep quiet about the *shetou*.

"Bullshit! I'm with Lieutenant Ash—and he ordered me to get you. He's got questions."

"The ashcan himself," I said. "You know I can't stand him."

"I know. And if you don't come, you'll dislike him even more."

No use arguing. "All right, Manny. Where are you?"

"I'm with Ash in front of 260 Mulberry Street. That's where the body was dumped."

"Lovely. I have to call the attorney handling the investigation, let him know what's happened, and tell him the police want to question me. The attorney may want to be present."

"Thanks, Shakespeare."

I hung up and looked at Stella. She had already guessed the Hwa murder was heating up.

"It's bad, isn't it," she said.

"Manny said they found the Uncle. Stabbed to death."

"Oh, God. Just like John Hwa?"

"Seems that way. I'm on my way to meet Lieutenant Ash."

Before leaving, I called Zeckindorff. "Brian, I got a call from the police. The owner of Asian Seas is dead. Stabbed to death like John Hwa. A homicide lieutenant wants to question me."

"Christ, another murder! Why does the lieutenant want to question you?"

"He thinks I may know something. I told Sergeant Ortiz you might want to be present."

"I'll let you handle the cop questions. They'll want to talk to Caldwell." Zeckindorff cursed. "Call me later. Can you meet me at my office around two tomorrow? I'm heading to IG International, and I want you with me."

"I'll be there." I told him about Stan's cold call with Ahmad.

"Very interesting. Send me a report," Zeckindorff said.

©©

The address was a short cab ride away, a small neighborhood of Manhattan known as NoLita, or North of Little Italy, bordered by the Bowery and Houston Street.

Manny didn't tell me where the body had been dumped. I would have guessed an alleyway or in the hallway of a building. When I arrived, I knew it had to be the green construction dumpster parked in front of 260 Mulberry; the building was under renovation.

The dumpster was girdled with yellow police tape that continued around either end to seal off the sidewalk as well as the entrance to the building. Uniformed officers were on duty to keep pedestrians from the crime scene. This block would have been perfect for dumping a body at night. The old St. Patrick's Cathedral across the street would have finished its evening service.

I paid the cabbie and walked toward the dumpster, a green open-top with front and rear doors on hinges. The dumpster's front door was half-open, enough so that I could see it had been a sad end for the Uncle. His body had been dropped off here, among a disheveled mix of plasterboard, metal pipes, broken bricks and cinder blocks, and sections of wood and nails; this refuse had been sent down a construction chute that stretched from a third-floor window.

I spotted Lieutenant Ash. He looked spiffy in a double-breasted blue blazer and gray slacks, and was standing next to the building and talking to Manny, in uniform, and Chris Harney.

"Glad you showed up," Ash said. He told an officer to let me pass through.

I signed the crime scene entry log sheet. The officer nodded and lifted up the crime scene tape. I thanked him and walked towards Ash, who turned his head and began talking to the others, even as I approached. I practically had to interrupt him.

"Good seeing you again, Lieutenant." Ash ignored me.

Mike Ash, the "ashcan," was the epitome of an in-your-face kind of cop. I'd known him since he was a detective third grade in the 5$^{th}$ Precinct and seen him turn a hardened hood soft after getting nose-to-nose with him and yelling at him like the drill sergeant he once was.

Finally, he turned to face me. "Yeah, Shakespeare, long time no see." He shook hands. "I'm out in force on this one."

"So I see," I said.

"Glad you could make it, Shakespeare," Manny said.

"We had trouble identifying him," Ash said. "No wallet. Nothing in his pants pockets. Just a middle-aged Asian male. He hemorrhaged to death from a knife through the ribs. My guess is he died quickly.

"I made some calls and learned there was a warrant for a fugitive fitting his description. I called Detective Harney, and he brought in Jenny Ling to identify the body."

Harney stepped around Lieutenant Ash. "Detective Wu said a Caucasian man and another Asian woman entered the building, stayed for a half-hour, and left. I assume that was you and another investigator," he said, glaring at me.

"There are eight million stories in the naked city." I tried to sound indignant.

"Stuff it, Shakespeare," Ash interrupted. "Jenny told us it was you."

"Look, I don't like your tone of voice. I'm not answering anything until you charge me with a crime."

"Two people have been murdered," Ash said. He took a step closer to me. His eyes bored into me like a laser. "Murdered, do you read me?"

"Loud and clear."

"Whoever killed Hwa also killed the Uncle. Any idea who the killer might be?" Ash asked.

"Maybe an Asian Seas client," I said.

"Yeah, like who?" Ash asked. "We know you talked to Jenny. What did she say?"

I slowly exhaled. I could no longer deny meeting Jenny. Nonetheless, I didn't like Ash's interrogating me in front of other people.

"I wanted to find John Hwa's killer," I said. "I've already given Detective Harney a list of cases Hwa tipped us."

"Yeah, thanks. Your continued cooperation is needed," Ash said sarcastically. "Now, once again, what did Jenny tell you?"

"We need to crack this—and fast!" Harney pleaded. "A dozen undocumented aliens from Asian Seas are missing and might wind up in body bags."

"I asked her about the strike. Figured conditions had to be bad for undocumented aliens to make such a move. She told me how terrible the Uncle was—how he kicked a pregnant woman. After that, everyone walked out on strike."

"Anything else on the Uncle?" Ash asked. "Does she know his real name?"

I knew the Uncle was a *shetou*, but had promised Jenny I wouldn't say anything to anyone about the snakehead. "No. She said John got her the job. She doesn't know anything about the Uncle, not even his name."

"How about the other workers? Does she know where any of them live?"

"Hwa told her not to ask any questions or get friendly with anyone."

"Did she say anything about a worker named Lucy?"

"Yes. I believe her last name is Zhu. She was the one who organized the strike."

"Anything else about Lucy?" Ash asked. He took a step forward, hoping to intimidate me by invading my body space. It was an old cop trick. I stood my ground.

"Nothing," I said.

Ash continued. "You said the IG sweaters sitting in Asian Seas are worth half a million dollars."

"That's my best estimate."

"Would the IG sweaters be reason enough to kill the Uncle?" Ash asked. "Someone paid for that order—and is pissed that it's never going to arrive. Any idea who?"

"Jenny didn't know any of the clients by name but mentioned a guy from India or Pakistan."

"Is that Musa Ahmad?" Harney asked.

"Could be. As you know, I'm meeting the FBI to discuss him—now maybe you can help me."

"Help you?" Ash was bemused. "You're in a ton of trouble, Shakespeare. I'm thinking about having your license yanked."

"What happened to the Uncle?" I asked.

"Somebody did a job on him," Ash said. "My guess is they killed him somewhere else, wrapped him in black plastic, and then dumped him late at night. They almost got away with it. A carpenter nearly dropped a load of plasterboard down the chute that would have buried the body. A mason jumped inside the dumpster and tore the plastic open. Boy, was he surprised!"

"Where's the body now?" I asked.

"Morgue," Ash said. "Jenny's in the station house."

"What's going to happen to her?"

"She's in protective custody and will be moved to a safe house," Ash said.

Both Harney and Ash fired away with questions about Musa Ahmad. Even Manny jumped into the fray with questions. *Twenty questions,* I thought. *Times up.* "Look, I've answered everyone's questions. Now, I'm running a business and need to get back."

Ash was exasperated. Of course, he wanted to continue questioning me, but I wasn't having any of it. Cops like to question you over and over to keep you talking. It's like therapy: they're hoping some fact will emerge from the subconscious, and then it's "Aha!" and more questions.

"I'll cooperate, but at another time. I'm running a business and have clients waiting."

Ash relented. "You can go. I've spoken to Officer Mark Chan. Do you know him?"

"I know him very well. We'll be working together on a peddler sweep."

"Yeah. Chan gave me the beef about Hwa and his role as an informant. How often do you work with Chan?"

"Once, maybe twice a month."

"I want to talk with you after you meet with the FBI."

"You know the number," I said.

© ©

I hailed a cab and returned to the office.

"How did it go?" Stella asked. I told her to wait until after I had phoned Zeckindorff.

"Ba-a-aby," he crooned. "I got hold of Caldwell. He shit a brick! You're lucky you don't have my job. What happened?"

"Lieutenant Ash thinks whoever killed John Hwa also whacked the Uncle. I told him Musa Ahmad might be an Asian Seas client. I believe Ash and Detective Harney are going to check into it."

"Musa Ahmad?" Zeckindorff paused. "I wouldn't be surprised. I'll mention this to the FBI ASAC."

After the phone call, Stella and I discussed the murder. She sighed when I told her about the Uncle's final resting place. "Sounds terrible, that poor man."

"Wait until the FBI hears there's been another murder," I said.

# Chapter Ten

THE PATH RIDE UNDERNEATH the Hudson River took fifteen minutes. As I headed home, I stopped to savor the smell of freshly baked pastries from Carlo's bakery, located near City Hall.

Josh was sitting on the living room sofa and reading a book.

"Dad, you're home," he said. "Look at the present Mom gave me."

It was a book about Andy Warhol.

"See, look at the nice paintings, Dad." Josh flipped a page and showed me the "Brillo Box" painting.

"That's great," I said, hiding my concern. Maybe I was prudish, but Warhol was gay and surrounded himself with transvestites and drug addicts. I flipped the pages, relieved the book was mostly about the controversial artist's pictures.

I left Josh to his book and went to see Linda. She wasn't in the kitchen. A pot was on the stove. I walked over and popped the lid. Beef stew, a favorite of mine.

Linda was upstairs in Josh's bedroom. She was standing by his bureau and folding clothes. She had changed into blue jeans and a cardigan sweater.

She looked up and smiled. "Theo, I'm glad you're home."

I walked over and gave her a hug. "How was school?"

"Great! Teaching is such a joy."

I asked her to sit on the bed with me. "Is anything wrong?" she asked.

"I was thinking about the premonition you had."

Before I could say another word, she cut me off. "Theo, I believe it was a bad dream. I got excited, and who wouldn't, especially on the anniversary of the terrorist attack."

"Honey, what about my family history?"

"Let's not get carried away." She turned her head away. "I don't want to discuss it right now. Maybe at another time."

I decided not to tell her about the murders. Besides, I was beginning to believe there was no connection to her premonition. Maybe she was right. I even hoped the family curse was much ado over nothing.

I realized George's death on that horrible day in September 2001 marked a break in the pattern. First, he could not be buried in the family plot at the cemetery because his body was never found. Second, George and I were brothers. Perhaps the death of one brother was enough.

I changed the subject. "Josh showed me the art book you bought him. I was wondering if Andy Warhol is too . . . decadent for a child."

She turned to face and said, "Nonsense. He's nearly eight. Kids his age know who Andy Warhol is." She gave me a knowing smile. "I was thinking about you when I bought the book."

"Me?"

She nodded. "I thought about you after looking at Andy Warhol's painting, *32 Campbell's Soup Cans.*

"You thought of me! What brought that on?"

"I thought of something unexpected while admiring his painting. I read the text, which said Warhol was trying to make a statement about commercial art being accepted as fine art. That's when I realized Warhol was talking about the Campbell's Soup trademark, not the cans. That's why I thought of you and trademark counterfeiting."

It was a fascinating connection. "Okay, I'm hooked."

"So you're interested in my idea?" Her blue eyes sparkled as she stretched out on the bed and leaned her head against a pillow.

"Very interested. Not only is the trademark protected but also the trade dress, which is the distinctive design of the packaging."

"That's my point!" She gave me playful push. "Warhol got his start as a commercial artist and believed that commercial art would replace fine art. The *32 Campbell's Soup Cans* was thirty-two paintings, not one, and are supposed to represent machine-replicated art."

"That's a bit crazy," I mused.

"Theo, Warhol was a gay Manhattan man who wore a blonde wig. How crazy is that?"

"Half the men in Manhattan fit that description." The thought of machine-replicated art was interesting—and frightening. I was intrigued. "Machine-replicated. So Warhol predicted an art world where everything comes from a machine."

"I believe that's correct. Or maybe it's commercial art stamping out fine art."

Linda's use of *stamping out* reminded me of how the counterfeiting problem was stamping out the legitimate market. That's why Jenny Ling was selling the real product to her friends in China.

I realized we had gotten into a heady discussion about Warhol. Heck, I was hungry. But something about Warhol lingered in my head.

After dinner, we took a walk to the waterfront. Josh was up ahead near the railing overlooking the setting sun, which glowed a rusty red. Linda and I were seated near a 9/11 memorial. Across the Hudson, the New York City skyline looked resplendent—until you realized the Twin Towers were gone.

I wanted to continue our discussion about machine-replicated art and trademarks, and then I realized something about the World Trade Center and the terrorist attack.

I had wondered why the terrorists chose the World Trade Center. The Pentagon, yes. But the World Trade Center? *Why the WTC when the Stock Exchange is a few blocks away?*

The terrorists chose it because it's the *symbolic center* of the country's business community.

After the destruction of the WTC, the economy took a nosedive, fueled in part by one business scandal after another. Enron, Arthur Anderson, WorldCom. Even Martha Stewart, the patron saint of the middle class, was being investigated for insider trading. The rotten core of the business community had been revealed by this monstrous act.

I had seen several doomsday TV shows that likened the Trade Center's destruction to a Biblical prophecy. I had thought these were bunk—but wasn't so sure now. My brother and so many innocents died that day. I had asked myself what was the reason? Now, perhaps, I knew.

©©

Everyone remembers what they were doing the day of the September 11th terrorist attack. I was in my car, traveling out of town on assignment and listening to the radio.

A plane crashed into one of the towers at the World Trade Center.

I thought of my brother George. I pulled out my cell phone and tried calling his office, but got the busy signal. I remembered reading about a plane that crashed into the Empire State Building during the 1940s. Maybe that's what happened.

More news reports. A plane struck the second tower. Now it was clear—an attack! I tried calling again and again. No answer.

Traffic had slowed to a full stop in both directions, and I was trapped in a sea of vehicles going nowhere.

Thank God, I got through to my mother, who was crying. Next, I called Linda. She was home with JJ. Classes at the Demarest School had been dismissed.

Hours later, I arrived in Hoboken. I parked on the street and bounded up the stairs. Linda raced to the door and hugged me.

"God, I'm worried about George," she said. Her blue eyes were watery. We returned to the living room, where Josh was watching the television coverage.

"I hope Uncle George is all right," he said. Josh knew he worked in the World Trade Center. I wondered if his young mind could comprehend that his Uncle George was probably dead.

Every half-hour the newscasters would start coverage from the beginning, including a replay of the second jet smashing into the tower. I must have seen that jet disintegrating a hundred times, as I prayed for my brother and the people trapped inside.

I took several days off to mourn and spend time with family. I posted pictures of George in Grand Central, the train stations, and the bus terminals. The poster had the word *MISSING* at the top, with my brother's name, picture, and a telephone number, imploring anyone who had information to call. My poster took its place beside hundreds of similar posters of missing persons who had vanished. We were desperate for an answer.

© ©

"Theo, are you all right?" Linda asked.

"I'm fine."

"Are you sure? You look like you've seen a ghost."

"Boy, Linda, I thought you were the one who saw ghosts, not me."

"Caliban, simple oaf. I told you it was a bad dream. Nothing else."

"Not a premonition?"

"Heavens, no. I know generations of Jones men have died violently. But that's not fate."

"It's more than a coincidence, isn't it?"

"Mathematically, yes." She looked at me, irritated. I knew she didn't like talking about this. "We shouldn't speculate."

I looked at her, momentarily spellbound. We had a closeness that came from acting together on stage, living other people's lives, feeling other people's feelings.

"Why have you been urging me to change careers? Is it because of George's death?"

"No, not entirely. I believe that's what you want."

Her words penetrated because she was right. I was unhappy and longed for a life in the theatre. Nonetheless, I continued to believe I was doing more good as an investigator than as a failed actor. Despite the threats and danger involved, I thought of the lives saved.

That night, after Josh was asleep and we were alone in the darkness, we held each other silently. I must have fallen asleep, because when I opened my eyes, the early morning sunlight filled the room.

I lay back with my head resting against the pillow. I couldn't bear to live if anything happened to my family. I thought about George, remembered how he looked after me. I was wild during my teens. I saw him for the last time in his apartment on Greenwich Street in Tribeca. It was a hot August day. I was wearing micro-fiber jeans to stay cool and a blue polo shirt. George was wearing comfortable white slacks and a button-down shirt.

"Hey, little brother." He hugged me. "Come on in."

He looked young for a man approaching fifty, his brown hair starting to show gray. He was a solid six feet and ruggedly handsome, especially in comparison to me. I was four inches shorter and balding. He had moved a month earlier and gave me a tour of his bachelor pad with its wide-screen television and abstract paintings lining the walls.

He brought back two Buds from the kitchen and joined me on the sofa, while oldie James Brown hits serenaded us on his sound system. He took a hit, set down the beer. "How's my nephew doing?"

"Growing up fast. It's hard to believe Linda's teaching him to paint."

"That's good; he's inherited your genes." We talked about baseball and friends. After a spell, he excused himself. He went into the bedroom and returned with a knockoff Rolex watch. "Go ahead, check it out. You're the expert."

I examined it. The trademark Rolex was blurry, among other defects.

He must have sensed my dismay, as I discussed the watch's flaws.

"I know I shouldn't have," he said defensively.

I didn't want to lecture him and handed it back. "Curious to know why you bought it?"

"An impulse. I spotted a street peddler selling knockoffs." He looked at the knockoff watch in his hand. "I remember you telling me this is a war. I've become a believer."

That was encouraging, because he'd disliked my profession. George sat back on the sofa. "You know, I envy you."

I thought he was joking. "What? You want to become a PI?"

With a chuckle, he confessed how he admired my passion for the work. "Theo, I'm making a huge salary and have all the creature comforts. But something's missing. It's all about money.

There has to be more in it for me. You have a purpose."

"Tell Linda. She thinks my job stinks."

"Don't get me wrong, I think your profession stinks. But I know you want to do something good—and you are."

I wondered what caused this change of heart. Was this his midlife crisis? And then I realized he might be thinking the family curse would come for him. He was older than Dad, who died at forty-six. Perhaps George was tackling the unknowable and searching for a meaning, like Dad before he died. A month later, George was dead. Did he have a premonition or an epiphany before 9/11? Or was his death an unfortunate occurrence? Many people died that day. George happened to be among them.

# Chapter Eleven

WHEN I ARRIVED AT the office, I discovered Saul Drake had left a phone message. He wanted me to call, said it was urgent, and left his private cell phone number.

"Stella, listen to this." I played it back on the speakerphone.

"It's Drake. Do you think he's on to you?"

"No, he wouldn't be calling. He'd be shredding documents, covering his trail. I'm going to find out what he wants."

I dialed the number, and Drake answered.

"Saul, I got your message."

"I'm glad you called. Listen, we have some unfinished business." As I expected, his voice was controlled, not angry.

"Oh? What's up?"

"A stock boy opened a box of IG International slacks—and the shipment is ruined. The color has faded from navy blue to peach."

"When were the pants shipped?"

"Several weeks ago. The shipment was lying in our sixth floor stockroom unopened until yesterday. Listen, you have to come immediately."

"I'm taking care of something right now. I can swing by this afternoon."

"The afternoon? Make it eleven o'clock; I'm very busy."

"I'll be there."

Although Stella thought it was a trap, I could hardly back down. I keep a blue blazer and tie in the closet for occasions like this. Matched with the gray slacks I was wearing, I was ready to meet him.

I had already met using a cover of an independent account rep looking to start up an apparel line. I left the office with a portfolio briefcase stocked with genuine shirts and socks purchased off the shelves; with the labels removed, they made excellent "samples."

Planning to take the uptown subway to East 68th Street, I walked through Washington Square Park, the heart of Greenwich Village, nearly empty at this time of day. I spied the Blue Note jazz club. I remembered enjoying cool jazz on a Saturday evening with Linda, then a struggling actress.

© ©

Those had been happy times. All that mattered to us was the moment. We'd head home after a night of good music and screw until the morning sun came up, sleep until noon, and have brunch and leaf through the Sunday *New York Times*. We had dreams of acting success, but a day came when I told her how George and I had learned about the family curse.

"Theo, I'm so sorry," she said. "Your father's death must have been traumatic. What does your brother think?"

"We hardly ever discuss it. How can we? It's too eerie for words."

She had given me space when George perished, and when I cried, she hugged and cried with me.

© ©

Like most department stores, Drake's tried to create a consumer fantasy world. I entered and walked through the main selling floor, in step with the steady boom-boom of a rock beat. A strobe light flickered on-off, on-off near a rack of designer Guess? jeans. Two roving fragrance spritzers approached. The man, dressed like a dandy in a lavender chalk-stripe suit and white tie, beckoned with an atomizer of Polo by Ralph Lauren, hoping to give me a spritz or two, while his partner, a demure waif with rouged cheeks in a fuchsia ruffle cocktail dress, smiled and gestured with Chanel perfume.

I brushed by them and the morning shoppers and walked through the cosmetics department, which had a nice mix of brand names: Shiseido, Revlon, and others. A young woman, possibly a student, was admiring her looks while receiving a facial from an Esteè Lauder saleswoman in a smock.

"Rick. Hey, Rick. How's my man." The floor manager was a young man with a shaved head and a dangling gold earring, easily identified by a white carnation in his suit lapel. I had met him previously.

Rick smiled. "Pleased to see you again, Mr. Winston." He wore a black three-button suit and caramel-colored shoes, a clothing combination that would otherwise have been ludicrous but somehow seemed right in the make-believe fashion world.

"I'm wearing an IG tie," he said. "See, check this out." He turned it over to show the stylized IG logo.

"Very nice. I sold two hundred ties to Mr. Drake. The product will be on the selling floor next week."

I took the elevator to the executive suite on the fourth floor. The receptionist, who was reading a magazine, looked up.

"I have an appointment with Saul Drake."

"Oh, yes, you were here before. Have a seat."

I sat while several minutes passed. I spotted Brenda Pills as she left the executive office. She walked down the corridor towards me. She was a runway fashion spread in a silk-wrap dress, with a generous display of cleavage—but nothing sassy. Real class.

"Winston, what are you doing here?" She looked perplexed.

"Me? I'm here to see John. He called and asked me to meet him here."

"John told me he left to meet you."

"You mean he's not here?"

She shrugged. "I don't know where he is. I'll call him." She returned to the office.

My cell phone buzzed. I knew this meant trouble. My staff knows to beep me, unless the matter is urgent.

I checked the incoming number. It was Stella.

"What's up?"

"Saul Drake was here asking for you."

"What?"

"I heard a knock on the door and opened it a crack. A man who introduced himself as Saul Drake said he was looking for Frank Winston. I recognized the cover name and said Winston left to visit a client."

The business card I handed Drake had no address, just a post office box number and phone number. The only people who know the exact address and suite numbers of the Chameleon Detective Agency are clients and other corporate investigators, including Bill Fogarty. Most business entities have a good idea what the competition is up to, and the private eye business is no exception.

"Bull Fogarty must have fingered us. What did you tell Drake?"

"He was suspicious of the boxes in the back of the office."

"You mean the knockoff watches and fake music CDs?"

"That's right. Course, Drake didn't know they were fake. I told him they were orders waiting to be shipped."

"Do you think he believed it?"

"I'm not sure. By the way, I researched Bull's cover."

"You have! What've you got?"

"I did a Lexis search on National Wholesale and learned it was purchased by Premier Financial Equities. Isn't that the firm that purchased IG International?"

"Yes, it is," I said. "That's odd. Bull and I seem to be working for the same client."

At that moment, the door to the executive office opened, and Brenda emerged and walked towards me.

"Stella, I have some business to attend to." This is a code message to alert the investigator on the other end of the line to end the conversation.

"Roger out." She hung up.

Brenda sat down next to me. "I phoned John. He's on his way back. He said he had to handle something unexpected."

"Thanks, Brenda. Oh, by the way, did you hear from Nick Carter?"

"Not yet." Her face tightened. I decided to press her for information.

"Yeah, Nick and I used to work together many years ago. I'll send you a bouquet of flowers, like I promised."

"Flowers? Whatever for?"

"For covering for me."

"Look, Winston," she said coldly. "Nick never asked about you, and even if he had, I wouldn't have given him any information."

"That's a relief."

"I told my uncle."

"Your uncle? Do I know him?"

"You should. His name is Saul Drake. I reported our little conversation to him."

"I see." I tried to hide my surprise.

She stood up and looked at me with contempt. "Saul will be here shortly. Nice seeing you again, Mr. Winston."

My eyes trailed her as she walked back to the office and closed the door.

I sat back, tried to relax. I had walked into that one. There was nothing to do but wait.

# Chapter Twelve

A HALF HOUR PASSED. I glanced up every time the elevator door opened.

Finally, it opened, and Saul Drake exited. His eyes narrowed when he spotted me. He was dressed in a blue serge suit and wearing a black yarmulke on his head. He walked to the glass doors, passed through, and continued to the receptionist. "Any calls?" he asked.

"No, Mr. Drake."

He turned to me. "*Shalom*, Winston. So good of you to come."

"The customer is always right." It was a tired phrase, and the words died a quick death.

"Would you like to have lunch, Winston?" He posed the question more like a command than an invitation.

"It's a bit early," I replied, wondering where this was leading.

He turned to the receptionist. "Tell Brenda I'm back and left for lunch with Mr. Winston."

He signaled for me to follow. In the elevator, he pressed the down button, then pulled out his wallet, and extracted a fifty-dollar bill.

"I believe this is yours."

"Oh, boy." I stuffed the green into my pocket.

"Don't ever do that again," he said coldly.

"I was trying to help," I replied, somewhat lamely.

We rode in silence to the ground floor and walked through the main selling floor.

"Good afternoon, Mr. Drake." It was Rick. "Mr. Winston, good to see you again."

"Good afternoon, Rick," Drake said. "I'm glad you've met Mr. Winston."

"Oh, yes, he's my main man."

I followed Drake through the store, as he greeted employees without pausing. We stepped outside. Across the street was a deli. The hostess greeted Drake by name and escorted us to a table for two in the back. He thanked her and took a seat. Neither of us said anything while browsing the menu. It was almost like a poker game, each waiting for the other to make a move.

A waiter arrived, and we ordered sandwiches.

"Do you know what you are?" He was smiling, obviously enjoying an inside joke. "You're a *momzer*. Do you know what that means?"

"A *momzer*? Isn't that someone who's a wise guy?"

"Very good!" he laughed. "You speak Yiddish? Are you Jewish?"

A typical question when I'm on assignment in New York City's garment district, a starting point for many immigrant Jews. Most of the top designers: Ralph Lauren (née Ralph Lifschitz), Donna Karan, Isaac Mizrahi, Calvin Klein, and Diane Von Furstenberg, to name a few, are Jewish.

"*Oy vey*," I replied. "I might as well be after fifteen years working in the garment district. I'm Irish."

"Oh, a Mick," he laughed. "Actually, the word means bastard."

"Hey! I thought we came here to talk about a shipment of bad pants."

"Don't play me for a *schmuck*, Winston. We both know why I left a message."

"Sorry," I murmured.

He gazed at me intensely, as if trying to give me the evil eye. "After you left, my niece told me you asked about Nick Carter. You know what she said, don't you?"

"Yes."

"Nick's been doing business with us for a month. He's retired, but works part-time."

"I didn't know that. I haven't seen him in years."

"We get along well. I told him what you told Brenda. *Oy vey!* Nick was angry. He told me not to trust you. He said you're a crook."

"Don't believe a word of it," I said indignantly.

"It's all right. *Auf tsuris.*"

"Yeah, trouble."

"In this business, I deal with all kinds of people," Drake said. "An hour later, Sammy Dubinsky tells me you handed him fifty dollars for the name of the distributor of the IG International sweaters on the second floor. Is that right?"

"I was looking out for everyone." I tried to sound sincere.

"I believe you." He leaned forward enough so I could smell expensive cologne. "Sammy was afraid you were a *shameus*. Do you know what that is?"

"Not exactly."

"The Irish spell it s-h-a-m-u-s, but the word is Yiddish, and it is spelled s-h-a-m-e-u-s. It means private eye."

I leaned back, my hand to my heart. "You think I'm a cop."

"No. I already told you what you are. You're a *momzer*. In this business, that's not so bad. It's almost a compliment. Maybe you and I can do business."

"That's great," I said, relieved that my cover was secure. "My associate called and said you checked me out."

Drake shrugged. "I've been around and dealt with snoops. I had to make sure you're legit. A few years ago I caught a snoop."

"What did you do to him?"

"I didn't do anything. A *shtarker* took him to a place and did a hospital job. Nothing serious, a warning." A *shtarker* is a Yiddish term for a strong-arm man.

Like most criminals, Drake and the people he did business with used fear and intimidation along with brute force. I wondered if that was why Sammy told Drake about me. Maybe he was afraid of Drake, or perhaps he's part of the counterfeiting ring.

The sandwiches arrived, thick with slices of pastrami served hot on rye bread with mustard and a sour pickle.

"It's good," I said.

"The best in New York. Screw the Carnegie Deli. This is better."

While we ate, he spoke reverently about his family and told me how the store was founded by his grandfather, Moishe Horenstein, who was born in a *shtetl* in Russia and opened the first store in the Garment District. During the 1930s, the patriarch changed the family name from Horenstein to the *goyishe* Drake because the Nazis were coming to power.

Drake's father entered the family business after World War II, when everything was ruled by the mob.

"If you were a small business owner and you wanted to stay in business, you paid protection money. My father refused to pay—and he got cut up bad. Still he refused to pay. So the crooks beat him, set fire to the store, and beat him again. Finally, the crooks left him alone, because he was too strong. My father was setting an example, and the crooks feared that."

"Wow, that's some story," I replied.

"Yes, my dad was strong. My family is from Russia and had survived pogroms. After that, what are a few beatings? But he taught me to be strong and to survive in this cutthroat business. He taught me how to finagle and to cut corners."

"He taught you well."

"Yes, he did. His favorite expression was *Ich bin ein baleboss*. Have you heard that expression?"

"Yes, I have. It means 'I'm the head guy and I look out for everyone.'"

"That's right. Come to me if you have a problem. Don't go bribing my employees."

"Fine, I was trying to help—before things turned into a *mish-mosh*."

Drake bristled. "From now on, speak only to me. Understand?"

"From now on."

"I cut a corner, got a deal on those sweaters, and made a profit. You've been around. Everyone's getting away with something."

"Everyone's getting away with something," I echoed.

*Everyone's getting away with it.* I wanted to smack him. I

have heard that excuse, or variations of it, countless times over the years.

"Maybe I can help you? What are you looking for?"

I opened the portfolio and removed the samples. I had mentioned on a previous visit that I was interested in starting up my own label, Hot Apparel, and talked quantities and prices. He had looked bored; but now appeared interested. My main hook was a genuine cashmere sweater with the Bergdorf Goodman label removed.

I handed him the sweater. He gingerly let his fingers run through the fabric, getting a feel for the hand of the fabric by direct tactile impression.

"This is very good quality," he said. "I can tell."

"I would like to offer a line of cashmere sweaters under the Hot Apparel product line."

"How big?"

"Lots of twenty. Men's and women's sizes. Two to three hundred sweaters for a bulk order."

"What's your niche?" Drake asked.

"Hot Apparel hopes to introduce brand label men's and women's clothing. It's a small collection, maybe two dozen SKUs, but the high-end offers stability to the collection and the innovative designs offer a marketing pitch to distinguish the brand."

Drake stroked his chin and looked at me slyly. "Do you ever have cabbage?"

I was hoping he would make the first move. Drake was a garment district *goniff*, a swindler from the *schmatte*, or rag trade as it's called. Many account reps surreptitiously deal in "cabbage." The term, from the Old French *cabuser* to cheat, originally referred to leftover pieces of cloth from commissioned suits that disreputable tailors made into clothes that sold at little cost to the tailor. Nowadays, the "cabbage" could be pirated designs, replicas, or outright counterfeits that looked as good as the real right down to the counterfeit brand label.

I laughed off his question. "Depends on who's interested and what they can do for me."

Drake chuckled. "I like the way you handled that. Maybe we can help each other out."

©©

My skill in working undercover came from my background as an actor as well as from years of bargaining with everything from street peddlers to white collar businessmen. Clients trusted me, and even allowed me to make deals. Usually, I was given discretionary authority to offer discounts of up to 10 percent over the standard wholesale price. This was in keeping with my cover, since so much of the business relationship involved haggling.

I continued to talk business, quoting favorable prices and huge discounts on Hot Apparel's designer apparel.

Drake smiled and handed back the sweater. "I know the owners of Raiments. I believe you already know one of them, Musa Ahmad. He imports fabric and does business with many designer brand labels here in the city. He subcontracts the manufacturing end for many small companies."

"I'd like to meet him."

"I'll be glad to introduce you." He reached into his pocket, retrieved a cell phone, and tabbed in some numbers.

"Hello, Mohammad. This is Saul Drake . . . Yes, how are you? Is Musa available? I want to talk to him."

While we waited, he looked at me and winked.

"Yes, hello. Is this Musa? Yes, it's Saul Drake. Good to talk to you. Listen, I'm having lunch with a friend of mine who's looking for a connection. His name is Frank Winston. He's starting up a line . . . Yes, that's right. He's sitting with me right now."

He handed me the phone.

"Hello, this is Frank Winston. Everyone calls me Winston."

"Pleased to meet you." A man with an accent answered. "My name is Musa Ahmad."

"I'm interested in purchasing cashmere for a line of sweaters."

"Cashmere? That's ambitious for a start-up."

"I have the cash, and the distribution is in place."

"I would be pleased to meet you. When are you available?"

"How about Monday or Tuesday?"

"Let's make it Tuesday, around nine-thirty."

"That works for me."

"Fine, Mr. Winston. I look forward to meeting you. Saul will give you the address and phone number."

While we ate, Drake schmoozed and told me about people, businesses, and fashions. I suspected he was suspicious and befriending me to keep a watch. He was an old school *macher*, or big shot in a business that had changed little since the days of the silk and spice trade, and a high level crook in the clandestine knockoff trade; seemingly respectable, yet unpredictable—and dangerous if involved in John Hwa's murder.

I asked how long he'd known Ahmad. "I've known Musa for about a year," Drake said. "I met him through the co-owners, Orlando and Pete Smith."

"Have you known the Smith brothers long?"

"About three years. They became partners with Musa about a year ago."

"Do you do much business with Raiments?"

"Musa calls from time to time with a deal. That's about it."

Drake expressed an interest in placing an order and offered me financial help, including assistance to obtain a letter of credit, if necessary.

I thanked him. I knew from experience that his offer of financial assistance might be for his sake, a ploy to implicate me as a legal defense if I did turn out to be an investigator. This tactic had been tried on me dozens of times without success.

He gave me a hearty handshake and said to call him after meeting Ahmad. I assured him I would.

# Chapter Thirteen

STELLA WAS SAVORING A cup of coffee and looked as relaxed as a lap dog on a lazy day. She looked up when I entered. Without a word, she opened a drawer, pulled out a sweater, and tossed it.

"Is this one of the sweaters?" I asked.

She nodded. "Just arrived. Stan has two more. How did it go with Drake?"

I sat at my desk and told her how I'd managed to turn the meeting to my advantage.

"So you've made an appointment to meet Ahmad," Stella quipped. "Nice work."

"Thanks." I said. "Get Stan in here."

While I waited, I examined the sweater, a man's large in black with the IG logo in superscript over the left breast. The FTC-issued number on the garment label caught my eye. I was familiar with the FTC-issued RN numbers of many big manufacturers and distributors in the area—including IG International. This number was a match. *Was the sweater genuine?*

He arrived shortly, with two sweaters under his arm. I inspected one of them. The blue sweater was a perfect replica, right down to the IG logo.

"From Musa Ahmad?"

"Right on schedule." He placed the other sweater on my desk and pulled up a chair.

"I recognized the RN number," I said. "It's a match with IG International's."

Stan nodded. "I noticed that, too. Do you think these sweaters are legit?"

"Maybe. Ahmad could easily obtain the number." I told Stan how Drake had introduced me to Ahmad.

"Wow, good work," Stan said. "Stella told me the Uncle's been murdered."

"Yes, this investigation is turning ugly, and Ahmad might be behind it."

"What about Drake?"

"He's going to get toasted. Zeckindorff has filed the seizure order by now. We'll take Angel out on this one."

I figured this seizure would be good experience for Angel. I had projects for him after this one, which would be his first in the field.

Before leaving, I decided to see if a truce could be arranged with Bull. We were rivals but had never been in a position where we were working the same case. If we continued to trade blows, the result could be disastrous for both of us.

I dialed the Madison Detective Agency and asked to be connected to Bull Boss, as he liked to be called.

"What do you want?" he bellowed. It was hard to tell if he was angry—or drunk. His speech was slightly slurred, and he was always angry.

"Calling to let you know your little trick didn't work, Bull Boss."

"Little trick, my ass! It's nothing compared to what you told Drake."

"I didn't tell him a thing. So blow it out!" Actually it was Brenda who told him, but I was having fun with my ex-boss.

"You rat bastard, I'm warning you."

"Okay, truce. I won't talk about you—you don't talk about me. Deal?"

"Yeah, we'll see," he said and hung up.

Same old Bull Boss, feisty and confrontational. At one time I found him amusing, even liked the guy; but that was before the demon rum caught up with him. I was saddened by his downfall, as well as by the stories of his dissipation. I knew alcoholism was progressive, even fatal. I said a silent prayer and hoped he would get into a program.

©©

I arrived at the law firm and found Zeckindorff waiting for me in the reception area. As soon as the elevator doors opened, he walked over and hugged me.

"What's in the plastic bag?" he asked.

"One of Ahmad's sweaters. Ahmad sent three after Stan cold called him."

"Great work!" He smiled as I handed it to him. This was the lynchpin. We had IG sweaters from every level of the distribution chain.

He usually broke into song at moments like this and began tapping a hand against his thigh and broke into a rapper's spiel.

*No borders, no boundaries*
*Are going to keep me down,*
*Cause I'm International, baby;*
*That's where I'm from.*
*I'm a ga-a-a-angsta,*
*I'm a pimp.*
*Don't take me for a simp.*
*Paid my dues,*
*Don't need no clues.*
*I'm International, baby.*
*Ga-a-a-a-angsta!*

"That's great, Brian. What do you do for an encore?"

"I'm saving that for the Gangsta. He'll be at the meeting."

We exited the building. Trying to hail a cab in Times Square is like trying to swim against a tidal wave of tourists, office workers, families with their kids.

Finally, Zeckindorff waved one down. On the ride uptown I told him about my unexpected meeting with Drake and introduction to Musa Ahmad.

"Fa-a-antastic," Zeckindorff crooned. "I'll let the FBI know. I've spoken with the ASAC. He knows about the second murder and Ahmad's possible connection."

The cab left us off at the Citicorp Center on East 53rd Street. More people. We made headway through the crowd, walked past a food court and a Modell's, and then we boarded a high-speed elevator that zoomed straight to the corporate offices on the 38th Floor.

The reception area had huge life-sized pictures of the rapper adorning the walls. In nearly every picture the rapper was wailing into a microphone and wearing jeans and an extra-extra large T-shirt with the ubiquitous IG logo.

The receptionist told us to be seated. While we waited, Zeckindorff elucidated on rap music's popularity.

"It's about revolution, about anti-establishment," he explained. "It's the modern day version of the 1960s. That's why rap music is so popular with white middle-class youth. They can't stand being white middle-class establishment."

His speech was interrupted by Caldwell, who walked towards us carrying a legal red weld folder under his arm. "Brian, good to see you."

"Ba-a-a-by." Zeckindorff stood up and shook hands.

Caldwell looked at me uncertainly. "Right, you're the investigator. Sorry, I forgot."

"No problem," I replied and shook hands.

"Zeckindorff told me the sweatshop owner has been murdered," Caldwell said.

"Yes, I spoke to the police," I said. "They believe it was in retaliation for a sweatshop strike Hwa's girlfriend arranged. The workers hated the owner who beat and cursed them."

"Let the police handle it. I want to focus on Raiments," Caldwell said.

We followed him to an opulent conference room with glass-paneled walls and lit by a dazzling crystal chandelier. A dozen double-plush, mid-back conference chairs, each with a telephone, were spaced around a twenty-foot long mahogany conference table.

Caldwell sat at the head of the table and picked up the phone next to him. He thumbed some numbers and hung up. "Gentlemen, the IG is on his way."

Zeckindorff handed him the plastic bag. "Musa Ahmad sent these sweaters."

Caldwell smiled. "That's what we've been waiting for." He took the bag, opened it, and inspected the sweater. "I'll turn these over to quality control after the meeting. Anything new on Ahmad?"

"I set up an undercover visit," I said.

Before another word could be spoken, the International Gangster walked into the conference room.

He was shorter in person. Nonetheless, I could see why his fans went crazy. The rapper had an unmistakable presence, like a mystical aura. He walked lithely on the balls of his feet. His long black hair was woven into dreadlocks that reached to muscular shoulders. He was wearing a leather tank top with the IG logo in the center. I recognized the denim jeans the rapper was wearing from the IG International clothing line.

"*Ayo,* gang-staah," Zeckindorff gushed. "Number one with a Bullet. All over it, yo!"

"Got that right, *fa'sho,*" the IG laughed.

Zeckindorff rose from his seat and extended his hand, the fingers closed into a fist. The IG reciprocated, closed his hand into a fist, and lightly tapped against Zeckindorff's in a fist-to-fist greeting or *pound.*

The IG looked at me suspiciously. "Who's the *busta?*"

I knew a *busta* in gangsta speak is a crybaby bitch.

"Theo Jones, he's the heat, a corporate detective," Zeckindorff said.

"*Boo-ya,* so you're the heat!" The IG extended his fist. I rose slightly from my seat, leaned forward, and gave the rapper a pound.

The IG sat next to Caldwell. "Show me," he snapped and held out his hand.

Caldwell opened up a red weld folder and pulled out the sweater sent by Detective Harney and placed it into the IG's outstretched hand. Next, he removed the sweater from the plastic bag and handed it over.

"Check 'em out," Zeckindorff said.

The rapper frowned and angrily tossed them to the floor. "This is gutter!"

The IG seemed to swell in size before my eyes. He slammed his fist on the table. To my surprise, Caldwell and Zeckindorff were unfazed.

"Major *dis*. I don't mind pimpin,' but not on my turf, dig? What's the name of these outfits?"

"Asian Seas, a sweatshop, and the distributor is Raiments," Zeckindorff said. "I got 'em sewed up."

"Yo, I want to be in the mix!" The IG roared and slammed his fist again. The table reverberated.

Zeckindorff tried to calm the agitated rapper. "Nigga, please, I'm the spin doctor on this gig," he said in a street drawl.

For one brief moment, the IG appeared to be ready to jump up and take a swing at him, but instead started laughing.

"Nigga *puh-leaze*. Did you hear that? This white boy is good. You should take a lesson in rapspeak from him before I fire ya white ass."

Caldwell shrugged. "It's all Greek to me."

"I represent many rappers," Zeckindorff said. "Kid Delicious, Baby Cool, Brother Thug, and a dozen scribes."

The IG smiled, clearly impressed by his clientele list. "You represent Kid Delicious? No way, don't jerk me."

"Known the Kid from day one."

I could see why Zeckindorff had so many rapper clients.

"Major cool." The IG grinned. "We gonna do some serious business."

Zeckindorff gave the IG the rundown on the seizure of Drake's and the possible connection to the murders, as well as the half-million in knockoff inventory at Asian Seas.

The rapper was annoyed and shook his head—but he exploded when the FBI was mentioned.

"The Feds are in the scene!" He jumped up and screamed, "Why the fuck wasn't I told 'bout this shit."

The irate rapper moved to the left, shifted quickly to the right as he ranted about the FBI and the danger to his clothing empire. It was as if he were performing on a stage. All he needed was a microphone.

The IG walked back to the table and slammed his fist on the table. He was standing next to Caldwell. Without warning, he slapped him on the side of the head. Caldwell yelped and jumped up from his seat.

Zeckindorff jumped in and calmed the nearly out-of-control

rapper. "Yo, keep it clean."

It was like a *Three Stooges* routine, with the rapper playing Moe, Caldwell playing Curly. That left Zeckindorff playing Larry. IG tried slapping Caldwell again and at one point roared, "You're such shit, I ought to fire you."

"Go ahead," Caldwell spat back. He rubbed the side of his head. "Let's see what the management at Premier Financial Equities thinks. I'm getting sick and tired of bailing you out."

"Bailing me out!" The IG made a move toward Caldwell, but Zeckindorff intervened, grabbing the rapper's arm. I rose from my seat, prepared to shield Caldwell if a fight broke out.

"Let's go in the other room." He escorted the rap star out of the conference room. Caldwell tried to follow, but he stopped him. "I need to talk to my man, here . . . Stay cool. We'll be right back."

I was left behind with Caldwell. "You all right?"

"Yeah, I'm fine." The young attorney straightened his tie and smoothed the hair where the IG had smacked him.

We both sat. The ferocity of the IG's outburst left both of us speechless. An odd silence filled the room. I didn't know what to say and presumed Caldwell was in the same predicament.

"So how long have you been in this business?" he finally asked, breaking the silence.

I doubted if he cared, but was making small talk. I told him I opened up my detective agency twenty years ago.

"Twenty years, nice. Is most of your work trademark counterfeiting?"

"Yes," I replied. "What's the word on the anti-counterfeiting unit?"

"We're working on it. My boss is putting the funding together."

Before I could say another word, Zeckindorff returned. He told Caldwell the IG wanted to speak to him alone in the hallway.

Caldwell looked puzzled but rose from his seat and walked past Zeckindorff, who held the door open and gave him a complimentary smile as he passed. Then Zeckindorff closed the door and walked quickly to the table and sat down.

Something big was happening. I looked at Zeckindorff, whose eyebrows arched upwards in a knowing manner.

A few seconds passed.

"You BITCH! PIMPHEAD! I'll make you cry!"

The IG was yelling so loudly I feared for Caldwell's safety. I rose and would have gone into the corridor to help, but Zeckindorff waved me off, motioned for me to remain seated. I sat back down.

The quiet was broken by a string of angry, demanding words from the IG. I couldn't make out what was being said but didn't need an explanation.

A minute or two passed before Caldwell returned to the room. His face was flushed like he had had sex. He slowly exhaled, before sitting.

"I guess you heard that little exchange out in the corridor," he said, embarrassed.

"Yeah, kinda." Zeckindorff knew the payoff was coming. He fixed him in a steely gaze.

"The sweater you brought will be examined. If it's fake, The IG wants the seizure order against Raiments filed. I'll be your main contact."

© ©

Zeckindorff hailed a cab. We jumped in and headed downtown to 4 Times Square. I chided him for his street drawl, telling him how foolish it was. He was unfazed.

"Theo, the legal business is all about clients. Getting them, keeping them happy, and billing. I represent more rappers than any other lawyer. You know why? "

"Because you can talk like you grew up in the projects."

"That's a gimmick, a secret language. I've never met a rapper who wasn't knowledgeable about copyright law. "

"I thought Leon Owen was a felon with a third-grade education."

"He is. But you talk about music piracy, fair use, copying— and surprise!—he knows so much he could give lectures."

I should have guessed as much.

He changed the subject. "The IG is scared to death of the FBI."

"I can see why," I replied. "I read in the newspaper that he may be indicted for getting into a shooting match with a rival rapper. He's probably facing weapons and assault charges."

"That has nothing to do with it—nothing!"

"Nothing? Are you kidding?"

He laughed at my naiveté. "You have so much to learn about the rap underground."

"I guess I do."

"Gun play and run-ins with the police are all part of the hype. Look at 50 Cent and Lil' Kim. Both of them are facing gun charges. When they're released, they're going to break the law again. The violent lifestyle is worth millions of dollars in publicity. It's business."

"So why is the IG afraid of the FBI?"

"Because now we're talking about intellectual property and branding. The publicity surrounding an FBI investigation and the murders would hurt the IG brand label. The IG understands all this. That's what he was ranting and raving about in the conference room, and that's why he smacked Caldwell."

Now it all made sense. The IG was in a fury over the FBI for the same reason that a client of Asian Seas, probably Raiments, broke up the strike at Asian Seas. It was all about bad business and negative publicity.

"The IG doesn't like Caldwell."

"Hates him."

"Can't the IG fire Caldwell?"

"I doubt it . . . Caldwell is the watchdog for the corporate eyes pumping millions of dollars into making the IG a superstar."

"One last question," I said. "Caldwell said the IG authorized the seizure at Raiments."

Zeckindorff shrugged. "Technically speaking, the IG is also the CEO. He had to give his approval anyway, especially with the FBI involved."

I sat back and tried to relax. The IG was shrewder than I realized. I thought he was a clown, but underneath his banter was a sharp businessman defending his turf.

I told Zeckindorff about Bull and National Wholesale. He shrugged it off. "Premier Financial Equities bought the company two days ago. When the in-house piracy unit is established, that will be the end of Bull."

# Chapter Fourteen

I WOKE UP EARLY, unusual for a Saturday. I showered and dressed while Linda slept. The morning sun filtered through the bedroom window. I looked professional in a blue business suit and tie for the International AntiCounterfeiting Coalition (IACC) convention being held in the New York Hilton. This was a must-attend event for anyone involved in the war against the counterfeits.

I parked on the street and walked to the Hilton. Inside, a throng of bellmen, businessmen, families, and tourists were crowded around the check-in. I walked past, moving slowly on the plush blue carpeting. Near the concierge was a video monitor with the location of the day's events. The IACC was on the second floor.

The floor was packed with conference attendees. I spotted familiar faces, mostly people who worked for companies I had done work for.

The day's agenda started with an address by the IACC president, who discussed the IACC's founding in 1979 by Levi Strauss and other companies with a counterfeiting problem. The main speaker was a United States Trade Representative who talked about the counterfeiting problem in other countries, a big concern for everyone.

I found Zeckindorff during intermission. "Ba-a-a-aby," he crooned and hugged me. We sat on a lounge chair. Conference attendees were milling around us.

"Caldwell called and said the FBI appointment is for Monday at ten-thirty," Zeckindorff said. "Can you make it?"

"No problem," I said.

"Meet us at the FBI's field office in Newark on Centre Street. Oh, yes, Caldwell sent me an e-mail last night and said the anti-counterfeiting unit will be up and running next week."

"I thought they were going to wait," I said.

"Never trust an attorney." Zeckindorff laughed. "It's Caldwell's boss. He doesn't want to wait another minute."

"Will I be continuing in the investigation?"

"For now," Zeckindorff said.

I nodded. "Maybe Raiments and Ahmad can be linked to the IG sweaters at Asian Seas."

"I'm sure the police would love to—but how? The business records at Asian Seas have been shredded. If the sample Ahmad sends matches, there's a connection to the sweatshop. That might be enough to arrest Ahmad and the Smith brothers, but I doubt if either of them will do jail time."

I told him there might be another way. "Ahmad would never tell the police he placed the order for the Asian Seas sweaters. But he might tell an undercover investigator."

He was silent for a moment. "Sounds dangerous. I know you're meeting Ahmad, but these guys could be killers. Look, Theo, the IG sweater Ahmad sent may be enough. If it's fake, I'll execute an immediate civil seizure. We may seize business documents that will prove a wide-spread counterfeiting operation."

"Brian, I'm only asking you to let me and my investigators infiltrate and snoop."

He stroked his chin. "Fine by me, but if you don't mind my asking, how do you and your investigators line up a company?"

"Simple. Most counterfeiters run a legit business. If someone calls them on the phone and offers to do business, he can't refuse. That would be suspicious. After that, we steer the deal making."

We parted. I decided to have lunch in the Horsemen's Lounge in the lobby. I sat at a booth and ordered a turkey sandwich and a Budweiser.

I heard an unexpected voice from behind, one I preferred to forget.

"Found your Christmas shopping?"

It was Bull, my old partner. I should have known he would be at the convention. "How are you, Bull Boss?"

"Fine." He sat next to me.

"Have a seat, why don't you?" I said sarcastically.

He looked unkempt, and I suspected he had slept in the black sport coat and gray slacks he was wearing, likely after a drinking bout.

"Thought I spotted you. How've you been, Theo?"

"Can't complain. How's the Madison Agency been doing?" I was baiting him. I knew business was bad and suspected that Bull, who was usually not that friendly, was hoping to pump me for information on my investigation into Drake Fashion.

"Fine, fine. We're getting new clients all the time."

I knew it was a cover-up; business had been sliding downhill for years. I felt sorry for him because National Wholesale would no longer need his services.

He ordered a shot of whiskey and a chaser, and I could see desperation in his eyes. I remembered the old Bull, an ex-policeman who was once a fine investigator. After decades of displaying a badge and demanding answers, most ex-policemen made poor private investigators; but he had the gift of gab and could talk his way through most doors. Much of what I learned about the field I learned from him.

"To your health—" Bull said, downing the whiskey and ordering a refill.

"How's Marty? Is he with the agency?"

"Marty? No, he retired several months ago."

"He was a great guy."

"The best," he replied and went to work on the refill. "Kind of like you, until you ran off with our clients."

"Hey, now don't go spoiling things," I shot back. "You were doing fine."

Bull's cheek twitched, a sign he was agitated.

He never forgave me for leaving the Madison. But he had no one to blame but himself. His stupidity forced me to go into business for myself.

© ©

I was with the Madison Detective Agency for two years. Trademark counterfeiting was an entirely new field. On one memorable assignment, Bull sent me into an apparel manufacturer without any cover. I tried to scam a manager, who listened to me for about three minutes before pushing me out the door. The investigation was blown, and I took the blame.

I vowed never to be humiliated again. I had my own business cards printed up and told people I was new to the apparel business and anxious to learn. Within a few months I had learned about import-export, FOBs, letters of credit, standard discounting practices, and quantity buying.

One day, after crap from Bull, I resigned. I called the clients I was working for, and as a matter of professional courtesy, told them I was leaving, and another investigator would be taking over. Most of the clients would not hear of it; they wanted me to continue the investigations. Shortly afterwards, I founded the Chameleon Detective Agency.

© ©

Bull polished off his drink and ordered another.

"Aren't you going heavy on the sauce?"

"Maybe I am. What do you care?" he huffed.

"You underestimate me, Bull. You gave me my first job and taught me. I'd like to help."

"That's decent of you to own up. Cheers." He downed the shot and was growing bleary eyed.

"You're so high-minded and all, Theo. I can't believe you'd turn against me."

"Come on, lighten up. I'm here for you, if you need help, Bull. You have a business and a career."

He slowly let out a breath. The smell of liquor, hot and musty, made me wince.

"If you're trying to do a seizure at Drake's, be careful." His voice rose and his eyes narrowed. He was trying to intimidate me, but I wasn't falling for any of it.

"Goddamn you!" I shot back. "You don't even know what you're talking about."

"Yes, I do. You're in too deep on this one, because Drake's into something deeper than you can handle. Do you know what I mean?"

"Christ, you've been drinking too much. You give me the creeps."

Something demonic flashed in his eyes. "Mark my words, smart guy. Drake is into something big, real big! So be careful."

A surge of fear swept through me. *What's he referring to? Is he threatening me?* Whatever the answer, this was not the man I once knew.

I reached into my wallet for a twenty, dropped it on the table and left.

# Chapter Fifteen

ON MONDAY I TOOK the New Jersey Turnpike from Hoboken to the exit for Newark. I travelled through the downtown area heading for the FBI field office and parked on Centre Street.

I entered Claremont Towers, showed my identification to the guard. He was surrounded by a state-of-the-art CCTV surveillance system, located behind him, and a digital camera for issuing IDs. He positioned me in front of the camera. My picture was printed onto an identification label and placed on my suit lapel.

In the twelfth-floor lobby I faced an imposing wood-paneled wall. An attractive brunette glanced at me from behind a receptionist window in the center. I stepped forward, introduced myself, and told her I wanted to see ASAC Tom Richardson.

As she dialed the number, I peered past her. Not much to see; the architect had anticipated snooping eyes.

"Tom is coming right out." She told me to enter through the door to the left.

A man with thinning hair emerged from what I thought was an office. He would have looked milquetoast—except for the shoulder holster and gun.

"Pleased to meet you, I'm Tom Richardson. The other two are already here."

I followed him through a layout that could have been mistaken for a typical business office where men and women sat at desks and typed into personal computers. We went into a large conference room. A round curved-end oak wood table took up much of the available space. Zeckindorff and Caldwell were seated next to each other.

"Ba-a-a-by," Zeckindorff said. "You're just in time."

Richardson sat at the head of the table, a pen and legal pad positioned in front of him. An IG sweater was in the center of the table. He picked it up and fingered the IG logo.

"You were referred by Detective Chris Harney," Zeckindorff said. "Known him long?"

"I've known Chris for years." Richardson smiled. "I used to be with the New York City field office and helped him on a big drug case."

He turned to me. "I was told you've identified the manufacturer and the owners."

"Yes, it's a company called Raiments," I said. "One of the owners is Musa Ahmad. The other owners are brothers, both ex-cons."

Richardson nodded. "I'm interested in Musa Ahmad because of his Middle Eastern background. Brian told me you've set up an appointment with him."

"I'll be meeting him tomorrow morning."

"That's what I like to hear. I'll want to see you after the meeting. Find out how big the knockoff operation is, how many people are involved."

He put down the sweater and picked up the legal pad. I told him about Stan's cold call with Ahmad and my introduction through Saul Drake.

"So Ahmad says he does business in source countries like Pakistan and India?" Richardson asked, as he took notes.

I nodded. "That's what he told my investigator."

"You think this guy is a terrorist?" Zeckindorff asked.

"That's what I intend to find out," Richardson said. "I'll be focusing on Raiments and Ahmad. Chris, who has no jurisdiction in New Jersey, will focus on Asian Seas and the murders. I'll let you handle Drake's department store. In fact, the judge has already signed the seizure order, hasn't he?"

"Yes, he has," Zeckindorff said. "I'm assembling a team of U.S. Marshals for backup."

"Good." Richardson turned to Caldwell. "Zeckindorff said you're inspecting IG sweaters from Raiments."

"That's right."

"And if they're a match, Raiments could be presumed to be at the center of the counterfeiting chain."

"That would be correct," Caldwell said. "If you don't mind my asking, who's on the task force?"

"Other FBI agents, as well as agents from U.S. Customs and select police officers from Newark and Jersey City."

"What about the murders?" Zeckindorff asked.

"The knockoffs may have nothing to do with them," Richardson said. "Chris believes it's in retaliation for his girlfriend's organizing a strike. So far, we don't have much on Ahmad and the Smith brothers. I could arrest them on a charge of trademark counterfeiting at the department store and the interstate transportation of counterfeit apparel, but the criminal case isn't strong. If I arrest them, the ex-cons might not even draw a sentence—and Ahmad would walk. That's why I want to join forces."

Richardson was relying on Zeckindorff's ongoing investigation to pave the way. He was familiar with the 1984 Act and said the FBI would be the backup when the Raiments seizure was executed. Richardson would arrest Ahmad and the Smith brothers when the *ex parte* seizure— seizure without notice to the defendant—was executed and question them. If the seized business records tied Raiments to the five-hundred-thousand dollar shipment sitting in Asian Seas, criminal charges could be brought against the owners.

Richardson resumed taking notes, but stopped writing when I mentioned that Ahmad might be alerted once the department store seizure was executed.

Richardson's forehead creased. "If Ahmad suspects either of you are PIs, you'd be in real danger. When are you planning on executing the department store seizure?"

"On Wednesday or Thursday," Zeckindorff said.

"How about the Raiments seizure?" he asked.

Zeckindorff turned to Caldwell. "I can't file the seizure until the sweaters have been inspected."

"That's right," Caldwell said. "We have to prove they're counterfeit."

"Make it quick," Richardson said. "National security might be involved. Gentlemen, our country is at war! We need to execute the Raiments seizure this week, if at all possible. I don't want any harm coming to Theo or his investigators."

"Don't worry about him," Zeckindorff said. He reached over and patted my shoulder. "The only person who could warn Ahmad is Saul Drake—and he's in big trouble. After we execute the seizure, Harney intends to question Drake about the murders and tell him he'll be arrested unless he cooperates."

I nodded and said, "Besides, I lost a brother in 9/11. I can't turn down a chance to nail a terrorist, even a suspected terrorist."

"Sorry to hear about your loss," Richardson said.

"I'm so sorry," Zeckindorff said. "I didn't know you had a brother."

"He was heading for work in the North Tower and never arrived," I said. "This investigation is personal."

"You'll have your chance to nail Ahmad," he said. "We're a team now. I want to meet tomorrow after you visit Ahmad. I'm gambling you'll find the evidence I need to nail him and the others."

Richardson walked us to the elevator. We split up after leaving Claremont Towers. I thought Caldwell would say something about the new anti-counterfeiting unit, but he jumped into his Cadillac and left without a word.

Zeckindorff insisted on walking me back to my car. The usually ebullient attorney was surprisingly quiet and appeared to be in one of his dark moods.

"That's too bad about your brother," he said.

"A lot of misery got passed around on 9/11," I replied. "His body was never recovered."

"You should have told me. I have contacts, important contacts. I might have been able to help."

"That's nice to know."

"I mean it. If you get into a jam like that, let me know. We're more than business associates. At least I hope we are."

"Thanks, Brian." I was embarrassed by this mixture of frustration and sympathy coming from this hardass attorney. I had never heard him express sympathy for anyone, including me.

He gave me a hearty hug and then got into his Mercedes and departed.

# Chapter Sixteen

I HAD CALLED LINDA and told her to eat dinner without waiting for me. The sky was faded gray when I arrived in Hoboken.

I opened the front door and paused. *Something's wrong.* I knew it right away. Linda's voice echoed down the corridor from the living room. I hurried down the corridor and stopped at the entrance. She was seated on the couch with Josh, her audience, sitting on the rug. Her hand was wobbly. Eyes looked wild. I had never seen her like this before.

*What happened?*

Unaware of the trouble, Josh jumped up from the couch. "Daddy!" he whooped and ran to greet me.

"Hi, tiger." I did a complete turnaround with the youngster in my arms, before setting him down.

"Honey, is everything all right?"

No answer.

"Did you hear me?"

She started shaking. Without a word, she rose and walked past me and into the kitchen. I got just a glimpse of her face, enough to see she was disturbed. *But what?*

"Josh, wait here," I said, trying not to sound alarmed.

I walked out of the room—and then rushed into the kitchen.

She was standing next to the microwave, with her back to me, and sobbing.

"Honey?"

She turned to face me, eyes watery. She was terrified. I took her in my arms and held her close. "It's all right," I said softly.

It was disturbingly like a climax in a play. No action, no dialogue. Her sobs breaking the silence in the room.

"Whenever you're ready," I said, trying to give her space.

Slowly she exhaled. "About five minutes ago I got a crank call."

I cursed and tried to hug her, but she assured me she was fine.

"It was such a shock. A recording! That's what it was. It mentioned you by name."

"A recording? Are you sure?"

"It was—terrible sounding . . . I don't know how else to describe it."

She did her best to mimic the voice and message.

*You're dead, Theo. Revenge! Motherfucker, I'll get you!*

I had to act quickly. First, I had to secure the perimeter, protect the house. To do that, I needed privacy. "Linda, go into the other room. Stay with Josh, while I make a call."

"Theo?" She hesitated.

"Go, now! I have to make a call."

She left the kitchen. I used my cell phone to call Stella at home.

"Stella, emergency! I need you in Hoboken to guard my family."

"Lordy, what's up?"

"Linda received a threatening phone call. She's shook up."

"Oh, no! Any idea who?"

"None. She said it was a recording."

"A recording? You mean a tape-recorded voice?"

"I think so. She said the voice was disguised. Hideous sounding."

"Maybe a voice scrambler was used," she said. "I wonder how he got your number?"

That was the question racing through my mind. "No idea. Let's talk about it when I see you."

"What time do you need me?"

"Early, before six."

"I'll be there."

Linda was sitting on the sofa with Josh, an arm placed protectively around his shoulder. I beckoned for her to return to the kitchen. She moved slowly, as if in a trance. After she had taken a seat, I told her Stella was coming to guard the house.

"Theo, is it that bad?" She ran her fingers nervously over her lips.

"I can't take a chance. We've been working with a security consultant, one of the best. I'll call him."

"What about the police?"

I told her we had had crank calls at the office—and used the police. "They asked questions about our investigations, contacted our clients without our knowledge, and did little."

"How about the telephone company?"

"I want Ray Mohanis to handle this. He's a former NYPD security technician."

I went into the living room, retrieved the number using caller ID, and returned to the kitchen. "Does this number sound familiar? It's a 717 area code—that's near Philadelphia. Is 717-655-0999 familiar?"

"I don't know anyone in Philadelphia."

I held her hand and shared a quiet moment. "The caller could be a college student. Most of the Internet pirates we pursue are college kids. They upload and download bootleg software and music. It's all we can do to keep up with them. Many of them have high IQs and backgrounds in computers and electronics."

"You think a kid is doing this?"

I nodded. "Could be. Most of them are skilled hackers and target law enforcement and Defense Department computer systems."

She was assuaged to know that a college kid might be the culprit. "Is he dangerous?"

"Maybe. That's why I want Stella here. I'll call the security consultant. Don't worry, we'll catch this nut."

We talked quietly for another half hour. Linda said she had been reading *Peter Pan* aloud to Josh when the phone rang. I was walking down the block at the time. *Was someone watching the house?*

Linda excused herself to put Josh to bed. I followed them upstairs and checked the windows for signs of entry. Outside, everything appeared peaceful. No sign a caller or anyone else was watching the house.

I went downstairs to the kitchen. Minutes later, she joined me.

"Honey, I want you to go to sleep. I'll be upstairs soon."

"I'm not sleepy."

I insisted and finally persuaded her. I switched the timer on the microwave and heated up the meatloaf. I tried to eat but was too angry to finish.

Someone had invaded my privacy and hurt my wife. Whoever it was had spent time to track me down and record his message. *A disguised voice.* What was that all about?

At eleven, I went upstairs. I opened Josh's door a crack. Fast asleep. I went into the master bedroom where Linda was lying in bed.

"Theo?" I heard her voice in the dark.

I fumbled for the lamp on the dresser. She had a pillow curled under her head. I sat next to her on the bed.

"Everything's fine," I said. "Josh is asleep. Don't answer the phone tomorrow. I'll call your cell phone if I need to reach you."

She sat up, swung her legs over the side of the bed. "Why don't you stay home? I can call in sick."

"I have to go to the office." I didn't want to tell her about my meeting with Ahmad or the FBI's interest in the investigation.

"Can't it wait?" She looked pensive.

"No. I have to warn the staff and call the security consultant. That's why I need Stella here."

She nodded. "When I picked up the phone . . . and heard that voice, I thought it was the same voice I heard in my dream. A voice of death."

Now I understood why she was so afraid. Her dream. The shrouds and the prediction of my death. She said it was the same voice—*identical.*

Although I hadn't heard the voice, I felt haunted, as if the supernatural was at work. It was uncanny how the caller had hit upon something so terrifying. *Can the caller reach into the depth of my soul? Uncover my darkest fear?*

"Is that why you were so upset?" I asked.

"Yes. I thought you were going to die."

"Baby, no. Don't even think something like that." I held her closer.

For one frozen moment, I remembered everything—from the 2001 terrorist attack to the day I was thirteen years old and Dad was gone. In a mind's instant, the faces of generations of Jones men passed before me.

©©

I remembered when Dad took me and my brother George to the Lonely Creek Cemetery, about a twenty-minute drive from our home in Deer Park, Long Island. I knew that Grandpa and several great grandpas were buried here. Other than that, the cemetery was never discussed. That was fine with me. I was young and had no reason to think about dead relatives.

I remember it was a hot summer day, great for baseball and going with friends to Carvel's for ice cream afterwards. George and I sat on the back seat while Dad drove the Ford station wagon. We got stuck in traffic on the Long Island Expressway. Hardly a surprise. Everyone was heading for the beach. I wondered why Dad had picked this day to take us to the cemetery, as if there was a special reason. It turned out there was.

He parked, and we got out and started walking. I had never been to a lawn cemetery and felt dwarfed by the vastness of its green grass and rows of engraved headstones.

We came to the Jones family garden and saw eight graves. Our father, whose name was Pete, said a prayer. Then he pointed to one of the headstones.

"This is where your great-grandfather, Matthew Jones, is buried. He died during World War I in the battle for Belleau Wood. His body was sent home on a ship."

He pointed to the headstone next to it. "This is your grandfather, Samuel Jones." Dad lowered his head for a moment of silence. "He was killed in a Kentucky coal mine accident, and his body was sent here by rail."

Grandpa, who died when I was four, was a distant memory. Shortly after his death, the family relocated back to Long Island. I had not thought about him until today.

As Dad continued, I began to feel queasy. I looked at George, standing rigidly, as his lips tightened. Death had not come easy for the men in the Jones family. Even sadder, the genealogy was not only violent but young, before the age of fifty. Grandpa had made it to age forty-six, and it dawned on me as I stood under the hot sun that Dad was the same age.

His voice faltered at one point, his eyes lingering on the reserved plots. In horror, I realized these were for us. I wanted to flee and never look back. But I couldn't. Instead, I stood transfixed. He said a final prayer; after that we walked back to the car. Two weeks later, he was killed when the scaffolding of the building he was working on collapsed.

Fear of an early death haunted me after Dad died. I rebelled by skipping classes, listening to the occult and horror-inspired lyrics of Ozzy Osbourne and Black Sabbath, and experimenting with drugs. Fortunately, I discovered acting, which became a constructive outlet to explore my inner turmoil.

I was inspired by the imagination of the Romantic poets—Keats, Shelley, Lord Byron—who all died young. I was intrigued by the Spanish poet Federico García Lorca, who was obsessed with an early, violent death.

I remembered one verse, in particular:

*When the pure shapes sank*
*Under the chirping of daisies,*
*I knew they had murdered me.*

Lorca must have had a vision or a portent of his own death.

In 1936, during the Spanish Civil War, Lorca was arrested by the Fascists. Tortured and executed, his body was never found

George distanced himself after visiting the cemetery. He looked down on my acting as a childish pursuit. Athletic and studious, he eventually received an MBA and became an insurance executive. He never married, possibly, I believe, because he didn't want anyone close to him—if the end came.

I didn't believe George's death was a coincidence, not with our family history. I was ready to believe supernatural forces were at work. I remembered Lorca's poem and found it spooky that my brother's body was never discovered, buried under enough metal and mortar to reach the sky.

I briefly considered selling my detective agency and getting into a less dangerous line of work. But somehow, I didn't see the revival of my acting career, such as it was, as a viable option, not with a family to support. Besides, I didn't think I had it in me to face those damned casting calls. Half the population of Manhattan Island showed up for parts that pay squat and have a single spoken line.

Maybe I didn't love being a PI—the long boring nights in my car, chasing after street peddlers, endless hours behind the computer—but I was good at it, very good, and no asshole casting director could cut me off in mid-sentence, with an insincere "Thank you. Next!" It never came to that anyway, not after Linda's premonition. I suspected my father and brother had premonitions of impending death. I knew how they felt, yet I refused to be resigned to that fate.

©©

Linda interrupted me. "Theo, you're scared, aren't you?" Maybe she sensed what was racing through my thoughts.

"A little," I said, trying to be honest.

"I'm scared, too."

"Let's not talk about it anymore." I was anxious to end the discussion.

I tried to sleep, but it was impossible. I wondered if I had been wrong about Hwa's killer. Were they behind this weird call? Then I realized a killer would never alert an intended victim. No, he'd simply go ahead and kill.

Around four o'clock, I got up, took a quick shower, and dressed. Downstairs I turned on the coffee maker, filled a cup, and moved to the living room for a view of Garden Street. Everything was quiet, not even the sound of early birds chirping.

While I waited, I tried to get a handle on the caller. Maybe the call was meant for me—maybe not. Was someone watching the house, following me? Would he target my family to get to me? And why?

Outside, I heard footsteps. Someone was walking up the block.

It was Stella!

She was early. I opened the door and hugged her. "Stella, am I glad to see you."

She looked different—not like the Stella who had stared down a street peddler wielding a baseball bat or wrestled another street peddler to the ground and held him until the backup could arrest him. Her eyes were tired and her cheeks puffy, and I wondered if she had stayed up all night, filled with worry for me and my family.

She was dressed in jeans and a jacket. After a hug, we went into the kitchen, and I poured her a cup of coffee.

"Are Linda and Josh all right?"

"They're asleep." I poured another cup for myself.

She drank coffee and listened as I told her about the call, timed a few minutes before I arrived home. Her eyes widened at the obvious connection.

"Do you think someone's following you?"

"He might be," I conceded, although I had been vigilant to safeguard my family.

She set down the cup and said she was impressed by the caller's research skill. The creep had to have spent hours accessing my personal information. The house, utilities, and phone were registered in the name of Jack Bell, Linda's father. As far as anyone knew, I was renting the house.

I changed the subject. "I haven't mentioned anything about my meeting with the FBI."

"Oh, she doesn't know."

"No. Now is not the right time to tell her."

"What time are you meeting Ahmad?"

"Nine-thirty. I'll be travelling to Whittier."

She bit her lip. "Theo, be careful."

# Chapter Seventeen

I DROVE DOWN THE New Jersey Turnpike, heading south for the Route 55 exit, better known as Veterans Memorial Highway. This took me southwest to the Delaware Valley. The landscape gradually changed from urban to rural, from row houses to deer grazing by the side of the highway.

Whittier was a hamlet, with a handful of single-story buildings and a post office flanking one end. I zipped through in a heartbeat, took a long drive up a steep hill, and parked when I had reached the top. I walked to the crest and felt dwarfed by the majestic mountains surrounding the Valley. The sweet pine scent of conifer trees was refreshing. The highway snaked into the distance, with homes dotting the landscape. I spotted a gas station far away in the distance.

An access road branched off from the highway to Raiments, a one-story brick building located at the base of a hill. The company name was visible in large block letters on a large sign. To the right of the entrance were two recessed loading bays for trucks.

Judging from the size of the main building, I guessed Raiments was using one or more offsite warehouses. I counted twenty-five cars in the parking area. I called the main number on my cell phone and asked to speak to Musa Ahmad. After a short pause, "This is Musa. Is this Winston?"

I recognized the accent. "I'm at the top of the hill. I believe Raiments is at the bottom, off to the right."

"That's us. See you soon."

It was nearly nine o'clock when I called Frank Mohanis, figuring he'd be in his office.

"Frank, its Theo." I told him about the recorded death threats.

"Recorded death threats? God, this guy is a weirdo."

"What's his game? What does he want?"

"Sounds like the caller is taunting you. Can you get me a copy of the message?"

"No, I got the number he used. Can you catch him?"

Frank paused. "My guess is he's using a throwaway cell phone. It's nearly impossible to identify the caller."

"I use throwaway cell phones myself. I have a stock of ten in the office."

"Maybe I can locate the store where the caller bought the phone or the location where the call was made. That's not much to go on. When did he leave the message?"

I hesitated, before telling him the call was made minutes before I opened the door. *Was someone following me? Watching the house?*

Frank agreed it was possible. "I'd like to drop by your home and perform a security check."

"Come around six. I'll have Linda take Josh for a walk."

© ©

After retiring from the NYPD, Frank started a security business. I hired him after receiving a letter death threat eight years ago. He sent it and the envelope to a forensics lab for fingerprints and installed a security alarm on the office windows. A year later, I picked up one of the scam lines and was blasted by someone on the other end shouting obscenities and threatening to kill me. Frank installed recorders.

I hung up and continued driving, trying to stay focused and trying to forget, for the moment, that my family was in danger.

I entered the parking area, found a vacant spot, and

walked towards the front entrance with my portfolio briefcase. Everything about Raiments looked respectable; one would hardly suspect skullduggery. I walked up to the front door and searched for a buzzer. Finding none, I turned the doorknob, walked through, and found myself in a display room that resembled a scene from the Arabian nights with thousands of fabrics, prints, and woven designs in an endless cornucopia of colors and textures. The bolts of fabric were stacked on shelves lining the walls separated by dividers.

A young man with a dark mustache and olive complexion sat behind a desk. He was wearing chinos and a sports shirt. A tape measure dangled around his neck.

"May I help you?"

"I have an appointment with Mr. Ahmad."

He smiled and stood. "Are you Mr. Frank Winston?"

"Everyone calls me Winston."

"I am Mohammad, one of Mr. Ahmad's assistants."

"Why don't you show me some fabrics before I meet him?"

"Glad to." Mohammad introduced me to his assistant, Harasha, a shy young woman sitting on a stool and partially hidden from view. She had a red dot in the center of her forehead and was cutting fabric with a scissors on a cutting board. She smiled and resumed work.

Mohammad gave me a quick rundown of the fabrics available to the walk-in clients: silks, cottons, and blends, available in myriad patterns and colors. He told Harasha to bring over a chenille print.

The young girl rose and removed a bolt. Harasha walked quietly, conscious of my eyes on her, and handed it to him.

"Feel this." Mohammad smiled, urging me to touch the golden white fabric. The cloth had a light satiny feel.

"Guess how much?" He was testing me, eyes bright with anticipation.

I quoted a price per yard that was surprisingly close. Mohammad seemed pleased and said it was a big seller, imported from Pakistan.

"Most of the outlets in Pakistan are small mom-and-pop, aren't they?" I wanted to pump him about Raiments' overseas connections.

"Yes, we do business with many small companies in Pakistan, as well as India and Bangladesh."

"I've done business with companies in those countries. Who do you work with?"

"You'll have to ask Musa."

I followed Mohammand to the back. He opened a large fireproof safety door. We entered into the Raiments warehouse.

Fabric dust was so thick it clogged my breathing. Stacked were hundreds of huge cylindrical rolls of fabric, each bigger than a man and held together by a band of wire in the middle. There were too many to count; some were stacked by the loading dock, others lined up next to a fabric spreader.

Two men, part of a four-man team wearing dust masks, were working on a roll of blue fabric and stretching it out onto the fabric spreader. I recognized the spread-end cutter system with its computerized cutter and pneumatic clamp, which pulled the fabric down an eighteen-foot-long table. One man operated the cutter, while another, the final man in the team, folded up the cloth and prepared it for delivery.

I noticed a pallet with boxes ready for shipment stationed on a forklift. A large burly man with a clipboard was instructing the driver. As we approached, I noticed a scar on his left check, identical to Jenny's description of her attacker. *This has to be the killer.* He spotted us and looked me over. "Is that him?" he growled.

Mohammad tried to humor him. "Now, Bruno, this is a client."

He spat in my direction. "You causin' trouble?"

Bruno was big and ugly like a soiled mop. He was obviously expecting someone—me.

"Tell that ape to back down," I said coolly.

"Who you callin' an ape!" He walked up to me, close enough to smell his breath, pungent and sour.

"You know who—" I looked directly into his eyes without giving ground. A fight might have erupted—if Musa Ahmad hadn't intervened.

"Bruno, go back to work. Do you hear me?"

I recognized the accent. Ahmad was chunky with a dark-olive complexion and a short mustache. He was standing in the doorway of a small office.

We walked over to him. Mohammad introduced me. "Everyone calls me Winston."

"Winston, I've been expecting you. I am Musa."

I shook hands with Ahmad, who reminded me of a squat, ugly beetle with jet-black hair. He ushered me inside and told me to take a seat. He sat and squirted two shots of mouth spray.

"You'll have to excuse Bruno. He had you mistaken for someone else."

"That's good to know." I did not believe a word of it. The meeting with Bruno was prearranged, a warning.

"How do you know Saul Drake? Do you do business with him?"

"I'm filling in as an independent rep for IG International. The department store is in my sales territory."

"Saul is a good friend. So how can I help you?"

"I'm hoping to branch out and open my own company." I delivered the usual spiel while looking around the office, hoping to spot business files and records.

"What Hot Apparel wants to do is to create fashion that is accessible and desirable," I said, continuing my pitch. "I want to offer clothing designs people across the country understand."

I opened the portfolio case on my lap and removed clothing designs; simple but professional looking and created using fashion design software. To complete my ruse, I handed him "samples," either purchased in department stores, labels removed, or donated from clients.

He thumbed through the designs. "The look reminds me of the designers Nina Perso and Michael Jacobs. They captured the same appeal for The Gap and turned The Gap into a brand name."

He explained how Raiments had obtained fabric for their collar-less trench coats, tweed-and-suede carpet bags. "Look what happened to the Gap; it's closing over a hundred stores this year."

"I read the trade magazines," I said. "The Gap was too focused on retail and lost market share to Old Navy and other discount sellers. The sad fact is that Americans are buying fewer clothes. Retailers across the country are closing stores, and clothing manufacturers are shipping less merchandise. The focus is on selling fewer pieces of clothing, but at higher profit margins."

"So where's your niche?"

"Hot Apparel will be a combination of high-end apparel at a good price with a mix of original, innovative designs. A small collection, maybe two dozen SKUs, with a high-end that offers stability to the collection and innovative designs for a marketing pitch to distinguish the brand."

"Interesting. I can supply you with the fabric... We completed an order for men's shearling sweaters for B&B Fashions. I ordered the fabric overseas and had the sweaters manufactured in India. The sweaters were shipped to a subcontractor who added the labels and embroidery and shipped them to the client."

"Here's what I want to order in quantity." I handed him the black cashmere sweater, the same one I had shown Drake.

He lovingly stroked the fabric with thumb and forefinger. "Aah . . . cashmere. This is good quality, forty or fifty denier."

"Yes, forty denier. I'm interested in selling men's and women's sweaters in lots of fifty."

"Lots of fifty? Sounds like a big order?"

"Three to five thousand piece minimum."

"Three to five thousand? You're talking twenty to thirty thousand dollars minimum, my friend. Cashmere is expensive."

It was a big order—big enough to loosen him up.

"I intend to keystone the selling price to justify the expense," I said. "I can set up an escrow account. Saul Drake has agreed to be my backer."

"Saul Drake?" He smiled knowingly. "Saul is backing you?"

"Yes, Saul wants to see more of my line, but you can call him."

"Don't worry, Saul has called me several times about you."

I suspected as much, but was taken by surprise anyway.

"Saul is impressed with you. He said you discovered the IG sweaters in the store."

"I was conducting—" Before I could say another word, he cut me off with a wave of his hand. He sat back and relaxed, before reaching for the mouth spray. After a spritz, he placed the atomizer on the desk.

"I work with many people. You know what this business is like. Everyone is looking for a deal. We manufacture IG sweaters, but use acrylic fiber instead of cashmere. No one knows the difference. A company we do business with gave us an order that later went sour. I made some calls and found a connection. Everybody was happy."

"Are the sweaters legit?"

Ahmad laughed. "Everyone's cutting corners."

"Yep, everyone's cutting corners," I replied. "Can I order some?"

"Give me quantity, and I'll give you a quote," Ahmad said. "IG sweaters are a big seller. My partners grew up with the rapper."

"Saul said you're a co-owner with the Smith brothers."

"Yes, Orlando and Pete. They should be back this afternoon."

"Let me call some clients and get back to you."

"I'm glad we met," he said. "Saul was afraid you might be an investigator, but you're a player. I can tell." The toad flashed a smile that looked genuine.

"Is that why you introduced me to Bruno?"

"Don't get mad. Just a precaution." Ahmad laughed, a high-pitched snort. "You're my friend. From what Saul said, I gather you know people in the business and have connections."

God, how I despised this arrogant beetle-skinned cockroach. Not only was he in the counterfeiting business, but he was hoping to network with me to expand his illegal operation.

Of course, there was a show of muscle and intimidation—something similar might have been shown to the account manager, Sammy Dubinski. That could explain why he reported my interest in the sweaters to Drake.

Ahmad opened up, told me about his business, how he traveled overseas and purchased fabric. I tried to keep him talking about his overseas connections and was not surprised to discover that he did considerable business in India. The apparel business is one of India's biggest exports thanks to the advent of computerized embroidery machines. A design can be e-mailed abroad and downloaded and copied exactly. Possibly the two personal computers behind Ahmad were used to send and receive designs and manufacturing orders.

He asked if I had a swatch of the cashmere for the sweater.

"No, but I can send one."

He asked if he could cut a swatch for a burn test. I agreed

and watched as he took a scissors and cut a two-inch square piece from the sleeve.

He opened up the desk drawer and inspected the cut-out swatch of fabric with a pick glass. He squinted through the eyepiece and commented on the tightness of the weave. Next, he used a long sewing needle to count the wales and courses in the fabric.

"This is a warp knit, forty gauge, likely produced on a tricot machine."

He unraveled several thread fibers from the swatch, then pulled out a lighter from the desk drawer and flicked on the flame. He held the threads with thumb and forefinger and positioned the flame underneath. A wisp of smoke rose as the thread reacted to the heat. His eyes followed the upward movement of the flames as the threads were slowly consumed. Finally, he dropped the threads into an empty coffee cup and watched the fabric disappear; all that remained was a blackened char.

"This is good grade cashmere," he said, "not a mixture of man-made fabric. I sell high quality cashmere like this, but not for my walk-in clients. It will have to be shipped from India. If you like, I can get you high-quality fabric like this, but allow me to make a few recommendations to save money on the order."

"I'm starting out, so I would appreciate your assistance."

"I see. So that's why you were interested in finding the source of Drake's sweaters?"

"Yes."

"I can obtain good grade cashmere, as well as any fabric you need. Just provide me with a spec sheet."

"Sounds good."

"Also, I can get you a significant price reduction for the cashmere and maintain quality by using a lightweight fabric. This is seven or eight ounces per linear yard; I suggest using five-weight."

"Fine with me."

"I also suggest going to 28 gauge in the production with a different finish and pressure dyeing. For basic black, no one will know the difference."

Ahmad outlined a *knockoff* strategy for the sample sweater.

Scrimping here, cutting there to bring down the cost to undercut the original manufacturer. There is nothing illegal under copyright law for producing a close copy of another designer's work. In fact, much of the apparel industry thrives on knocking-off a competitor's design. If a fashion designer comes out with something hot, everyone else will try to knockoff the design by substituting different fabric or subtle changes in the pattern. Several years ago, the late designer Gianni Versace came out with a rubber mini-skirt that sold for three grand, but before Versace could market the product in the United States, competitors sold knockoffs in vinyl for three hundred dollars.

"You could save a bundle by using acrylic fiber," Ahmad said.

"For now, I'll stick with cashmere. If I order fabric in bulk, I'll need a warehouse. Any suggestions?"

"Raiments can warehouse it."

"You can? Do you have enough room here?"

"No, you're right. There's a storeroom in our production department. It's on the right past the swinging doors, past the cutting department. We do stitching and cropping, finishing and checking, packing and loading, but we have to outsource. We own two warehouses, but even that's not enough space, so we rent."

I questioned him about the warehouses, but he was evasive. After all, this was where their inventory, including knockoffs, was stored.

The deal was nearly finished. He said if I provided him with a spec sheet and design for the sweaters, he would provide me with a production quote for a cut-and-make-trim agreement, otherwise referred to as a CMT.

I asked for a list of references. Ahmad nodded. He turned to the personal computer, typed on the keyboard, and the pages flowed into the printer. He handed them to me.

I reviewed the references. *Bingo!* Asian Seas was at the top.

"I noticed you do business with Asian Seas. That's a sweatshop in Brooklyn. The owner was murdered."

Ahmad was speechless.

"A client asked me to contact you with a deal. He believes he has something of yours."

"A-a-a deal? Something of mine?"

"A load of IG cashmere sweaters left behind at Asian Seas," I said.

Ahmad straightened up; he was blown away.

"Wha—what are you talking about? A client of yours? What's going on?"

"You heard me! My client will hand over the sweaters. In return, he wants to buy all IG apparel, including any orders ready to ship. He'll pay cash, dollar for dollar what anyone else has paid."

Ahmad's jowls were shaking. "Good God! Who are you?"

"Like I said, a client wants to do business. There's a catch. The deal has to be completed within the next forty-eight hours. Understand?"

"Forty-eight hours! It can't be done," Ahmad huffed. "Maybe another brand?"

"No, IG International," I insisted. "You've got orders to be shipped. I know you do."

"Yes, but these are for clients" Ahmad said. "Everything I have is on order."

"Fuck 'em. My client will pay cash for whatever the clients are offering. Cash! Upon an inspection of the goods. After delivery, my client will arrange to send you the IG sweaters. It's a win-win deal."

"Tell me," Ahmad said, "how you got those sweaters from Asian Seas first."

"Never mind how. Now do we deal?"

Ahmad was quiet, obviously trying to figure the angles. "Why is your client being so generous?"

"It's all about connections," I said. "He wants to do business with you after the deal."

The toad demanded to know the client's name. I glared at him. The atmosphere in the cramped room was getting steamy.

Finally, he continued. "I can't complete this order without consulting my partners."

"You mean the Smith brothers? I'll call later. Remember, forty-eight hours or its goodbye sweaters. My client tells me the retail price is around a half-million dollars."

"Yes," Ahmad said. "That's about right. What's the rush?"

"The fucking sweaters are hot! Damn it, there's a police

investigation. My client has to get rid of those sweaters fast."

"How do I know this is not a set-up?" Ahmad said boldly.

"You'll have to trust my client. Besides, they're your sweaters. You ordered them—and had them on order prior to the murder. Isn't that right?"

"Well . . . yes. I keep the records right behind me in the filing cabinets."

"You can cover yourself. So how can you be set up?" I pushed the question back on him.

Ahmad let out a breath. "I have to talk to my partners before I can give approval. You won't be disappointed. We've got six orders for IG apparel. We can consolidate them into one huge order."

"That's what I like to hear. I'll call this afternoon. And remember the deal has to be completed in forty-eight hours. Or those IG sweaters are history."

Ahmad grimaced. "And what about Hot Apparel?"

"I should get a nice commission for this deal. After that, we'll talk again."

©©

I followed Ahmad out of the office. As we walked back towards the door, I realized he was steering me towards Bruno. I was ready.

"Uh, excuse me," I said as we walked. "I have to make a phone call."

I reached into my pocket and retrieved my cell phone. I pretended to punch in some numbers as we approached. Bruno glared at me.

"You've already met Bruno," Ahmad quipped.

"Unfortunately, yes." I positioned the cell phone and took his picture.

"Hey, what's that for!" Bruno yelled.

"Something to remember you by."

Bruno rushed forward and tried to grab the cell phone.

I quickly shoved it down my pants. "Yeah, come and get it!" I leered, gesturing toward my groin, where the cell phone rested snugly inside my underwear.

Bruno scowled, but I knew he would not pursue it, not with his boss standing next to me.

Ahmad took my arm and ushered me away. "Why did you take that picture?"

"For protection, in case something happens to me," I said bluntly.

"Don't do anything like that again." He told me to erase the picture.

"Look, you started it. Ordering that goon to scare me."

I walked ahead of him as he continued to demand I erase the picture. I felt safer after I had passed through the door and entered the display room. Mohammad was assisting a customer. I said a quick goodbye and left.

# Chapter Eighteen

I WAS HEADING TO Newark when Stella called. I knew this was trouble. I switched on the emergency blinkers, veered onto the shoulder, and parked.

"Stella, what's wrong? Where's Linda?"

"Linda's fine. We got a weird telephone message at the office."

"Oh, shit! When?"

"Late last night. It's the same guy. Has to be. He left a telephone message on a scam line."

"A scam line? Jesus, what a creep. Did the message sound like it was recorded?"

"That's what Stan said. He knew you were tied up with Ahmad, so he called me."

"What time did Linda leave for school?"

"About eight."

"Good. Linda would have stayed home with Josh if she was afraid."

"What do you want me to do?" Stella asked.

"Stay put. This will have to wait until after I meet Richardson."

Two calls had been made last night. Whoever was doing this knew where I worked and where I lived. I vented my anger and frustration at Ahmad. A counterfeiter, maybe someone like Ahmad, had to be making these calls.

I returned to the Turnpike and headed for Newark.

The ASAC wanted Ahmad as much as I did. Not only had this toad and his goons tried to intimidate me, but he was up to his neck in dirty deals and not above using violence. I wanted him fried.

I took the exit, drove through the downtown until I came to Centre Street. I found a parking spot across from the FBI field office. I passed through security and took the elevator. I told the receptionist Tom Richardson was expecting me.

He arrived shortly. After a quick handshake, I followed him into his office.

"How did it go?" he asked after I was seated.

I told him how I baited Ahmad into admitting the sweaters in Asian Seas belonged to Raiments. Although Ahmad never admitted to knowing the Uncle, he had to have done business with him, maybe even knew the mystery man's identity. Then, I explained how I leveraged him into a deal for the remaining IG knockoffs and how Bruno threatened me twice.

"Threatened you?" He perked up.

"Nothing that would stand up in court, just words."

I took out my cell phone, thumbed to the picture, and showed it to him. He laughed when I told him where I hid the cell phone.

He studied Bruno's face. "Cute, but he doesn't look familiar."

"Notice the scar? Jenny Ling said an attacker had a scar on his cheek."

"So this might be the killer?" He again reviewed Bruno's picture. "He looks tough enough. Can you get me a copy?"

"Sure, I'll have one sent to you."

"I want Ahmad," he said firmly. "I took over this task force because I lost friends in 9/11. Will Evans was a special agent with the New York field office. He wanted to help and ran to the Twin Towers. No one ever saw him again."

I remembered civilians rushed to the Twin Towers to assist during the 1993 terrorist attack. This was likely a fatal move in the 2001 attack. Evans was probably buried alive.

"We've investigated Ahmad," Richardson continued. "He was born in the United States and took over Raiments from his father who started the company in 1945. I've checked with Homeland Security about Ahmad's importing apparel from Pakistan, India and Bangladesh. We know all about the co-owners, Orlando and Pete Smith. Real sweethearts.

"I've met with an assistant U.S Attorney who plans on prosecuting Ahmad and the Smith brothers. Now that Raiments can be tied to Asian Seas, we may have enough evidence to arrest Ahmad on a charge of murder. Are the fakes being stored inside the company?"

"No. I've already inspected Raiments. The business records are there, but the knockoffs are being stored somewhere else. I've got to get Orlando to take me to the location."

Richardson nodded. "It's shaping up like a buy-and-bust drug operation. In many operations, we have to wait until the bad guys make the exchange before arresting them."

"Most seizures I've worked on are like that," I said. "The fakes are stored in a custom bonded warehouse, a rented basement, an abandoned factory. I won't know until I show up with the cash."

"How much is the deal for?" he asked.

"I haven't negotiated it." I checked my watch. "I'm supposed to call him this afternoon."

"Let me know what happens." Richardson smiled and said, "Maybe when this is over, we can go out to dinner."

"Sure, I'd like that." I was getting to like Richardson. He was personable, a family man with a picture of his wife and kids on the table. He had a boyish face and looked preppy in chinos and a button-down shirt. An average Joe, except for the shoulder holster and Glock.

He leaned back in his chair. "What kind of guy is Caldwell?"

"Funny you should ask." I chuckled. "He's basically a pain in the ass to work for. Zeckindorff doesn't like him, and the Rapper IG beats him up."

"Beats him up, no way!"

I told him about the fistfight in the corporate office.

He laughed. "I've got a ten-year-old who listens to his rap. What's this world coming to?"

"I've got a seven-year-old. Luckily, he's too young."

Richardson walked me to the elevator and insisted on riding down to street level. I sensed he was unhappy in Newark and longed for New York. I commiserated, told him New Yorkers were never far away. We shook hands, and then I headed for Hoboken.

# Chapter Nineteen

I HEADED HOME, MY family's safety uppermost in my thoughts. *Another phone call.* If the caller wanted to strike fear in me, he had succeeded. I considered myself a failure as a husband and father. I had been so worried about my own safety and the family curse that I had neglected the ones I love. I arrived home, opened the front door, and was greeted by the soft sound of the pop group ABBA coming from the living room. Linda and Stella sat on the sofa; Josh lay on the carpet with drawing pen in hand, his attention focused on a sketch pad.

"Theo, you're home." Linda looked refreshed and had changed into jeans and a cotton shirt. I walked over, gave her a kiss on the cheek.

I turned to Josh, engrossed in his artwork. "And how about you, my little man?"

"Stella helped me—" His brown eyes sparkled, as he proudly showed me the Western scene and pointed to the horse that Stella had colored.

"Stella helped you? That's great."

"Lordy, I did what comes naturally."

I leaned over, gave Stella a quick hug.

"I had a wonderful time, Theo. Do you want me to stay?"

"No, we'll be fine."

I escorted her outside. She looked tired, not like her usual self. Her eyes were puffy. I remembered she had travelled from Brooklyn to get here before six o'clock.

"How did things go?" I asked.

"Mostly boring . . . Linda and I shared coffee. I think she's too embarrassed to talk about it. After they left, I watched television, stayed calm, and waited."

"Does she know we got hit at the office?"

"I didn't tell her."

"This is my fault." It was a tired voice that spoke those words. I had been on the go longer than her and nearing an emotional breaking point.

"You feel guilty, don't you?" Stella asked.

"Yes, I'm supposed to protect them, but I don't know what I'm up against. Maybe Hwa's killers are making these calls?"

"Theo, you're too hard on yourself. Ease up."

"I want Stan to make a copy of the caller's message. I want Linda to hear it."

"First, I want you to hear me." Stella's no-nonsense tone stopped me in my tracks. "You're feeling bad because you're family's been hurt . . . well, we're all family on this one."

I paused, as her words rolled around inside. Maybe I was moving too fast, putting too much pressure on myself.

"Thanks, I appreciate your concern, but I want Linda to listen to a copy."

"Fine, Theo. She's a trooper like your son Josh. He's my hero, you know."

That remark made me smile. "I called Frank Mohanis. He's never encountered anything so weird and wants a copy of the recorded voice. He's coming at six to inspect my house."

She nodded. "I'll get him a copy. So what happened with the FBI?"

"The ASAC took notes as I told him about visiting Ahmad." I showed her the picture on my cell phone.

"He looks nasty," she said "Who is he?"

"Name's Bruno, works for Ahmad. We believe he's the killer. I want you to make copies for distribution. Send two to the ASAC."

I checked my watch. "I'm supposed to call Orlando over at Raiments and negotiate a deal for the IG knockoffs."

"Do you want some privacy?"

"No, you can listen in. This could be fun."

©©

"Hello, Musa. It's Frank Winston."

After a long pause. "Yes, Winston. I discussed your offer with Orlando Smith. He wants to talk; let me switch you."

Another pause. "Yo, it's Orlando."

"Orlando, Frank Winston. Everyone calls me Winston."

"Been expecting you. What's this about Asian Seas?"

"I told Musa I have a client that has something of yours. A half-million dollars in IG sweaters. Want 'em back?"

"Hell, yes. First I want to know how you—or your client—got them."

"Look, the client has 'em. Are you ready to deal—or not?"

"Bullshit! I know the cops have Asian Seas padlocked. So what are you trying to pull?"

"Sure, the place is padlocked. But the cops aren't guarding the store. Dig?"

"You mean?"

"That's right—the client pops the lock and removes the sweaters. *Bada bing.* The operation will take twenty minutes. After that, he's got to unload fast."

A long pause. "I think this is bullshit."

"Fine. Why don't you go to the cops and claim the sweaters? Because the cops will ask questions you'd prefer not to answer. Right? Now do we deal or not?"

Dead silence, then "Here's the deal, Winston. I've got twenty thousand IG T-shirts in mixed colors, boxed and ready for shipment. Another four thousand IG sweatshirts that retail for fifty bucks each; mixed colors, boxed and ready for shipment. All told—that's half-a-million bucks retail."

"Sounds cool."

"The inventory is in children, teenagers, men and women, in lots of forty. Small, medium, large, extra-large, and double and triple XL. Got that. It's a one hundred box count.

"All right, I'll inspect the goods. You ship to me."

"No, you pay us, pick up the load, and disappear. Cash and carry."

"Understood. Where's your warehouse located?"

"We'll take you there."

"Hey, come on. I have to bring my own truck and hire someone. At least give me an idea of the mileage."

"We'll let you know," he said flatly. "Besides, how do I know you aren't taping this conversation?"

"You think I'm a cop?"

"I don't know what you are, so I'm playing it safe. Have a truck ready."

"Fine. So cut to the chase," I said.

"I was getting to that. We got a half-million-dollar inventory. Standard discount, the goods wholesale at fifty percent, we'll give you the load for one hundred and fifty grand, payable in cash."

"You've got to be joking."

"Hey, I'm serious. That's a great price."

"Not for me." I huffed.

"What the fuck! Are you trying to back out?"

"Settle down, we both know I'm not going to pay that much."

"Fuck you! Fuck you!"

I loved this part of the game, the haggling. Never mind what Donald Trump and the other experts tell you about the "art of the deal." Most of the backroom deals I make are full of curses, even outright threats. Orlando was one of those players who became abusive, as if you were offending him.

"Settle down! I'll give you fifteen grand for the load. Cash and carry, after I inspect the goods."

"What kind of chump do you take me for?"

I let him talk me up to thirty thousand in cash. Orlando wanted the sweatshop sweaters included.

"After we complete our business, you'll get them."

"I want them when we meet," he insisted

"No can do; that's my security blanket."

"Security blanket? What the fuck?" He was angry.

"How do I know I can trust you? As long as I'm holding those sweaters, you can't rob me."

"Rob you? This is bullshit! Do you hear me?" He was really angry now.

"Whatever! I said this is a win-win deal. You pay cash up front. After the exchange, you get sweaters. Deal?"

"Deal."

© ©

When I ended the call, Stella congratulated me on a job well done.

After a hug, I watched her walk up the street to her car. She waved and then drove away.

Back inside, Linda was sitting on the sofa.

"Want to go into the kitchen?" She nodded and followed me. We sat down at the dining table. "A security consultant is coming tonight. I want you to take Josh for a walk around five."

"Can he catch the caller?"

"I hope so." I told her that Frank had helped us with other threatening calls.

"Theo, is this necessary? I'm not some namby-pamby. I'll admit I was upset over the caller. Who wouldn't be?"

"Don't apologize," I said. "We can't take any chances."

© ©

Frank Mohanis arrived at six. He was a certified Technical Surveillance Countermeasure Specialist, better known as TSCM. He arrived in a Chevy Express Cargo Van that had been converted into a surveillance truck. Frank had showed me the inside and told me how he and an associate had installed paneling, carpeting and a lighting system, and well over two hundred thousand dollars worth of electronic equipment, including video and audio recorders. The windows were tinted and had blackout curtains.

Frank carried a large canvas bag that contained the tools and electronic equipment. Frank is a tough guy to look at, with a pock-marked face that resembles the craters on the moon. We went into the kitchen. I poured coffee, as I told him about the recorded messages.

"Wow, this guy's too much!" Frank said. "You said the latest message was left on an answering machine?"

"Yes, on an office scam line. I'll send you a copy. The call was made using a New Hampshire area code. Does that mean anything?"

"Nothing much," Frank said. "The caller purchased a cell phone and asked for an area code in that state. Sorry about your family. How's Linda?"

"Shook up. The scrambled voice freaked her. She's better now. I had her take Josh for a walk. Thank God, JJ doesn't know what's happened."

"Any idea who the caller is?" he asked.

"None. I told Linda it might be an Internet pirate. Many of them are kids who are computer literate hackers."

"You think this is a prank?"

"I'm not sure," I said.

"The caller has to be using a throw-away cell phone," Frank said. "They're popular because you don't sign a contract and can pay in cash."

"Can you track him?"

"Unless the caller uses the phone again, it's a dead end. If he does, I can use cell-tower information to pinpoint the location of the call." Frank paused, shook his head. "If he throws the phone away, it's impossible; even the FBI couldn't find him."

I was surprised by his mentioning the agency. "What's so special about the FBI?"

"Ever heard of CALEA?" Frank asked.

"Doesn't ring a bell."

Frank explained that CALEA was the Communications Assistance for Law Enforcement Act of 1994. It was passed after the Justice Department complained that digital technology, cellular phones, and features like call forwarding made it difficult for law enforcement investigators to conduct wiretaps. CALEA allowed the FBI to develop DCSNet.

"Hardly anyone in the public sector has heard of DCSNet," Frank said. "It's a software surveillance system developed by the FBI that collects and stores phone numbers, outgoing calls, trap and traces to record incoming calls, text messages. A throwaway cell phone, used once and discarded, can defeat it."

Frank looked around the kitchen. Security to him was like chess, a two-way game with variables and openings and gambits. He scrutinized everything for a weakness, an entry or avenue for prying eyes and ears.

"You're experienced with stalkers and telephone threats," I

said. "What's with this guy? Do you think he'll get violent?"

"Probably. He's trying to prove how smart he is. I'm afraid he might escalate."

"We've probably busted him. That's how he knows about our scam lines."

"Would you recognize the caller's voice if it was unscrambled?"

"I've trained as an actor, which gives me an edge. I thought about reviewing past calls, but I've got thousands."

"A voice descrambler might help, if I can filter away the scrambling."

"Can you do that?"

"I can try. However, it's a dead end if the caller is using encryption technology."

"Shit! Who's going to all this trouble?"

The caller appeared to know *everything* about me, even my deepest fears. Had he been secretly listening the night Linda had the dream, or the conversations we had had about George's death? How was his call timed minutes before I arrived home?

Frank said, "There's something new on the market that might help."

"There is? What?"

"It's called lossy compression, the same technology used for the MP3. It filters away unnecessary data so that a computerized music file can be compressed. Using lossy compression, the scrambling can be filtered away to create a master voice print."

"What happens next?"

"Hopefully, you'll recognize the voice. If not, we can compare the voice prints on your recorded messages and hope for a match."

"Will it work?" I asked.

"It's a big job with technical hurdles," Frank said. "I'd have to use an outside company. Are you sure you can afford it? We're talking five figures. Maybe more."

"Frank, he threatened my family."

"I understand, but I had to let you know."

I agreed to pay for the voice analysis.

I had been working with Frank for many years. I liked him, respected his expertise, and decided to confide in him about my brother's death, and how it had opened a painful past. It was a side of me that I rarely discussed.

He listened attentively. "Sounds spooky," he said at one point.

"After my brother died, Linda had a dream ... a premonition. A voice warning her of my death."

"Your death?" He set down the coffee cup and regarded me ominously.

"Frank, all of the men in the Jones family have died young, including my brother George. Linda's been after me to get out of the business since he died."

"She's worried you'll die young, like George?"

"Yes. Truthfully, I have thought about getting out of this line of work."

"I know how you feel," he said. "I retired from the police force after my partner was killed in the line of duty. We were as close as brothers. His death made me realize how dangerous the job is, and I got out for the sake of my family."

"Do you think Linda's right?"

"I don't know what to make of Linda's dream," he said. "I do know that getting out is your decision."

©©

Frank figured the caller had to be watching me to garner so much information. After finishing his coffee, he inspected the inside of my home and found nothing suspicious. We went outside and inspected the home's perimeter for a location to install a security camera.

"I'll put it here to cover the front entrance." Frank pointed to a spot above the front door.

"Thanks, I feel better. Frank, would you come to the office and talk to the staff."

"Sure, I'm free next week."

"I'll call you, and we'll set up an appointment."

# Chapter Twenty

I DROVE THE CAR into New York the next day and parked in the garage on Sullivan Street, three blocks from the office. I walked to Thompson Street, entered the building, and took the elevator. Usually I would have stopped in at the front office; instead I went directly to the boiler room to see Stan. Everyone looked up when I entered.

I spotted Stan and walked towards his cubicle; Kimberley and Angel rose from their seats and followed.

"I want to hear the recorded threat," I said.

He nodded and brushed aside the reports on his desk. He pressed a tab on the phone's console. There was a whirr—and then:

*I'm waiting . . . waiting FOR YOU!*
*Ha-ha-ha-aaaaaa!*
Theee . . . Theeeeeeo Jones
MOTHERFUCKER!
Die! Die! Die! Die! Die!
RevennnnGGGGGEEEE!
*Hate you!*
*Hate you!*

*HATE YOU!*

It wasn't so much the message that was terrifying—but the recorded voice.

Like a screech from hell.

Kimberley winced. "Any idea who this is?" she asked.

"None . . ." I remembered a verse penned by Lord Byron:
*Forests were set on fire—but hour by hour*
*They fell and faded—and the crackling trunks*
*Extinguish'd with a crash—and all was black.*

A vision of a world without life. That's how I felt. My family's safety and the safety of my investigators were more important than my own. *How could I live with myself if anything happened to them?*

Yet, something terrible had happened. My guess was increased violence was coming.

The caller's message reminded me of the threats mailed by Jack the Ripper and signed "from hell"—a taunting invitation to catch him. To catch the caller, we had to enter his realm, play his game.

I told everyone I had hired Frank to inspect my home, and then I asked Stan if copies of this threat had been made.

Stan nodded. "I re-recorded onto a CD and burned five copies. Stella has them."

"Is it possible Ahmad could be behind the calls?" Kimberley asked.

"Not too likely. Anyway, the net's closing on him. I met with the FBI. The ASAC wants Ahmad and his henchmen prosecuted."

"What about Saul Drake? Are we going ahead with the seizure?" Stan asked.

"Full steam ahead," I said.

I told Angel to follow me into the other office. He was wearing jeans worn low, an extra large CK polo shirt, and Adidas sneakers. I hoped this death threat wouldn't spook him.

I sat behind my desk and told Angel to be seated. Stella, who was seated at her desk, handed over my cell phone. "I downloaded the picture and printed out ten copies. I also have CDs of the death threat."

"I listened to the recorded message," I said. "It's hideous. Send three pictures to the FBI ASAC, and then send a picture along with a CD of the recorded death threat to Frank. Tell him the mug shot is part of an ongoing investigation and may have nothing to do with the death threat."

Angel remained silent, waiting for my instructions.

I felt protective because he was barely out of his teens. He was coming on fast as a private investigator. Although he had grown up in a tough neighborhood, I had to be sure his mental condition wasn't impaired by being exposed to murder and death threats.

"Your mother wants me to look out for you," I said.

"Yes, I know," he said sheepishly. "She told me to listen and learn."

I had hired Angel because his mother Dorita told Linda she was concerned he was hanging with the wrong crowd. I spoke with him shortly afterwards and told him I'd hire him if he'd complete a three-month course on investigation taught at La Guardia Community College.

I opened a file folder and handed him the letter threat. The words, each of them, had been cut out of the newspaper and pasted onto a sheet of paper and photocopied. The photocopy was placed into an envelope and sent to an agency mail drop.

The young investigator looked mystified. "Who is this guy, Theo?"

"He could be anyone. Most likely, it's a counterfeiter with a grudge, trying to scare us."

I could tell he understood our situation, which was not pleasant to contemplate. "Remember when Stan told you this was a war?"

He nodded.

"It's a war much like the drug war. Instead of drugs, it's fake products."

"*Bien*, I feel bad for Linda. *Da mi pésame por ella.* (I extend my condolences.)"

"*Gracias.* When someone targets your family, it's war. Now you understand.

"*Si, es la guerra.*"

Although Stella had run over the operation with Angel, I ran over it again.

"I'm ready, Theo." His voice was calm.

"Good," I said. "Go see Stan. The two of you will work as a team."

The next order of business was the thirty grand. I left for an appointment with Zeckindorff to discuss this before the seizure. I drove uptown, parked in a garage, and walked to 4 Times Square.

I arrived in his office to find him in an upbeat mood. "Caldwell wants to meet us at Fashion Week this afternoon. After we meet, he'll join us at the department store."

"*Fashion Week*? Why meet there? The place will be packed with people."

"The IG is unveiling his new line. Caldwell has to be there."

"What about the thirty grand?"

"A bank account with the money has been set up. Caldwell will give us the account number and bank location."

I had never attended Fashion Week, held twice a year in Bryant Park, not far away. I followed Zeckindorff outside, and we started walking uptown. We passed the W.R. Grace Building with its dramatically sloping profile.

Rock music blasted from outdoor speakers. Tents housing the fashion event were located across from the historic Radiator Building, an eighteen-story tower sheathed in black brick. The top of this building, clad in gold *terra cotta*, resembled a glowing radiator coil when illuminated at night.

Crowds milled between the tents that stretched for yards like elongated sausages. Security personnel in red blazers and walkie-talkies were strategically positioned. Fashion Week was invitation only.

Zeckindorff headed towards a table where two young girls, flanked by security, were seated. I guessed they were fashion interns. One girl, a bleached blond with a pierced ear, handed us an itinerary. Her associate, in corn braids, crinkled her nose and looked at us wide-eyed, obviously hoping we were celebrities. "Name, please," she said.

"Mine's Brian Zeckindorff, and this is Theo Jones."

"Zeckindorff . . . Let's see."

"We're with Robert Caldwell. He probably made the invitations this morning."

She pulled out a notebook and reviewed the hand-written

names. She smiled, gave us nametags to fill out, and instructed us to go to Tent 5.

I recognized journalists, celebrities, and socialites whose faces graced the tabloids and television. Some, like Cindy Crawford, looked different in person. Everyone seemed to have an air about them, as if their presence here was staged, which to a degree it was.

The security guards at Tent 5 gave us a cursory look over. One had a clipboard, checked our nametags and ushered us inside. Rock music reverberated from speakers positioned on the rafters. The runway for the models stretched nearly the length of the tent.

Most of the audience appeared to be African American, likely part of the IG's entourage. The stadium-style seating units, set up in a tier arrangement, were filled.

The guard escorted us to the front row, where Caldwell was waiting.

"Robert, Ba-a-a-a-by!" Zeckindorff crooned. Caldwell told us to be seated.

"Glad you could make it," Caldwell said loudly, trying to speak above the boom-boom music beat. He cupped his hand, placed it close to Zeckindorff's ear, and began talking. They enjoyed a lively, if muted conversation, about Baby Phat, the clothing line popularized by Kimora Lee Simmons and her husband Russell Simmons, co-founder of Def Jam Records. Kimora, a former top model, merged the world of hip-hop culture and couture with marketing campaigns and high-profile fashion shows that had hip-hop and rap music provided by her husband.

I couldn't hear everything the two said, but wasn't listening either. I was interested in the guests, the glitterati, whose faces were instantly recognizable.

"Welcome . . . Welcome . . . Welcome," a female voice droned from the overhead speakers.

On cue, beautiful models entered in sequence wearing clothes that were decidedly ready-to-wear: jeans and T-shirts with the IG logo. They paraded in that exaggerated foot-first over foot-first gait copied by drag queens and known as "vogue-ing," and popularized by Madonna in a song. Flash bulbs popped as they vogued down the catwalk in tune to the IG's rap music.

Models came and went in a stupefying procession of clothes. Then the IG himself—the rap star and clothing designer—came onstage.

*Dowutchalike.* I'm here to sta-a-a-a-y.

Be free, be me, be *wutchawa-a-a-nabe,*

Ga-a-a-ngsta-a-a . . . International Ba-a-a-a-by!

It was dizzying. The IG was using a cordless microphone and rapping away while he walked up the runway in tune to a scratch beat blaring from the overhead speakers. The audience went wild. People swayed and clapped.

The rapper posed for pictures. He wore a bulletproof vest and leather pants and a black leather baseball cap.

Caldwell leaned over. "Time to go."

Zeckindorff and I headed for the exit, as the IG thanked everyone and posed with several models. We followed Caldwell, as he cleared a path through the crowd.

Outside the tent, Caldwell used his cell phone to order the rapper's car.

Within minutes, a Rolls Royce Phantom rounded the corner of Fifth Avenue and Forty-Third Street. I recognized the car from pictures I'd seen of the six-figure machine in *Car and Driver* magazine and knew it was a favorite play toy of rap and hip hop royalty.

The Phantom was jet black and identifiable by its sleek European silhouette. The car stopped at the curb where Caldwell was waiting.

Caldwell opened the rear door. Being a British model, the door swung outwards right to left, the opposite direction to U.S.-made cars. The interior was luxurious black leather. We moved into the back seat while Caldwell slid into the front seat and introduced the driver, a heavy-set dark man wearing sunglasses and dressed in a chauffeur's uniform.

The driver turned, lifted his sunglasses enough for us to see his eyes. "Pleased to meet you."

"*Ayo*, mah man," Zeckindorff chimed. "I'm Brian, and this is Theo."

Caldwell gave us the name of a bank executive at the Easy Commerce branch in downtown Whittier. He'd wired thirty thousand dollars to an account.

"Good," Zeckindorff smiled. He turned to me. "When will the Raiments seizure go down?"

"Whenever the money's ready," I said.

"The money's ready." Caldwell handed an envelope to Zeckindorff. "The account number and contact info are inside. Don't lose it."

"Don't worry." Zeckindorff tucked it into his suit pocket.

"The IG is on the way." Caldwell said he had to return to the office and would meet us at the department store at one o'clock. That's when I'd scheduled a meeting with Saul Drake, only we'd be arriving in force.

Moments later, the IG left the tent surrounded by a phalanx of security guards in red blazers who shoveled a path through the bystanders.

Caldwell got out and held the door open for the rapper, who slid into the front seat, and departed. The engine revved with a surge of power as the driver stepped on the gas pedal and roared away.

The IG looked over his shoulder. His face glistened with a slight sheen of sweat. "Trippin', ba-a-a-by! Everything's cool." He leaned over and extended a fist.

"Number one with a bullet!" Zeckindorff crooned and gave him a pound. I followed with a pound. "You were fabulous, ga-a-a-a-angsta-a-a-a. We got the Raiments investigation wrapped up. Gonna nail dem punks, big time."

"Damn right!" the IG snapped. "*M'fo's* set me down. Want 'm wired shut." He looked at me, "You the heat, ain't you? The bag man?"

"I guess you could call me that," I said.

The rapper looked me over. "I likes to help people helpin' me."

I sensed something had transpired between the two, because the rapper was grinning and Zeckindorff was flashing a gold-plated smile he reserved for special occasions.

"Me? I'm doing my job."

"Been talkin' to your man, here," the IG said and reached out and extended an open palm. Zeckindorff reached over and gave him an open palm "high five."

"Ah'm lookin' for talent for my next video. Y'know, true to life, stuff. Thought I could use you."

I could not believe what I was hearing. "Me, in a music video?"

"Damn right! Wha' d'yu'all say?"

I felt silly, like the butt of a friendly joke. Zeckindorff assured me otherwise. "He means it," he said and broke into a rap song, serenading me:

*Dowutchalike. I'm here to sta-a-a-y.*

*Be free, be me, be wutchawaanabe*

*Gangsta-a-a-a-a!*

"When did this all come about?" I asked.

He continued tapping his hands against the upholstery and, without missing a beat, said, "I told the IG you used to be an actor."

"So you're to blame for all this," I chided him good-naturedly. "I should have known."

With the two of them goading me, I reluctantly agreed.

The thought of getting an acting assignment was thrilling. Zeckindorff offered to take care of the contract negotiations *pro bono*, while the IG laid out the details for the video.

We almost forgot the upcoming seizures. Zeckindorff assured the rapper they would be going down, first, Drake's department store and then Raiments.

"Tha's what I likes to hear," the IG cheered.

I was curious about the Smith brothers, who claimed they used to run together in the old days.

"Half of *Crooklyn* claims to know me," the IG spat. "These guys are jerkin' you. Ain't a word of truth to it."

We were dropped off at 4 Times Square and returned to Zeckindorff's office. He sat back in his chair and looked at me coyly. "When this is over, you've got an acting job waiting."

"C'mon, this is all hype," I protested.

"No kidding, this is on the level. The IG was drooling after the PR treatment I gave him. Many cops sideline as actors. Remember *The French Connection*? Eddie Egan, the cop who handled the bust, had a supporting role."

Although I was skeptical, he assured me the offer was genuine. "The rapper approached me about the video, and I gave him the pitch. Go for it. That's what friends are for. I'll handle the negotiations, no charge."

# Chapter Twenty-One

AFTER LUNCH WE HEADED in separate cars for Drake's Department Store. Zeckindorff arrived first.

"Ba-a-aby! We're set to roll," he gushed. "I've got my camcorder in the back seat." He got out of the Mercedes, opened the rear car door where a shoulder-mounted RCA camcorder rested on the back seat. He lifted it out and held it in both hands like a rifle.

"Real sweet." I reached into my jacket for my cell phone and called Stan for an ETA.

"We're on our way," Stan said. "Angel's driving. The Marshals are right behind us."

We waited on the sidewalk by the entrance. The agency van arrived within minutes. Right behind was the Marshals' patrol car, a black Chevy Impala with strobes and the familiar "Eagle Top" five-sided star in circle in white on the doors.

Both vehicles parked at the curb. I hadn't seen either Fred Paxton or his partner Tad Mahoney in months. Both were beefy, experienced Marshals. Sometimes they were loaded down with bulletproof vests, Kelvar helmets, and assault rifles. No counterfeiter in his right mind would dare to resist. Today, however, Fred and Tad wore dark blue slacks, and their neck chains had the familiar "Eagle Top" five-sided star in circle badge. Their raid vests were emblazoned with the word U.S. MARSHAL in large white block letters in the center. They were wearing kit gun belts and packing .9 mm Glocks.

"Theo, good to see you," Fred said. He walked over and shook hands.

"Here we go again," I laughed and greeted Tad who was right behind.

Caldwell arrived by taxi, completing the seizure team, which numbered seven strong.

I intended to serve Drake on sight. Serving documents on a counterfeiter is a pleasure. I have this practiced way of throwing the manila envelope with a copy of the seizure order at the counterfeiter, as if swatting a cockroach. I called Drake on my cell phone.

"Yes, hello. Brenda, it's Winston. Yes, can I speak to Saul . . . Saul, its Winston . . . Good, I'm on my way."

Puzzled shoppers and salespersons stared as we moved by them in a blur and boarded the elevator. I was the lead man with a Marshal on either side, forming a three-man front. Stan and Angel, each carrying a bundle of cardboard boxes, followed behind. Zeckindorff and Caldwell took up the rear. The plan, once the actual seizure began, was for Zeckindorff to move to the front and begin filming. The Marshals' job was to ensure the seizure was executed without interference. My job was to serve Drake and supervise the boxing of records. I couldn't wait to see Drake's face when he realized I was a PI.

We exited the elevator. Leading the way, I rushed forward and pushed open the doors. The receptionist, the same girl I had previously seen, jumped up from her chair.

"What's going on?" Her mouth was open and her head bobbed as she looked first at the Marshals—then at me, at Angel and Stan, and at Zeckindorff, who shouldered the camcorder and began filming.

"This is a court-ordered seizure!" I shouted. She shrank into a ball and sat down. "Drake, we're coming for you!"

I marched down the corridor with the Marshals at my side. Alerted by the commotion, office workers emerged from their offices.

"Out of the way!" I yelled at one worker and gave him a push.

Drake stormed into the corridor, dumbfounded. Brenda was standing behind him.

"Winston? What's going on? I thought you were coming to discuss business."

"Yeah, that's a laugh. Here, scumbag, this is for you. Catch!"

I walked up to him and slapped the manila envelope against his chest. I wanted him to catch it—and he did, his right hand rising instinctively.

"What the hell is this?"

"It's a seizure order!"

"Winston, I don't understand?"

"Scumbag, you've been served! My name isn't Winston, I'm an investigator. Can you figure it out now? I'm here on behalf of IG International."

Angel and Stan followed, as I brushed past Drake. "All right, let's get started."

Stan removed the thin plastic strips binding the cardboard boxes and quickly assembled a box. I opened the top drawer of the filing cabinet. The files were arranged alphabetically in folders. I removed a handful and gave them to Angel who shoved them into the box.

Drake was stunned. Everything was happening too fast. He watched helplessly as I removed folders. Meanwhile, Zeckindorff, who had maneuvered into position with the camcorder, began filming.

"My name is Robert Caldwell, in-house counsel for IG International," Caldwell said. "We've been investigating you, Drake."

Drake was speechless. His fists clenched, his face turned red, and he angrily threw the manila envelope to the floor. "Stop what you're doing!" he yelled. "Stop!"

Drake charged. Instead of heading for Zeckindorff, who was filming everything—he came directly at me.

The two Marshals moved to intercept him—but they were too late. Drake delivered a slap that echoed in my ear like an exploding firecracker. I remained rigid as stone and took the blow without flinching.

I ignored the pain and glared at him with controlled hatred.

He looked at me, stupefied.

Fred, the burlier of the Marshals, wrapped his arms around him in a bear hug, while Tad took out handcuffs. Drake put up no struggle as he was cuffed. With a Marshal holding each arm, he was escorted away.

Brenda was sobbing. "Oh God . . . Oh God."

I ignored her and turned to Zeckindorff.

"Did you get it on tape?" I muttered and gingerly tapped my right cheek.

"Don't worry, I caught it," Zeckindorff said. "We'll nail the bastard."

"*Madre Mia!* That was something." Angel said.

I stared at him. "Keep working, move!"

"Yes, boss." He reached into the cabinet and continued to remove files.

"Are you all right?" Caldwell asked. "Can I get you anything?"

"I'm fine, never mind about me." I touched my right cheek, which felt raw. Brenda appeared to be in shock. "You can go home now. Don't worry about locking up. We're taking everything."

Flustered, she took her sweater and headed for the door, nearly bumping into Caldwell. He smiled appraisingly as she waltzed past.

The two investigators continued boxing up files, while office workers timidly looked on.

Fred returned and elbowed his way through the crowd. "Drake is secured. Tad's guarding him." He noticed the red mark on my cheek and whistled, "Man, that's some shiner you got. Don't worry, this guy's going to pay."

I ducked into Drake's private restroom and turned on the light. My cheek was flushed red. Fortunately, there were no scratches.

I was once punched in the face by a street peddler wearing a diabolical looking ring with devils and horns on the sides. A glancing blow, but I began bleeding profusely, and it took several stitches to close the wound. I later learned he'd used a fighting ring.

I splashed cold water to relieve the stinging and gently patted my face dry. When I returned, seventeen boxes of business documents were ready to be taken away.

"How's your face?" Zeckindorff asked.

"Feels like hamburger sizzling on a grill."

"You're too much, b-a-a-by."

# Chapter Twenty-Two

"I'M GOING TO LEAVE with Tad," Fred said. "We'll take the prisoner downtown and book him. We can come back, if you need us."

Zeckindorff rested the camcorder on Drake's desk. "Why do both of you have to escort Drake downtown?"

"Procedure. One of us has to guard the jerk, while the other drives in case he gets frisky."

Zeckindorff asked Fred to stay behind until the knockoff sweaters on the second floor were seized. Fred agreed and contacted Tad on his handheld radio.

We heard footsteps out in the corridor. Next, two men entered the office. One was a uniformed security guard; the other, an older man in a business suit.

"What's going on here?" The older man furtively regarded each of us in turn—until he noticed Fred. "I saw you and the other officer take Mr. Drake away in handcuffs."

Zeckidorff moved in. "My name's Brian Zeckindorff, attorney for IG International. I'm in charge of a court-ordered seizure."

"Je-e-e-zus. I'm Matt Knowles, head of security for the department store."

"And I'm corporate counsel for IG International." Caldwell

pulled out his wallet and handed him a business card.

"Pleased to meet you." Knowles put the business card in his pocket.

Zeckindorff pointed to my right cheek. "Drake slapped him. I got it on film."

"I'm sorry, real sorry about this." Knowles shook hands with me.

"It's all right. I'm used to it by now."

"Is there is anything I can do to help?"

Zeckindorff picked up the manila envelope. "Inside is a copy of the seizure order."

"What should I do with it?"

"Give it to Drake when he gets back," Caldwell said. "IG International is suing him."

"We could use your assistance downstairs," Zeckindorf said. "We're going to seize counterfeit IG sweaters from the second floor."

"On the second floor?" Knowles moaned. "What about the shoppers?"

"Keep them out of the way."

"Fine, fine, I'll cooperate. I hope I don't lose my job." He motioned to the uniformed guard. "Help these people. Do whatever they ask."

Each of us took two boxes and carried them to the elevator and rode to the first floor and walked single file through the selling floor. We stacked the boxes on the sidewalk next to the van. Stan opened the rear door and slid inside, and then we handed him the boxes, one at a time.

We made another trip inside to remove the remaining boxes. After the boxes were in the van, Zeckindorff and I walked to the patrol car. Drake was seated in the back, head bowed. Tad rolled down the window.

"What's up?" Tad asked.

"I want to speak to Mr. Drake in back." Zeckindorff eyed Drake.

"No problem." Tad looked over his shoulder at Drake. "Hear that? The attorney wants to have a word with you."

Drake shook his head without answering.

Zeckindorff handed me the camcorder and walked to the

other side of the car, opened the door, and sat down in the front seat next to Tad. Drake remained speechless.

"You're in big trouble," Zeckindorff said. "We're working with the NYPD on two sweatshop murders. Musa Ahmad may have ordered the hits."

Drake was stone-faced. Finally, he said, "I want a lawyer."

"Yeah, you're going to need one. We'll talk again."

We returned to the department store and rode the escalator to the second floor. Zeckindorff shouldered his camcorder as we assembled boxes and began removing the IG sweaters. Knowles and the guard took up position and dispersed the shoppers.

Angel had been quiet for some time. "How's it going?" I asked.

He tried to smile. "Oh boy, whew!" He continued to remove sweaters from the rack.

"Saw some action, didn't we?"

"We sure did. I can't believe he bitch-slapped you like that."

"He's going to be booked for assault. Zeckindorff got the attack on tape, so he has no defense."

"What's going to happen?"

"He's in big trouble. After he's booked for assault, the police will interrogate him about the murders and demand his cooperation."

My cell phone buzzed; it was my home phone number.

"Hello, Linda?"

No answer.

"Hello! Hello!"

"Theo, its Linda."

Her voice. Something was wrong. "Linda, are you all right?"

"The weirdo called. I spoke to him."

"What? He called the home phone?"

"He called my cell phone."

*The cell phone, damn it!*

"When did he call?"

"A half-hour ago. I didn't know how to get in touch. I'm using the phone in the living room."

I cut her off: "Don't say anything—he may be monitoring it. I'm on my way. Dial 9-1-1 if anything happens."

"Wait, don't hang up—not yet."

"What is it?"

"Theo, you're not listening. I said he spoke to me. It wasn't a recording. He threatened to kill Josh."

"Josh! Where is he?"

"Here with me, he's safe—" Her voice started to crack.

"I'm on my way."

*Damn, damn, damn!*

Both investigators had caught snippets of conversation and knew something was up. I told them the caller had struck again and instructed them to finish loading up the boxes and not to tell Zeckindorff what had happened.

I brushed past the attorney, with a quick "something unexpected came up." He hardly had time to blink, let alone respond.

Outside, I jumped into my car and risked a call on my cell phone and contacted Stella. I quickly filled her in—and then stepped on the gas. There was the usual stall at the Lincoln Tunnel before entering Hoboken.

I bounded up the steps, opened the door. It was deathly quiet inside. "Linda?"

"She's not here," a man's voice answered.

It was Jack! What was he doing here?

I rushed into the living room and found him sitting on the sofa. He was wearing a cardigan sweater and blue jeans. His face was grim, like he had something terrible to tell me.

"Where's my family?" I was expecting the worst.

He stood up to face me. He looked right through me and said Linda left for Riverdale with Mattie.

"Jack, I want to see my family."

"Son, please wait—"

"For Christ's sake! I want to see her now!"

I had a mad impulse to get into my car and drive to Riverdale. Jack must have read my mind. He told me to stay calm and have a seat.

I was overwhelmed but managed to sit on the couch. Jack had his hands clasped, imploring me to go easy.

My heart sank when he told me Linda called him first.She had arrived home from school, when the stalker called and threatened Josh.

Jack realized it was an emergency. He and Mattie drove in separate cars to Hoboken and split up. Mattie returned with Linda and Josh, while he waited for me.

"She had calmed down by the time we arrived."

"What about Josh?"

"We told him his mother isn't feeling well."

"He doesn't know what's happening?"

"No."

"Thank God." Knowing my son was safe helped me relax.

"Son, we know how dangerous your work is."

"Jack, I need to speak to Linda right now! Please call her."

I told him to use his cell phone. I waited impatiently. After a pause, he handed me the phone.

Relief swept through me at the sound of her voice. "Theo, I couldn't wait . . . I had to get out."

"I understand, how's JJ?"

"We're safe. Theo, I spoke to him."

"You told me."

"It wasn't a recording, he knows my name. He knows the name of our son."

I silenced her, told her we were coming and hung up.

Before we left, I checked the house for signs of entry. All clear. I checked the windows, but found nothing suspicious, saw no one lingering outside.

I returned to the living room and asked Jack if I could use his cell phone to call Stella. She told me she'd contacted Frank Mohanis, the security specialist. I thanked her, silenced her questions, and promised to call again.

Next, I called Frank and told him about the latest phone threat.

"Linda said she spoke to him. It wasn't a recording. He threatened my son."

"Damn it, he's growing violent—and getting sloppy."

"Can you track him?"

"Maybe. He's slipping up. There's paper on him if he's using a police scanner to monitor your cell phone calls."

Finally, good news.

"The caller likely has some law enforcement or military connections. Theo, be careful. The scanner probably has a range of twenty miles. He's close by, maybe even watching the house."

"He's not watching the house. I checked." All of a sudden, I realized that the call occurred after Linda and Josh had entered. *He had to be watching the house to know that.*

"He's got to be there," Frank said.

"I've checked. Whoever he is, he's good."

"If you can't spot him, then I want you to get out. I'm heading to Hoboken to do some snooping. The scanner may be leaving an electronic footprint that I can pick up."

"I'm leaving right now to see Linda."

"Call me later."

I was glad I didn't know the caller's name, because I was angry enough to kill him. How long had this creep been eavesdropping, watching my home? He knew Linda's name—threatened my son's life.

He was becoming violent. Unless we caught him, it was a matter of time before he struck again. I remembered Frank's project about using voice analysis to identify the caller. Maybe ASAC Richardson could help. I decided to call and make an appointment after things quieted down.

©©

Riverdale is about three miles long and part of the Bronx. I followed Jack through Spuyten Duyvil in South Riverdale to Broadway. He made a right turn onto Chambers Street. I followed and parked behind him.

We walked up the steps of his house. Rosco, their Dalmatian, began barking as he opened the door. The dog jumped up and began licking him.

"Easy, Rosco." He playfully petted the dog.

"Hey, fella, remember me?" The dog barked and sniffed my hand.

"Shhh, Rosco." It was Aunt Mattie. She walked towards us, gave Jack a kiss.

"Theo, good to see you, dear." I gave her a kiss on the cheek.

"Where's my family?"

"Josh is in the kitchen drinking hot cocoa. Linda's upstairs."

"Let me see Josh."

I followed Mattie into the kitchen. Josh was seated at the table. "Dad!"

"Hey, JJ." I rushed over and gave him a hug. *Thank God he's safe.*

"Mom's not feeling well."

"I know . . . How are you?"

"Fine, I want to go outside and play with Rosco."

"Finish your cocoa first, Jack will go with you."

I left everyone in the kitchen and went upstairs to the guest bedroom. I opened the door and peeked inside. Linda was lying on the bed. Her head was resting on a pillow, but she was awake. I went inside.

"Linda, how are you?"

She smiled weakly, as I sat down beside her. "Are you all right?" I asked.

She sat up, put her arms around me. *What a relief to hold her.*

"We're going to catch this nut," I said. "He slipped up. The security consultant thinks he can track him down."

She seemed to be in another world. Puzzled, she reached out and touched my cheek. "What's this?"

"A scratch. A bad guy got playful. Does it look bad?"

"I've seen worse." She looked petulant. I changed the subject and asked about the caller.

"I checked the number, before answering." She covered her mouth with her hand. She appeared to be dazed. "It was your number, I'm sure of it."

"The caller used a trick. A cell phone is like a computer."

She nodded. "The voice was different. Then I realized I was speaking one to one."

She hesitated, as she tried to recall the conversation. I urged her to continue.

"He addressed me by name, said he was following me and was going to kill Josh. Oh God!"

I took her hand in mine. "Do you remember the specific words?"

"No. For a moment I panicked, thought about hanging up. Until I remembered this was a teenager. Maybe he's trying to communicate, reach out. I remembered what I had been taught in my self-defense class on how to deal with rapists—*talk to him, try to establish contact, make him realize you're a person.* I asked what his name was . . . I asked why he was doing this—but he hung up."

Her eyes turned watery. I hugged her again. "It's all right, I'm here. I'm proud of you."

"He's a sick person . . . It was scary."

"Jack said you were upset, nearly crying when you called him."

"I'm ready to cry now—"

"No, baby," I whispered. "Relax, everything will be fine." I held her tightly for a moment, and then asked if she wanted to return home tonight.

"I'm not sure if I can ever go back."

"Honey, don't say that." I tried to reason with her.

"Things have to change before I can return."

"Things will change, honey. We're going to get him. Please come home."

An empty silence was my answer.

"Linda, please."

"Theo, someone wants to kill you. He's threatened your son, threatened me."

"I'm sorry. You weren't supposed to get hurt."

"I've lived in your shadow, your career. I need time to rest, to find myself in all this."

"We'll move. I'll do whatever it takes."

To my great relief, I heard her laugh. God knows how much I wanted to hear her laugh again.

"Remember when we were living in the Village," she said.

"I remember it all."

"You said we'd be together forever. You said nothing could touch us."

"I remember. I thought our love was so strong that nothing could destroy it."

"I know if one of us goes, our love will be destroyed . . . Please get out of this business before it's too late."

"Linda—" I pleaded, but she interrupted and told me to leave.

# Chapter Twenty-Three

I WALKED DOWN THE stairs in a devastated state and wandered into the kitchen. Mattie was standing by the stove, a yellow apron tied around her waist and her attention riveted on a pot simmering on the stove. I sat down at the table.

She turned to look at me and sensed I was troubled. "Theo, are you all right?" she asked.

"How's Linda?"

"Mattie, she blames me for everything," I said half-heartedly. "Maybe she's right; I'm a terrible husband."

"Don't even think that!" She turned off the heat, walked over, and sat down next to me. She smiled tenderly. "Linda loves you. She's upset about the caller."

"She said she won't go back to Hoboken."

She placed a finger to her lips to silence me. "A stalker called and threatened her child. She's reacting like a mother. She'll settle down and return home, I know she will. She told me so."

"She did?"

"When we were alone in the guest room, she said she wanted to be there for you if something happened."

I found this news reassuring.

"Thanks, Mattie." I said but was numb.

"Whoever called is a sick individual. You need to slow down, take care of your family."

She suggested I go outside and find the others. I took her advice. Outside, the early evening air nipped. The two of them were in the distance. Josh had Roscoe on a leash and was laughing and running to keep up. The thought of someone threatening my son was unbearable. *What kind of person threatened a child?*

I caught up with Jack. Josh was far ahead, affording us some privacy. I thanked him for his help.

"We all want to help, son." He was curious to know about the caller.

"We believe it's a kid, possibly a music pirate with advanced computer skills."

"A kid? You mean a teenager is causing all this trouble?"

I reassured him by mentioning the FBI.

"The FBI? Goodness."

"I'm working a case with them. I'm hoping they'll help catch this creep."

"Linda didn't tell us anything."

Josh headed in our direction. "We'll talk again," I whispered.

Dinner was ready by the time we returned. Linda was dressed in corduroy slacks and a sweater. Mattie put her to work setting the dining table.

Jack took Rosco into the basement. I took Josh into the dining room and took a seat with him next to the bay window.

"How are the men in the Jones family?" Linda asked, as she selected flatware and serving plates from the country French buffet.

"Fine," I replied. Jack, who had returned, sat next to me.

Linda and Mattie served platters of rolls, mashed sweet potatoes, salad and steaks.

Afterwards, we retired to the den, a small room that appeared larger because of a kilim rug whose geoconcentric pattern stretched wall to wall. We listened to slow jazz, as Josh talked about school and little league. Around nine, Linda took him upstairs, leaving me alone with the Bells.

"Mattie, Theo says the FBI may get involved," Jack said. "Maybe they can catch this nut."

"The FBI is getting involved?" Mattie looked at me in earnest.

Linda returned and down beside me. She was floored by the news. "The FBI? Why didn't you tell me?"

"The FBI isn't involved yet," I said. "I plan on asking for their help."

I asked if she'd return home tomorrow morning. "Theo, is it safe? Maybe I should stay here with Josh for another day. I'll call in sick tomorrow."

I was unable to persuade her. I felt our marriage slipping away. In a moment of complete surrender, I said, "Honey, I will retire from the profession after this investigation."

Jack was shocked. "Why, Theo?"

"I have to. If that's what it takes to hang onto my family."

"What!" Linda gave me a gentle push. "Are you doing this for me?"

"Yes, for you. And for Josh."

"Oh, you stupid Irishman," she sighed.

I explained how the caller was a catalyst, not a cause for my decision. Mattie and Jack tried to dissuade me, while Linda was silent. I sensed Linda was uneasy about my quitting like this.

We debated my quitting for another hour, until I agreed to think it over. At that point, Linda agreed to go back to Hoboken but wanted Mattie to drive her and Josh to Hoboken. I agreed to this because I would be leaving before seven a.m.

When we went to bed, my mind was drained, like a deflated balloon.

Linda scolded me by telling me my decision to quit was embarrassing. She was by the bed, the half-light showing off her curves.

As she continued to admonish me, I found her half-nakedness seductive. Overwhelmed with passion, I took her in my arms and silenced her with a kiss—a long passionate kiss.

She moaned, held me closer. "You stupid Irishman, is that all you can think about?"

"I like it when you're angry," I whispered. I got lost in her, overwhelmed with desire, holding her close, feeling her breasts, the sultry warmth of her mouth. We tried to keep our lovemaking silent, but it was difficult . . . so difficult.

Afterwards I lay in bed, exhausted. She was asleep, her

breath undulating. Thinking about the caller kept me awake. God, how I hated him. I had dealt with many creeps over the years, but this bastard was in a class by himself.

©©

Nighttime, the highway nearly deserted. I drove into Hoboken and parked in front of my home. I entered and turned off the security alarm.

I had never been alone in my own home. The silence made me feel like an intruder. I checked the windows, the doors, and the closets. Nothing suspicious.

Sunlight peeked through the windows. I went into the kitchen and fixed a breakfast tea. I despaired over the possibility Linda and Josh might leave me.

I wondered if this was the meaning of Linda's dream. *Death?* The artist in me knew there were many types of death besides the corporeal. There was a spiritual death, a death of the spirit.

This much I knew: I couldn't bear to lose my family. That would be more painful than dying. Could I turn my back on my PI work? I didn't think so. I was caught in a whirlpool of fate and following a destiny that began long ago with the death of my father and my father's father before him.

Claudius expressed it best in *Hamlet*:

> *But you must know your father lost a father,*
> *That father lost, lost his, and the survivor bound*
> *In filial obligation for some term*
> *To do obsequious sorrow.*

The truth is I loved being a PI. Although dangerous, the work was electrifying and placed demands on my craft I had never experienced, real life-and-death dramas, walking a tightrope without a safety net, where one slip might be fatal. This paled when compared to the make believe of a stage. I felt compelled to continue, even if I fulfilled a destiny that destroyed me.

I snapped out of the depression and finished the tea. I went upstairs to shower and change clothes. Before leaving the house, I called Frank.

"Theo, I've been expecting your call. Where are you?"

"Home in Hoboken. I'm leaving soon."

"I canvassed Hoboken yesterday in my van, hoping to pick up a footprint of the scanner. Nothing."

"Is it safe to use my cell phone?"

"It's probably safe, but be careful. I spoke to Stella. Everyone's worried."

"My family's safe. I'm heading into the office."

# Chapter Twenty-Four

I DROVE INTO MANHATTAN, parked in the garage on Sullivan Street, and headed for the office. Stella was waiting in the boiler room with the other investigators.

"Theo . . ." She walked over and hugged me. "How's the family?"

"They're fine." I told everyone my in-laws had taken them to Riverdale.

"We were so worried," Stan said.

"Frank thinks the creep is slipping up. The caller used a police scanner to monitor my cell phone calls. If he did, then Frank may be able to track him."

Stella balked at the price after I explained Frank's plan to track the caller.

"I have to do this," I said.

Stella sighed and nodded in agreement. "Do you want Linda to hear the message on the answering machine?"

"Yes, I'll take a CD home with me tonight."

"What about Chen-Kuo?" Kimberley asked. "Do you think he knows anything about Hwa's murder?"

"I wouldn't be surprised," I said. "Right now, the cops have zilch. Chen-Kuo must have heard something."

Stella said copies of Bruno's picture had been sent to Richardson's attention. She gave me a manila envelope with a picture to show Chen-Kuo.

©©

I was looking forward to the peddler sweep in Chinatown. Before we left, I took Angel aside and told him about the violent Asian gangs that once ruled the knockoff market in Chinatown. Their favorite weapon was an M-80 firecracker, equivalent to about a quarter stick of dynamite.

"My back was turned once, and an M-80 exploded near my head," I said. "I was knocked off my feet and later had to see a doctor."

Angel was awestruck and mentioned the gangs in Spanish Harlem.

"This is different, trust me. After the police formed Asian units to combat the street gangs, most of them disappeared."

Everyone was ready. Stan sat shotgun in the front seat next to Angel, who was the driver. He was wearing a dashiki shirt and a kufi cap for his cover as a Senegalese street peddler. He was fingering a string of prayer beads to complete the ruse.

The Senegalese street peddlers were an anomaly in New York City. Most of them were from Senegal or from other African countries. They moved in groups and could be found near the bigger department stores, fingering prayer beads and selling knockoff Louis Vuitton bags, Gucci watches, and pirated music CDs.

I sat in the back next to Kimberley, who looked forbiddingly fashionable in a leather jumpsuit. I was the odd-man out, a *gringo*. Asians on Canal Street had a natural aversion to the *Wai Guo Gwei* [Foreign Devils]. I had to work harder at this cat-and-mouse game. My favorite ruse was the good ol' boy Southerner.

We were not after street peddlers this time, but moving up a notch and targeting vendors who rented space in the numerous open-air markets and small boutiques. These vendors used an effective tactic of displaying a small selection of knockoffs, so only a small quantity would be seized.

Our job was to talk a big deal and show flash money. If successful, we'd be told to return later, only we'd return with a police backup. The vendor would be issued a desk appearance ticket or DAT.

As Angel drove down Broadway, he caught a sideways glance at Stan, absent-mindedly rolling prayer beads in his palm.

"I have seen you with these beads before," Angel said. "Are you praying?"

"Angel, you know I'm an atheist," Stan replied indignantly.

"*Si*, I know. You are a philosopher. A man without God."

"That's right." He continued to play with the beads. "Truth is, I'm practicing."

"Practicing?"

"To conduct a philosophical inquiry."

Angel took his eyes from the road. "You kiddin' me, man?

Kimberley jumped into the fray and reprimanded Stan "This is his first time out. Do you want to jinx him before we've even started?"

She looked like an avenging angel in black leather. When she gave an order, people obeyed.

"It's the nihilist in me." Stan apologized and turned to Angel, "I'm practicing with the prayer beads, so I can pass as a Senegalese street peddler."

Angel smiled. "Yes, I have seen the Senegalese in groups selling counterfeit goods. I have seen the clothes they wear and their beads."

"They're called worry beads." Stan replied as he began to manipulate the beads. "A man fingers them to calm himself or to pray to Allah."

While watching Stan demonstrate, Angel stayed steady with the downtown traffic. "You're good. I am sure you'll fool the Chinese."

"Kimberley and Theo are the masters of this game," Stan said.

Angel glanced at us in the rearview mirror. "I can tell Kimberley is ready for business. *Chiquita*! She'll have the men crawling. But Theo, what's your plan of action?"

I replied in a neat Southern drawl. "Shucks, son. Ah'm from New Or'lins. We speak a diff'nt language down there . . . If y'all know what ah mean."

"That was great!"

"Theo's the best of the best," Kimberley said. "We've all received acting lessons from him."

"When will you teach me to act?" Angel asked excitedly.

"Soon, *mi hijo.*"

Angel stopped at the intersection of Broadway and Canal Street, overflowing with shoppers, mostly Asians. A powerful pungency hovered over the wood troughs where fish, shrimp and butchered pork rested on ice in wood troughs. Many of the restaurants had tasty roast ducks hanging in a row in the window; while inside, people were seated and ordering steamed pork buns, dumplings, soup, or fried noodles.

The street peddlers were everywhere. They sold their wares in freezing cold or steaming hot weather, and were a throwback to Biblical times. Some hawked vegetables like bok choy and string beans; others sold inexpensive jewelry, water pipes, and magazines. By far, however, most hawked knockoffs. Street peddlers were the most numerous and successful counterfeiters. They triumphed by their numbers and lack of an efficient legal remedy.

Canal Street is the counterfeit watch capital of the world. John Hwa had been one of the many vendors who sold knockoff watches from a briefcase, ready to pack up and run. In the war against the fakes, this was a battleground where the genuine and the fake co-exist, where shoppers picked and haggled, and then pocketed their watches.

While Angel drove, Kimberley leaned forward and elucidated on her former neighborhood for his benefit. She knew where the turf battles between rival gangs had occurred.

"Gang members wore black jeans, white sneakers, and most had spiky hair with dyed highlights," she recalled. "Others wore nylon bomber jackets with a dragon stitched on the back."

She spoke about past places and people. Angel sat, transfixed, mumbling, "*Dios mio,*" from time to time.

"There, over there—" She pointed to a building with a pagoda roof plumb on the intersection of Mott Street and Canal Street. The Taiwanese flag waved from the rooftop.

"That's 83 Mott Street, where the On Leong Chinese Merchants has its headquarters. This is the Tong. It rules Chinatown through its hold on Mott Street. At one time the

White Eagles gang helped the Tong consolidate power. When relations frayed during the mid-1970s, the Tong sanctioned a takeover by the Ghost Shadows. Many people were killed."

Each of us had designated areas. Stan was assigned to the eastern end of Canal Street, Kimberley the middle. I had the western stretch.

Angel pulled over to the curb so Stan could depart. Several blocks away, he pulled over for Kimberley. As I exited, I instructed him to continue traversing up and down Canal Street until contacted for a pick-up.

I blended into the crowd and strolled into an open-air store, where vendors rented space and sold incense, back scratchers, fans, and other trinkets. It was long hours and small profits, prompting many to sell knockoffs.

I had no trouble spotting a suitable target, an old Asian man sitting behind a display of two dozen knockoff Rolexes, arranged by design inside a wood box. There was no cash register. All deals were for cash. He was one of six vendors inside the store.

"Y'all selling watches—now ain't that somethin.' Nothin' like this in Georgia. Say where's Mistuh Tam?"

It was a good opening gambit. I had conducted seizures in nearly every store in Chinatown and remembered a defendant named Tam who sold counterfeit sneakers here.

The vendor, a short squat man, shook his head dumbly.

"Golly me . . . he was mah man. Course, last time I wuz here was several years ago. Yes'm, that was before the terrorist attack. Shame 'bout "dat, yes'm. You was here, wasn't you?"

"Who me?" The Asian smiled politely.

"Terr'ble, terr'ble thing. I saw it on the TV and thought of all the dyin' and it made me and muh wife sick to think of it, yes'm."

I tried to find a safe line of communication that had nothing to do with counterfeits. The World Trade Center attack was a good topic for an out-of-town tourist.

"Oh yes, terrible. You like watches?"

*Bingo. Now to reel him in slowly.*

I inspected several styles. I picked up a Rolex, a Daytona replica that was much lighter than the genuine; another defect was the absence of a sweeping hand. Thirty bucks, the usual asking price.

"Y'know, I want to take some back home. Surprise the hell out of everyone. How much will three thousand bucks buy?"

The old man gave me a quick once over glance, as if trying to see through me. "Can't sell . . . Can't sell."

"Can't sell? Why not?"

"Only have these—" he made a gesture indicating that what was on display was his entire stock.

"Perhaps y'all know someone who can sell me Rolexes. I can pay cash." I pulled out my wallet, thick with seed money.

*Bingo!* The man's eyes lit up. Within minutes, I had a deal for five hundred counterfeit Rolex watches for three thousand dollars.

I haggled over a down payment. Eventually I forked over thirty dollars. The name on the receipt was Mr. Ho. He told me to come back in two hours.

I walked out of the store. I entered a retail outlet a few blocks away. There were hundreds of vendors. I walked from stall to stall until I spotted one selling counterfeit Rolexs.

I went into my good old boy routine but he was not easily swayed. He replied in an indignant, arrogant voice.

"Who you boss? A cop?"

"Yes'm, ah'm a cop all rightie!" I barked, reaching into my pocket and drawing out my wallet. I pulled out a twenty dollar bill and slapped it down. "Here's mah social security card!"

I pulled out another twenty and slapped it down hard. "Here's mah driver's license!"

Now I pulled out a fifty and slapped it down hard. Real hard. "Here's mah badge!"

"Okay, boss, okay." The young man looked around nervously. I had deliberately spoken loud enough to attract attention, forcing him to settle me down.

The counterfeiter offered me a deal for two thousand watches. "No down payment," he whispered. "Come back in two hours. Ten thousand dollars cash."

I thanked him and left. It was an easy day: two contacts, two deals. Sometimes, I had to make five or more contacts for a deal.

©©

I called Angel and caught the van at the corner of Centre Street. I reached for a notebook and recorded the time and location of the deals.

"Theo, when can I go out into the streets?" the youngster smiled. This was an adventure he wanted to join.

"First you watch and listen. Later, I'll give an acting lesson."

"Acting, I can't wait for you to teach me!"

I took out a counterfeit watch and instructed him on its flaws. "See, a real Rolex has a sweeping watch hand."

He listened intently while he continued to steer through traffic. At one corner, he pointed to a crowd of pedestrians: businessmen and secretaries on their lunch break buying knockoff watches, tourists searching for fake Hermes scarves, and mothers holding hands with their children while inspecting knockoff Louis Vuitton handbags.

"Theo, is all this counterfeit?"

"Yes, most of what you see being sold on Canal Street is fake."

"All counterfeit." He shook his head and I knew the sheer enormity of the crime had made an impact.

"Yes, Angel. And the problem is even worse overseas. I've visited shopping malls in Thailand and Hong Kong where people stand in line to purchase counterfeit goods stacked to the roof. Department stores filled to the ceiling with fakes.

After some thought, he asked what was causing this?

It was nearly an existential question and one I had asked myself. I had a simple answer:

"Human greed. The Spanish have a way of saying it, *"Con esperanza no se come."*

He smiled sadly. The English translation means "honor buys no meat in the market."

Within the hour, both Kim and Stan had returned. Now it was time to visit Chen-Kuo.

# Chapter Twenty-Five

SOME MEMORIES NEVER GO away. Ten years had passed since Kimberley worked in a sweatshop. Sadness crept into her voice whenever she recalled how they docked a half-hour of pay for a minute of lateness, and how even a single phone call could lead to being docked a half-day's pay.

Her worst job was in a sweatshop with a Chinese street gang for a client. The brazen gang members extorted money from the owner and forced him into providing knockoff apparel. They would come at any time and intimidate the seamstresses for sexual favors.

I met her while executing a seizure order in which the gang members were arrested. She became an informant like Hwa, while continuing to work as a seamstress. She quit after I offered her a job.

We walked the five blocks to 115 Mott Street. As we ascended the steps to the second floor, I tried to imagine the tired hands and sore limbs of those who had trudged these stairs to the drop-in center. Chen-Kuo disliked the term "labor center" and had organized it as a friendly, family-oriented drop-in center. This was his second location; the first was destroyed by a firebomb.

The children had a play area conveniently located next to a soft-drink machine. The sound of their laugher echoed; their mothers, seated at a large table nearby, talked and drank tea. Closer to me were old men playing Chinese checkers on a bridge table. Several youths watched the game, some seated on an iron settee with a view, the others standing.

When we entered, curious eyes looked us over and centered on Kimberley, no doubt because of her fashionable leather attire.

The indefatigable Hur Chen-Kuo was in his office. He waved as he rose from behind his desk and came out to greet us.

"*Ni hao, shao mei*," he said.

"*Hao, ba-ba*," Kimberley replied and embraced him.

Chen-Kuo turned to me. "We meet again, brother."

We shook hands. He had aged little since we last met. He was small and thin like a rail with sandy white hair. I sensed something troubling underneath his happy smile.

"Kimberley dresses so differently these days," Chen-Kuo laughed. "You should have seen the clothes she wore when I first met her."

"Thanks, *ba-ba*." Kimberley laughed. "Thanks for your help—we need it again."

"Please come into my office."

Little had changed, with stacks of paper piled high on the desk and on the floor. After the first office was destroyed, he decided not to purchase new furniture. His wood desk was second-hand, while the filing cabinet had rust patches. However, the pictures on the wall were genuine: workers on a picket line or at a picnic get-together. His favorite was of him receiving an award from the Chinese Business Association.

Kimberly and I sat on metal fold-up chairs. He sat down and clasped his hands before him on the desk.

"Kimberley said you're investigating the murder of John Hwa. I know you are trying to help but you must leave this alone."

"How well did you know Jenny Ling?" I asked.

"I cannot answer because of the police investigation."

"*Ba-ba*, you must trust us—" Kimberley said.

"It is not a matter of trust," he said firmly. "There are other workers involved."

"But their lives are in jeopardy," I said. "The owner of Asian Seas has been murdered."

"I know. Brother, please remember we do things differently in Chinatown."

I knew him well enough to be frustrated by this speech about different cultures, often used to meander around an issue. I interrupted and asked what he knew about the Asian Seas sweatshop.

"Nothing that Jenny and Sergeant Ortiz haven't already told you," he replied.

"You've spoken to Jenny?" Kimberley asked.

He nodded. "We spoke yesterday. She's cooperating with the authorities . . . Let the police handle this."

"How long have you known her?" I asked.

"Not long."

"Did you meet her in person or speak on the phone?" I asked.

"I cannot say anymore."

"*Ba-ba*, what will the *shetou* do if Jenny doesn't pay?" Kimberley asked.

His eyes darkened. "How do you know about the *shetou*?"

"She told us," Kimberley said.

"You know little about the *shetou*, little sister." A knowing smile crossed his lips.

"Forget them. I have had run-ins with the *shetou*, but they respect me and know I am trying to help my countrymen."

The room grew quiet. Chen-Kuo had managed to answer our questions without giving us much. I suspected he was hiding information. To break the deadlock, I told Kimberly to show him the picture.

"We believe this man may be the murderer," I said, as she handed it to him.

As he scrutinized it, his eyebrows arched. "This man was there the day of the strike!"

"You were there that day," Kimberley said, making the obvious connection.

"Yes, I was there. I saw this man's face before he pushed me to the ground."

Chen-Kuo was on the picket line and barely got a look at the assailants because of the hoodies. He tried to stop the leader, who had pushed and punched several people, and grabbed his sweatshirt. He tried to hold him and saw his face for a moment before being pushed to the ground. The assailant had a nasty scar on his cheek, like Bruno's.

"Could this be the man who murdered John Hwa?"

He nodded. "It could be. Who is he?"

"His name's Bruno. I managed to take his picture while investigating undercover."

"*Ba-ba*, why did Jenny become upset when we mentioned your name?"

"To protect me because I helped organize the strike. I worked with Lucy Zho who told me about the unfair labor practices and knockoffs. I met with other workers, including Jenny."

"Why did you tell her to contact the trademark infringement unit?" I asked.

"Use all the weapons at your disposal. The others were afraid to call and Lucy has a criminal record."

"A criminal record? For what?" Kimberley asked.

"Lucy worked as a prostitute to make payments to the *shetou*. After she was arrested by the police and released, she found work at Asian Seas. The owner is a former client of hers."

"My god, so Lucy knows the owner's real name," Kimberley said.

"Yes, but she is the only one who knows his real name. Even I do not know it. The Uncle wanted to continue having relations with Lucy, who was not interested. Perhaps there is more between these two, but I agreed to help."

"So you went for trademark counterfeiting," I said.

"That's all I had at the time to hurt Asian Seas."

Showing him the picture had opened him up. Everything about the strike and Jenny's involvement were beginning to fall into place, except that Hwa was murdered shortly after she contacted Sergeant Ortiz.

"An unfortunate coincidence," he replied. "Sergeant Ortiz is trustworthy, so I believe John Hwa was killed because Jenny is new to this country, easier to intimidate."

"Why kill the husband, not Jenny?"

"Not sure. Perhaps killing a man, particularly a loved one, would cause great fear among the female workers."

"Any idea how the killers tracked the Hwas?"

"None. The killers can answer that."

"Could the same people who killed Hwa also kill the Uncle?"

"It's likely."

Next, I wanted him to testify and took a chance by discussing the FBI's upcoming raid. His face brightened like the sun coming out after a thunderstorm. "The FBI! Wonderful!"

"A seizure of IG knockoffs will be going down at a company called Raiments," I said. "Bruno works for this company."

"Brother, it is so rare that justice is achieved," he said happily.

"The police and the FBI need evidence for a murder charge," I said. "Your testimony and eye witness identification of Bruno would help."

"It is out of the question." His eyes turned downcast.

"Why not?" I asked.

"The police are not my friend," he said. "I would be asked questions that I cannot answer without hurting the people that seek my assistance. Many are illegal; others have problems and no one to turn to."

"But you know Sergeant Ortiz," I pointed out.

"I know of him," he said. "I would never call him myself."

"You can help put a murderer away," Kimberley said.

"Show Jenny the picture. She will testify . . . I cannot."

Chen-Kuo smiled, but it was a sad smile. He looked at each of us in turn and his gaze was firm. I had managed to open him up and got a much clearer picture of the strike and his involvement. I decided to step up the pressure.

"Look Chen-Kuo, a murderer may walk free," I said.

"I know, I wish I could help."

"Bull shit!" I said. Kimberley took my arm. "Please Theo, don't."

This was our version of the "good cop-bad cop." I got angry and threatening and she calmed me down and urged the suspect to cooperate.

Alarmed, Chen-Know said, "Brother, you dare to threaten me."

"Damn right you're going to help us!" I leaned forward menacingly. "Or so help me, I'm going to the police."

"Please Theo," Kimberley wailed and looked toward Chen-

Kuo. He sat there with a look of defiance. He didn't bluff easily.

"What about the *shetou*?" Kimberley asked. "Jenny and the others aren't working. Are they in danger?"

"I don't believe so," Chen-Kuo said.

"We want to be sure," I said. "The *shetou* must be hiding them. Give me something to work with and I'll back off."

Chen-Kuo sighed. "All right, I will help you. There is someone you can talk to. His name is Joey Qin. He runs a dry cleaner about two blocks from here.

© ©

It was a small store with a plate glass front and the words *Qin Dry Cleaners* in English and in Chinese script. I hesitated before entering, not entirely sure what to say or expect. The man seated behind the counter was of average height and wearing glasses. Next to him was a cash register. A small television rested on a nearby stool. To the left were racks of dry cleaned clothes on hangers and wrapped in plastic. A few feet behind him were curtains that sealed off the back.

Qin was watching television and looked up. "May I help you?"

"I hope so. We're friends of Chen-Kuo's," I said.

That caught his attention. He turned off the television and stared at us. His eyes lingered on Kimberley, apparently not knowing what to make of her, dressed in scintillating leather.

"Who are you?" he asked.

"We're private investigators," I said. "Do you want to see my license?"

His eyes lingered on Kimberley. "That won't be necessary. What do you want?"

"We want to talk about Jenny Ling."

He frowned and yelled something in Chinese. Within seconds, a woman emerged from behind a curtain. Qin introduced her as his wife. She was short and rail thin. She took over, while we followed him into the rear.

We passed by stacks of clothes, a small table with a hot plate and packs of ramen soup; further back, a sink, and a sewing machine resting next to a basket filled with clothes. Against the back wall was a large table flanked by four chairs; obviously a meeting place. Qin sat at one end; Kimberley and I took seats facing him.

"You're too pretty to be an investigator," he snickered and brazenly eyed Kimberley. "What's with the leather, huh?"

She pouted and batted her eyelids. "It's for smart guys like you, *fang-pi*."

"*Fang-pi!*" He laughed raucously and turned in my direction. "Hey, do you know what this smart bitch called me?"

"We're not here for games," I said curtly. I knew she had called him a smelly fart.

"Yes, yes . . . that's good. *Fang-pi*." He licked his lips and smiled. "Now, please tell me your names."

"Mine's Theo. Hers is Kimberley."

"Theo and Kimberley. Pleased to meet you. It is such an honor to meet someone so beautiful . . . Now what did Chen-Kuo tell you about me?"

"He said you're *shetou*," Kimberley said.

"*Shetou*?" Qin tried to act surprised. He laughed but stopped short when neither of us joined him. "Is that what he told you, pretty one? Look around, I run a dry cleaning store."

"We're concerned about Jenny Ling," I said. "We're working with the police to find the killer of her boyfriend, John Hwa. Jenny must have mentioned me. I was his friend."

"Yes, Jenny did mention a Caucasian friend. Maybe it was you. I am familiar with the term *shetou*, the snakehead. A serpent with a thousand limbs. Is that what you mean?"

"That's right," I said.

"Then I am *shetou*. So is Jenny Hwa, so is Chen-Kuo, and many who live in Chinatown are *shetou*."

"I don't understand," I said.

"I think I do," Kimberley replied. "Qin is referring to *guanxi*. To connections."

"That's right, pretty one. The snakehead is different things to different people. It all depends on *guanxi*. I am a low man and take assignments from others. For that I am paid."

"What kind of assignments?" she asked.

"Like speaking to you, pretty one."

Qin loosened up about his past.

©©

*I was born in the big city of Fouzou in Fujian province. My family had run an agricultural equipment business for decades, but after the Second World War, the factory was taken over by the state. The business continued as before, except that the state took most of the revenue. However, my family, which had imported machine parts for tractors, got involved in assisting people to move out of the country—and thrived because it was a way of life in Fujian Province, strategically situated to Taiwan, and because of corruption, which meant paying this official or that official to look the other way. For a price, a person could be moved across the straits to Taiwan, and from there travel to other countries. Many people wanted to flee the Communists.*

*Large families in China were legal when I was born. My four older brothers got involved in the family business of smuggling people overseas. From an early age, I knew I would eventually be involved with the family business; but when I was young, President Richard Nixon established diplomatic ties and everything changed. As democracy slowly crept across China, people wanted to move to America. I was selected to travel to the United States and to serve as a liaison with others already in the human smuggling business. I asked for political asylum and became a legal citizen. After opening a dry cleaning establishment, I continued to work with people whose sole business was smuggling people into America.*

©©

"I have contacts that I cannot discuss with you or even Chen-Kuo," Qin said. "Although the *shetou*, as you call them, are engaged in a criminal enterprise, they are not criminals. Jenny owes money, but arrangements will be made for her to pay off her debt."

"Isn't the INS looking for the people who smuggled Jenny into the country?" I asked.

He nodded. "The police and the INS questioned Jenny about how she snuck into the United States. She has been coached on what to say."

"How about Lucy Zho and the other workers?" Kimberley asked.

"I don't know any of them . . . I know Jenny. I cannot tell you anything more."

"Tell us the truth." I glared at him. He was up to his ears in human trafficking, otherwise Chen-Kuo wouldn't have referred him.

I continued, "You must know where some of the workers are hiding. The police are looking for them because their lives are in danger."

"I told you I don't know any of them," he said.

"You little shrimp, two people have been murdered." I rose from the chair as if going to pummel him.

"No need to get nasty." His voice quavered. "I didn't know two people had been killed."

"You didn't know about the Uncle?" Kimberley asked.

"Yeah, don't lie to us," I said.

Qin squirmed uneasily in his seat. "You mean the owner of the sweatshop where Jenny worked?"

Kimberley nodded. "He's dead. Murdered."

"Have you ever seen this man?" I told her to show him Bruno's photo.

He gave it a once over, then shook his head. "No. I have never seen him."

"We believe he's the murderer who killed John Hwa and the Uncle. I'm going to leave you this picture. And don't fool around with me or I'm coming back here. Understand?"

"I told you I don't know this man."

"Yes you do. You know I'm a friend of John Hwa's and I want answers."

I stood and tried to grab him by the shirt lapels; Kimberley held me back.

Qin tried to act tough but his body was shaking. "I cannot tell you anything."

"Then let us speak to Lucy Zho." Kimberley said, softening him by acting the good cop to my bad cop.

He frowned. "No. It cannot be done. Too dangerous."

"You can arrange it." I pointed my finger at him like a gun. "You better if you know what's good for you."

"Qin, please arrange something." My acting lessons had paid off. Kimberley gasped, as if she couldn't control me, while I let my voice rise. "If I know she's safe, then I know the others are safe."

This went back and forth for a few rounds. With me getting angrier, Kimberley trying to settle me, and Qin refusing to get involved.

We wore him down and he agreed to arrange a meeting with Lucy Zho. "I speak to you now because you know Chen-Kuo and Jenny. The people who helped Jenny arrive in this country are more concerned with her safety than money. I have answered your questions and trust what I have said will remain secret."

"You have my word," I said.

"You will hear from me."

©©

"What happened at Chen-Kuo's?" Stan asked when we returned.

"Let's talk about it when we get back to the office," I said. "It's complicated. Besides, Officer Chan is on his way; don't mention any of this to him."

I reviewed the inventory sheet. A total of eight thousand watches would be seized. The rendezvous with Chan was to take place at three-thirty at the corner of Elizabeth and Canal Streets.

On schedule, a blue and white patrol car pulled over. Officer Chan exited and joined us on the sidewalk. He was in his early thirties, could speak several dialects and was an asset when dealing with the Asian peddlers, some of whom couldn't speak any English.

"That's the one good thing about this detail." Chan smiled and looked Kimberly over. "I get to check out Kimberley. Lookin' good."

"Oh boy," she pouted. "If checking me out is your idea of fun, then you should join a monastery."

"You won't have to put up with me much longer," Chan said. "I'm getting out."

"Getting out? You mean you've taken another job?" I asked.

Chan nodded. "Yeah. I decided to take another career path. "Ten years. I should have made detective by now but I'm doing this shit work."

I knew what he meant. Chasing knockoff street peddlers was low level and did not offer a career path.

"Lieutenant Ash said he questioned you about John Hwa," I said.

"Yeah, I'll miss Hwa. I told the Lieutenant what I knew about them."

"Them? I didn't know you'd met Jenny," I said. "Did you know she was an undocumented alien?"

He shrugged. "No, but I'm not surprised. Being undocumented in New York City is a non-crime . . . I hardly knew her."

"What's your interest in Hwa's murder?" Chan asked.

"I feel like I owe him . . . maybe I even feel responsible. I'm trying to figure out whether he was killed because he was a snitch—or whether he was killed in retaliation for Jenny's involvement in the strike."

"I heard about the strike at the sweatshop," Chan said. "I didn't even know she had a job."

We headed for the old Asian man. The four of us entered and surrounded him. There were two plastic bags near his feet. The Asian's eyes drooped when he saw the uniformed officer.

"Are you Richard Ho?" Chan asked. "Do you have identification?"

The old man nodded. He reached into his pocket for his wallet and then handed over his driver's license.

"We're private investigators," I said. "We're seizing those watches. Understand?"

"You good," he said and managed a half smile. "Fool me, good."

Stan walked behind the counter and pushed the old man aside. He grabbed one of the plastic bags, Kimberly the other.

Chan handed him the DAT. "You're to appear in Court on the date and time indicated. Now who delivered those watches to you?"

"A man, I don't know his name."

"How did you contact him?" I asked. "Come on, cooperate. You could go to jail."

"By phone."

"What's the phone number?"

He hesitated before answering. "212-997-8992."

"Is that the right number?" I asked. "If it's not, you're going to jail."

"That's the number." He glared at me.

As we were leaving, I saw him pull out his cell phone.

"He's going to call everyone he knows," I said.

Chan nodded. We knew news of the raid would spread like the wind. However, we hoped to execute the seizures before the vendors and peddlers on Canal Street could hide their knockoffs.

We continued to the next vendor, and after that, the next one until all of the watches had been seized and the cargo space in the back of the van was filled. Some of the watches were in plastic bags; others in cardboard boxes.

When we were finished and ready to depart, I told Chan I'd miss him and wished him luck.

"Thanks," Chan said. "I'm too burned out. There's no end."

He gestured up and then down Canal Street at the endless peddlers, lined shoulder to shoulder and hawking their counterfeit goods. Our sweep was only for Rolex watches.

"I know what you mean," I said. "That's why I call it a war."

He laughed. It was a gripe of mine he had heard many times. "Maybe you're right," he said and we shook hands for the last time.

# Chapter Twenty-Six

LINDA WAS IN THE living room, seated on a couch and reviewing papers for a class. "Theo, glad you're home," she said.

I sat next to her, gave her a quick kiss. "Where's Josh?" I asked.

"I think he's upstairs . . . probably drawing."

Perfect. I didn't want JJ present when we listened to the CD. There was no easy way to tell her, so I jumped in, "Honey, someone left a threatening phone call at work. It was a recorded voice."

"Another recorded threat?" She looked at me in disbelief.

"That's right." I told her how Stan had discovered the message, delivered at nearly the same time.

"This is . . . sick." She cringed. "Who is this nut?"

"I have a copy of the message with me."

"Yes, I want to hear it."

I removed the CD from my briefcase and inserted it into the CD player next to her. I put the sound on low and pressed the play button.

There was a whirr—and then.

Linda gasped, "My God, that's the voice! It's the caller."

I shut off the CD player. "Now do you remember what he said?"

"It happened so quickly, but I believe this message is identical."

"He may try to call again," I said. "That's why I had a security consultant inspect our home security and telephones."

"Security cameras, telephone threats!" She shook her head. "Theo, what's our life going to be like?"

"It won't be like this much longer."

©©

I awoke at six the next day and headed into Manhattan for a rendezvous with Stan. I was excited by the prospect of working with the FBI on a high profile seizure.

The rental truck, an Isuzu NPR, was parked in front of 236 Thompson Street. I took the elevator to the second floor, stopped for a moment to greet Stella, and then went next door to the boiler room where Stan was waiting. He was wearing jeans and a dark sweatshirt. As for myself, I was wearing brown tropical wool slacks and a white button-down shirt. A far cry from my usual good ol' boy garb of Western boots and indigo jeans.

"We're ready to tackle Raiments," Stan said. "How's your family?"

"Thanks for asking, they're fine." I told him my wife had listened to the recorded death threat and said it was a match.

"Does she have any idea who's behind this? What's he trying to prove?" Stan was exasperated.

"We have to hang on," I said. "Stay focused. Don't let these calls rattle us."

I took a moment to review the operation. Satisfied, I called Zeckindorff.

"Theo, ba-a-a-by. All set?"

"We're ready on our end."

"Good. What happened at Drake's? Why did you leave?"

"An emergency. But it's all taken care of. Did you get a chance to talk to Drake?"

"Yes I did; Harney joined us. Drake was scared when the detective questioned him about the murders. You won't have to worry about him tipping off Ahmad."

"Good, because we're getting ready to leave."

"Wait, Drake said something interesting."

"Yeah?"

"He admitted to selling knockoffs from time to time—but get this; he said the IG sweaters are genuine."

"What! He must be crazy. Didn't you tell him the sweaters were analyzed?"

"I told him. But he insists that the Smith brothers are tight with the rapper and have an agreement to manufacture IG apparel. Caldwell is familiar with the IG International licensed vendors and said Drake is lying to save himself."

"What's going to happen to him?"

"He was booked for assault and made bail. As for the license, I agree with Caldwell. Drake's lying to save himself."

"What about the Raiments seizure?"

"Richardson wants to discuss it. I was about to leave for Newark."

"I'll meet you."

"Wait, before you hang up—"

"What?"

"Drake's sorry. He lost his temper when he realized you're an investigator. He wants you to call so he can apologize."

"That's big of him."

Stan, who had overheard my conversation, wanted to know more about Drake's story.

"Zeckindorff and Caldwell are in big trouble if the Smith brothers have a licensing agreement with Raiments," I said. "The legal term is 'groundless and without merit' for the department store seizure we executed. Drake can countersue for damages."

"Are we going ahead with the seizure at Raiments?" Stan asked.

That was the obvious question. It would be suicide to continue if Raiments had an agreement with the rapper, who was the trademark holder and the perfunctory president of IG International.

"Zeckindorff will discuss it with the FBI," I said. "Let's presume it's a go."

We left the office. Stan drove the truck. He questioned me some more about the legal problem. I knew he was trying to understand how our side could suddenly be in trouble. Truthfully, so was I. However, trying not to sound philosophical, I gave him a piece of wisdom honed by two decades in the field.

"I bill by the hour and never get too involved with the legal issues." I said. "What's *fake* is sometimes *real* in this business. And vice versa."

Stan chuckled and kept steady with the Turnpike traffic. I reminded him why I had to inspect the knockoffs before the backup swooped in and the defendants were arrested. "I've had investigations where the fakes were genuine. Either an overrun from a licensed vendor, gray market goods, a fire sale or goods that wouldn't fit onto a shipping container."

"Shit happens," Stan said. I knew he understood.

We drove through the Holland Tunnel and onto the New Jersey State Turnpike on our way to see Richardson at his office. Stan parked the truck across the street from the FBI field office.

Stan and I crossed the street, passed through security, and took the elevator.

Richardson greeted us. I hardly recognized him. Instead of a business suit, he was wearing black jeans and boots. A Glock pistol was holstered to his duty belt. The word FBI in block letters was on the front of his baseball cap and on the back of his windbreaker.

"Is that your corporate look?" I joked. He wasn't amused. The friendly preppy was replaced by a stern visage.

I introduced Stan. After that, we followed him into the conference room where Zeckindorff and another special agent waited. His name was Zack Wilde who was part of Richardson's task force. He was an older man with gray hair.

Zeckindorff managed a smile and crooned, "Ba-a-a-by." I could tell the attorney was anxious. His shoulders drooped and he slouched in the chair.

I introduced Stan and, after some quick handshakes, we sat down at the conference table opposite Zeckindorff and the agents.

Richardson glared at Zeckindorff. "I need to know the seizure we're about to execute is on the level. Where's Caldwell?"

"According to his secretary . . ." Zeckindorff paused to compose himself. "He's out of town."

"What?" Richardson snapped. "Isn't he supposed to be here?"

Zeckindorff slowly exhaled and nervously looked around the room. I felt sorry for him, tongue-tied and unable to offer a credible explanation.

"He never said he was coming . . . I presumed he'd be here."

"Oh Christ," Richardson's voice rose.

Zeckindorff laid out the legal problem. "According to Drake, Orlando Smith and his brother grew up in the same neighborhood as the rapper. They've done business with him and supposedly have an agreement to manufacture IG apparel."

"So, what's the problem?" Wilde asked.

"The Raiments sweaters may not be counterfeit," Zeckindorff said. "Doesn't matter if acrylic fiber was used instead of cashmere. Last night, I leafed through the seizure order and reviewed the two affidavits Caldwell signed. One as in-house counsel for IG International in which he stated Raiments has no licensing agreement and is illegally manufacturing sweaters and possibly other apparel with the IG brand name. In the other, he identified himself as head of quality control and detailed the sweatshirt's flaws."

Richardson pointed out a discrepancy. "I've never heard of an in-house counsel in charge of quality control."

Neither had I. Quality control audited fabric and inventory, conducted factory visits. The person in charge usually had a background in apparel merchandizing.

"Yes, I noticed that myself," Zeckindorff said. "I believe Caldwell signed off as head of quality control to cut corners. He had to produce this document within hours so I could meet in chambers with the judge to amend the seizure order and post bond. I asked him about this, but he said from a legal standpoint nothing's wrong."

"No, I guess not." Richardson paused. I knew this was the moment of truth. The ASAC had the authority to call off the seizure.

Finally, he said, "Caldwell's signed affidavit is the bottom line. If anyone's lying, it has to be Drake." Richardson pointed a finger at Zeckindorff. "I'm depending on you and that fancy pants attorney. If this backfires, I'm going to look like an idiot. My superiors will have my head—and if the press gets hold of this, it's front page news."

"Ba-a-a-by," Zeckindorff tried to turn on the charm. But Richardson wasn't interested. "Let's get moving," he said curtly.

Richardson handed me a cell phone. This was no ordinary phone but had state-of-the-art features that would allow the ASAC to monitor me via a global positioning system and also had a radio frequency transmitter relaying conversation to a recording device.

He instructed me to keep the cell phone turned off to avoid detection by the Smith brothers who might search me for a wire. I was to turn it on when it was safe.

"Is the cell phone hooked into the DCSNet surveillance system?" I asked at one point.

Richardson looked at me with suspicion. "What do you know about the Red Hook?"

"I'm a PI. I have connections. I'm supposed to know these things."

I didn't tell him how I knew because I didn't want to get Frank Mohanis in trouble.

Richardson said the cell phone was hooked into the DCS-3000, also known as Red Hook.

"That's impressive," I said. For the first time, Richardson smiled. "The FBI prides itself on being the premier law enforcement agency in the world."

The ASAC had contacted the Cumberland County Sheriff's office. Two armed deputies from a tactical operation unit had been assigned and would be meeting us at the bank. Richardson walked us through a safety check and procedure. Most of it was familiar to Stan and me.

I led the discussion on the operations end of the seizure for the FBI agents.

"Tail us when we leave Raiments," I said. "I'll try to give you a coded message by cell phone after I've inspected the fakes. I'll serve the defendants with the seizure order when you arrive."

"What about Stan?" Richardson sat back in his chair and looked at him. "Won't Ahmad recognize his voice?"

Stan nodded. "Yes, but that was last week. Ahmad's never seen me in person."

"You guys will be alone with these creeps," Richardson said. "I don't want anything happening to either of you."

Zeckindorff came to our rescue. "These guys are good. Theo's a former actor."

Richardson smiled. "Fine, I'm convinced."

We left the room with the ASAC in the lead. The five of us fit inside a service elevator in the back of the office. It was an old elevator that had to be manually operated. A mechanical whirr, as Wilde worked the lever, and we descended, floor by floor, to a subbasement. Wilde opened a safety door that led to a dimly lit underground parking garage.

The sound of our shuffling feet echoed as we walked past rows of cars, including Zeckindorff's Mercedes. He had driven into Newark this morning and parked it here.

We continued. The air was stale and smelled of gasoline. We arrived at the FBI's car fleet, an area sealed by a chain link fence. Wilde used a key to remove the padlock.

The ASAC pointed to an unmarked black Ford Victoria Police Interceptor, sometimes called a CVPI, and showed us the inside. The dashboard had a command console in place of a glove box. I had never seen anything like it and was reminded of the car gadgets James Bond used. He pointed to the digital monitor which would be used for GPS tracking and another outlet he'd be using for eavesdropping and recording my conversations.

"Impressive," I said. The five of us got inside. With Wilde behind the wheel, we drove out of the parking garage, rounded the corner to the front of the building, and parked behind the truck.

We departed with the truck in the lead. When we hit the Turnpike, I looked into the rearview mirror and saw the backup vehicle following behind. I did a cell phone safety check. Satisfied, I sat back and tried to relax.

"What's up with Caldwell?" Stan asked.

"Beats me." I looked out the window and watched the traffic. "He's disappeared. Let's hope nothing's wrong."

Stan drove in silence as we headed for Whittier. We took a pit stop after two hours on the highway. I offered to drive, but Stan said he was fine.

Back on the road, he joshed me about my acting gig. "Never thought you'd get a role, did you?"

"No, I never did. It feels good to get back into it."

"This is a fabulous start. The International Gangster is big time. Zeckindorff has connections and can get you work. You'll see, Theo. You're on your way to acting fame. It will fall together."

Deep down I wanted to believe I could still perform. Sitting there, I began looking at my professional goals though a different lens. Maybe I could follow Linda's advice and move to another career, set my star for my life's first ambition. Perhaps sell half the business and work part-time. A world of possibilities lay ready to me.

As we proceeded on the highway, famous brand names flashed by in a blur—McDonald's, Burger King, Gulf. An endless and hypnotic monotony that left me feeling like the lead role in a surrealistic movie.

I had forgotten those happy, if futile days. If I sold the business, money would not be such a burden—but would anyone hire a middle-aged actor? Maybe I could get a break like the actor Joe Pesci, who was in his late thirties when Robert De Niro called and offered him a starring role in *Raging Bull*. Harrison Ford was another actor in his thirties and doing carpentry work when he got a role in *American Graffiti*.

I toyed with the fantasy. I had wanted to believe I was using my acting skills for a good cause, but now that my wife had been hurt, I feared the price was too high.

We rolled into Whittier at eleven-thirty. Stan parked the truck across the street from the Easy Commerce Bank. The backup vehicle parked in front of us. Zeckindorff opened the car door and waved as he crossed the street and entered the bank.

I got out and walked over to the CVPI. Richardson said he'd received a call from the deputies and expected them shortly. Everything was going smoothly. I walked back to the truck, where Stan was waiting, and got inside.

"What's up, boss?" Stan asked.

"The deputies are on the way," I said. "We'll be leaving shortly."

I spoke too soon. The minutes ticked by. Ten minutes became twenty.

"I wonder what's keeping Brian?" Stan mumbled.

"I don't know," I replied. "We have a timetable to keep."

I spotted a white and blue patrol car with Cumberland County markings pull up behind us. Two uniformed sheriff deputies got out.

I told Stan to stay in the van. I got out and walked back and introduced myself to the deputies. Richardson and Wilde joined us. We discussed the operation, as another ten minutes passed by. A pedestrian, walking across the street by the bank, stopped in his tracks and stared at what had to be an unusual sight in a small town like this before moving on.

"What's keeping Zeckindorff?" Richardson said impatiently.

Zeckindorff finally emerged looking utterly defeated. He crossed the street and walked over to us. Richardson introduced him to the deputies.

"Something's wrong," Zeckindorff said. "I met with my contact, a manager named Borchak. He's familiar with the account—and closed it on instructions from Caldwell. I tried to get hold of Caldwell to confirm. No luck. He's out of town."

Richardson was flustered. "I don't like this . . . It's starting to stink." He turned to me and said, "We may have to cancel. Maybe you can reschedule."

"Reschedule? No way. If we cancel, the deal will fall through."

Richardson pointed out the obvious. "What are you going to show the Smith Brothers? I'm sure they won't accept a credit card."

"Relax, these things happen. I can come up with several thousand to use as seed money."

"Will that work?"

"Trust me. We'll get the job done."

Although skeptical, I convinced him we should continue. We were too close to back away. Finally, he agreed. I walked back to the truck to talk with Stan. He rolled down the window so we could have a word.

"The bank account with the money was closed," I said.

"Closed? What happened?" He was flustered like all of us.

"Not sure. Zeckindorff tried to get hold of Caldwell, but he's conveniently out of town."

"Sounds like a setup."

"Let's hope not."

Stan was exasperated and shook his head as if reeling from

a bad dream. "I can't believe he'd close the account. What's up with him?"

That was the same question running through everyone's mind. "Maybe the rapper changed his mind about the money, and Caldwell had to close the account. "

"What are we going to do, Theo?"

"Improvise. Come up with a suitable ruse to fit the scenario. Hopefully, this is a minor screw-up, the kind of thing that happens in the field."

We always carried four or five thousand for unexpected expenses.

I pooled our cash, including the five thousand dollars flash money. Most of it was in hundreds and fifties. Bundled up, the wad was as thick around as a roll of toilet paper. Richardson walked over to us and offered to have money wired. I told him to forget it. We were already late.

# Chapter Twenty-Seven

STAN DROVE THE TRUCK, leading a convoy of three vehicles. He retraced the route I had taken earlier to the hill with its sweeping view of the Valley.

He pulled over onto the shoulder. I got out and walked to the crest and pointed to the access road that led to Raiments.

"We'll wait here," Richardson said. "I have binoculars, and I'll be monitoring what's being said."

"What about us?" one of the deputies asked.

"Both of you will follow my lead," Richardson said. "We can't get any closer without being spotted."

"Fine, we'll get ready." The deputy walked to the back of the car, opened up the trunk, and removed two Kevlar bulletproof vests and two shotguns that were secured on a trunk carrier. Stan's mouth fell open at the sight of the two armed deputies. We did a final safety check before Stan and I departed.

We drove down the hill and onto the access road. I noticed something odd when we got close. The parking lot was empty, except for a blue Lexus.

"I'm sure there's a good reason," Stan said.

"I'm sure there is," I said. "I don't think it's good for us."

I retrieved my cell phone and called Richardson. "Tom, its Theo. I noticed something odd. One car in the parking area; there were a dozen the other day."

"Sounds suspicious. Hang on." I heard him discuss the situation with Wilde. "I'm not sure what the reason but it may be good. Less people, less odds."

I was about to say that if we were going to be ambushed, the Smith brothers wouldn't want witnesses. I held back and told him we were going in.

Stan parked next to the Lexus. We exited and walked to the door. I opened it, and we entered the display shop.

Mohammad and Harasha were gone. Instead, two white guys were waiting. One was over six feet tall; the other was shorter but a mass of bulging muscles and sporting a shaved head.

"Which one of you is Orlando?" I asked.

"That's me," the tall man said. "This is my brother. Who's that with you?"

"My driver," I said of Stan. "Where's Musa?" I insisted.

"In his office. He wants to speak with you before we take you to the warehouse."

Orlando waited for us to pass and then followed behind. I didn't like this at all. I decided to wait before turning on the cell phone in case the ex-cons checked for a wire. Richardson had explained that the transmitter in the cell phone sent out radio waves, sometimes referred to as "harmonics," that could be picked up by a nonlinear junction detector, a device that looked and operated like a metal detector.

We entered the production area. Dead quiet. The fabric spreader and forklift were silent. Not surprising, because no one was here.

"Where is everyone?" I looked around as we proceeded.

"I sent everyone home," Orlando said. "Gave them the day off with pay, so we could conclude our business in private."

"That was thoughtful of you." I tried to control my nervousness. "Where's Musa? He's not in his office."

Orlando stopped. "His office?"

"Yeah, that office over there, where we met yesterday."

"That's not his office," Orlando said. "That's the shipping room, where we handle warehouse production. Our business office is in back. Follow me."

Orlando led Stan and I through the warehouse to a door in the back. He opened it and walked inside. The lights were on but I didn't see anyone.

Now I saw them. Off in the corner was Bruno and another man. Bruno was leering like he'd won the lottery.

Orlando's brother closed the door.

There was absolute silence in the room.

"What's going on?" I asked.

"We know you punks are investigators," Orlando growled.

It was a setup. Someone had ratted us.

"I don't know what you're talking about," I said coolly. "I came here to purchase a load of IG apparel."

"Bullshit!" Orlando barked. He reached behind the desk for a baseball bat. Pete and the other accomplices charged.

Hoping to distract the attackers, I grabbed Stan's arm. "Goddamn it, you must be a cop!" I slapped him on the side of the head with my other hand.

"Jeezus," Stan wailed, instantly guessing my plan. "I don't know anything about this."

"You bastard," I slapped him again, hard. My ploy momentarily confused Orlando and the others. I recognized the man with Bruno. I'd seen him at work on the fabric spreader. He looked different now, ugly and tough in work jeans and construction boots. I realized he helped Bruno break up the strike and was likely there when Hwa was stabbed.

I pummeled and cursed Stan, while he protested his innocence. This had to be convincing. I slapped and then belted him so hard he fell to the floor.

"Quit fooling around," Orlando yelled. "We know you guys are investigators."

Orlando ordered his men to break us up. I exploded in anger—real anger!—and ripped free. I ran to a desk, yanked the phone free from the wall jack and warned everyone to back off.

Meanwhile, Bruno wrestled Stan to the floor and grabbed hold of one arm, while the henchman joined him and secured the other.

Orlando ordered me to put down the phone and moved in with the baseball bat.

"You bastards are not going to rob me." I refused to back down, knowing that if I gave in, we were done for.

"Come on, I'll smash your head in!" I raised the phone, ready to hit him. I pointed to Stan. "Look, he's the cop, not me."

Stan and I were trapped in a room with four angry counterfeiters.

My best chance to get through this was to make them believe Stan was the cop. He continued to claim his innocence.

I sensed a weakening in Orlando and the others. They certainly did not want to tangle with me. I was an insane man. I was fired up enough to take out Pete, that muscle-bound freak show, with one punch.

"Look, settle down." Orlando tried to entice me into dropping my guard.

"Stay the fuck away from me," I roared. "You guys got the wrong man. If anyone is a cop, it's that slime bag."

"You mean you don't know him?" Orlando said, motioning for his brother and the two other goons to back off. "What the hell are you doing here with him?"

That was the question I was waiting to hear.

"Someone from Fashion X gave me his name and number. Maybe it was the cops. Let's call Luther Pine at Fashion X. He'll straighten this out."

"Fashion X? Is that the client that's got the Asian Seas sweaters?" Orlando asked.

"That's right . . . Luther spoke to Musa and wants to do business with Raiments."

"I don't like this, it's bullshit." Orlando hissed.

"If I was a cop, would I be carrying this?" I reached into my pocket and pulled out the seed money. I held up the thick wad and waved it.

"Oh, shit," the goon, whose name was Donald, whistled.

"If anyone is a cop, it's that asshole over there. Come clean, you're a cop, aren't you?"

Stan continued to protest his innocence and said he was an independent trucker who handled apparel and anything else. He said Luther Pine, his contact at Fashion X, had used him before.

"Stop this shit," Orlando demanded. "We know one of you guys is an investigator."

"He's the cop! Hey, cop, if you are who you say you are, give us names of people you've done business with."

The ruse was beginning to work. Suspicion had shifted from me to Stan. Now, I could rely on Stan's cover to get us out of the jam.

"Please don't hurt me," Stan pleaded. "Sure, I'll give you some names. Let's see, I've done business with Allied Apparel in North Carolina. Call and ask the owner if he knows Ben Barine."

That was quick thinking by Stan. He was using the alias Ben Barine for several ongoing investigations.

"We've got to think this over." Orlando motioned for Pete to come with him.

"Watch these two," Pete growled and went outside.

Donald released his hold on Stan and walked over to guard me. I looked at Stan, who was lying defenseless on the ground, with Bruno hovering over him.

"Lousy cop, you're in for it," I snarled. Stan continued to protest in vain.

Now was my chance. I reached for the cell phone with my free hand and turned it on.

"Hey, no phone calls!" Donald scowled.

"Fuck you!" I said. "I have to call my wife and let her know I'm fine."

"I said no phone calls!" Donald yelled and headed towards me. I raised the telephone and was about to strike him when Bruno called for Orlando and Pete, who came rushing into the room.

"We caught this creep trying to make a phone call," Bruno said.

"No phone calls!" Orlando barked.

I put away the cell phone and felt safer knowing that Richardson would be listening. I had merely to utter the word "cough," a code phrase, and the FBI backup would race to the rescue. I thought about calling them in, but felt the situation was under control. I knew no one had a gun.

The two left the room. We waited . . . and waited. A long stretch of time, which gave me time to think this through.

I tried to figure out who had set us up—and why?

There were two suspects. The rapper who wanted me in a video and Caldwell. I believed it was Caldwell. *But why*? What could he gain by setting us up?

Then it hit me! Perhaps Saul Drake called the Smith brothers.

A clock on a desk showed that two hours had elapsed since we first arrived. Two hours trapped in this room felt like an eternity.

Finally, the two returned. I was holding the phone, ready to use it if anyone tried to rush me.

I pointed to Stan. "What are you going to do with the cop?"

"We're going to use your suggestion," Orlando said. "If he's a trucker, then he can supply references."

"I can supply references," Stan replied, meekly. "I hope I can remember everyone's telephone number."

"Yeah, I hope you can." Bruno laughed. He reached down and grabbed Stan's wrist. "Otherwise, you're mine. I want you all for myself. You know what I'm going to do with you?"

Bruno twisted Stan's wrist. "Hey, not so rough," Stan said.

"Don't hurt him for now," Orlando said. "All right, cop. Put up or shut up. Give us names and some numbers. Or you're dead."

"All right, all right. I've done business with a company called Allied Apparel in North Carolina. The sales manager is Joe . . . Joe Doaks. His number is 223-432-7835. Ask for Joe Doaks."

Orlando picked up the phone on Pete's desk and began dialing.

"Hello, my name is Orlando Smith. Can I speak with Joseph Doaks . . . Hello, Mr. Doaks. My name is Orlando Smith. I'm the president of Raiments, located in Whittier, New Jersey . . . Fine, thanks. The reason why I'm calling is because your name was given to me by a Mister Ben Barine, who says he's done business with you."

I could barely hear the reply. Doaks said he had been doing business with him for years. What a break! For whatever reason, he was doing Stan, who had spoken to him on the phone but never met him, a favor.

Orlando thanked him and hung up. His face paled.

Hoping to break all resistance, I said, "Come on, fucker. Give us names!"

"Why don't you call Luther Pine over at Fashion X?" Stan said.

Stan gave Orlando a number and told him to dial it. The number was one of our scam lines. If Orlando dialed it, Stella would pick up and say that Luther was out of the office, but she was available to answer questions.

"No, I don't like this," Orlando said. "There has to be a better way to check out these guys."

"Who else have you done business with?" Bruno twisted Stan's arm. "Give us another name."

"Ow! You're hurting me! Try this number, 305-477-6898. That's the number for Terror T's. The owner is Louis Pixel."

"What does this company manufacture?" Bruno demanded.

"It's a silk screening operation."

"I have an idea," I said. "Check out Terror T's in *Thomas Register*. If it's a legitimate company, then it would be listed there; so would Allied Apparel."

Orlando stroked his chin. He looked at Pete, who agreed.

"Check it out," Orlando said. Pete walked to the shelf and pulled out the directory. He thumbed through the pages.

"Yeah, here's Terror T's." He flipped more pages. "And here's Allied Apparel."

Pete gave Orlando the number for Terror T's from the directory listing. The outfit was counterfeiting sports and designer T-shirts. Orlando dialed the number and asked for the owner. There was complete silence in the room as we waited. I couldn't hear what was said, but Orlando appeared bewildered. Finally, I realized the man admitted to having done business with Ben Barine. That did it. Orlando and the rest of his crew were done in. Stan's cover was secure.

"There's been some kind of mistake." Orlando looked at me angrily and barked, "Put down that phone."

"Put down the baseball bat first and call off your watch dogs," I replied firmly. I was not about to drop my guard with these cockroaches, not for a second. Not even with a backup support that included the FBI and Cumberland County Sheriff Deputies close at hand. Orlando tossed the bat into a corner. It landed with a clatter and rolled around on the floor. He told Bruno to release Stan.

"Jesus, you guys are crazy," Stan wailed and rubbed his arms with the palms of his hands. "I don't know anything about this."

I ordered Pete and Donald to back off. Orlando nodded and told them to step back.

"That's better." I put the phone back on the desk. "What made you guys think we were investigators?"

"None of your damned business," Orlando growled. "I want to get this over with. Don't try any funny stuff, either."

"You creeps are a fine bunch. If either of us were cops, you guys would have been busted by now."

"Shove it, cowboy," Bruno said. He took a step in my direction.

"Easy, take it easy," Orlando said. "I need to talk to you outside."

Orlando told Pete and Donald to guard us, while he and Bruno walked outside.

"I still think you're a cop," I said bitterly.

"Screw you," Stan replied and rubbed his arms.

"Shut up, both of you," Orlando's brother said. "You're lucky we didn't kill you guys."

The two were gone for a long time. I glanced at the clock on the desk. I thought I was dreaming: it was nearly nine o'clock. Was it possible we had been trapped in this room for five hours? I figured our backup was waiting for me to give the code word. At this point I decided to hold off because Orlando and his crew were about to take us to the warehouse location.

Orlando and Bruno walked back into the room. Orlando was smiling. He walked over and offered to shake hands. "You guys are clean."

"Hell of a way to do business," I replied sullenly and shook hands.

"I want you to lead the way," Orlando said.

We walked back into the production area. To my surprise, the room was dark. The machines, barely visible, looked like sinister forms waiting to spring to life. The nighttime blackness filtered through a large window.

Orlando told us to stay put. He walked away and disappeared into the dark, with only the shuffling of his footsteps. I heard a click. The ceiling lights came on and forced me to blink.

"That takes care of that," Orlando said. "Come on, let's get out of here."

# Chapter Twenty-Eight

STAN'S RIGHT CHEEK WAS red where I hit him.

"I'm sorry I belted you," I apologized. "That muscle-bound freak had me seeing double."

"Let's get this over with." Stan wearily rubbed his cheek.

I followed Orlando, who was in the lead. We walked past the punch cards and out the door. Outside a light drizzle greeted us. Specks of rain tapped against my forehead, ran down my cheek. I raised my hand to wipe my brow and discovered my hand trembling.

Two overhead lights on the roof illuminated the parking area. I tried to catch a glimpse of our backup. Everything was dark and shapeless in the night.

"Damn rain," Orlando mumbled as he walked to the Lexus.

Stan and I were split up, with me in the back seat of the Lexus, Stan the driver for the truck under escort with Donald.

Orlando sat in the back next to me. His brother drove with Bruno riding shotgun. No one said a word. It was unreal, like being on stage, with an audience watching and waiting for my next move.

We left Raiments with the truck in the lead. Pete followed, keeping a distance behind.

I kept track of our direction, heading northeast on a road parallel to Rye. I glanced in the rearview mirror. To my great relief, I spotted the unmarked CVPI. That had to be Richardson! I couldn't see the Cumberland County Sheriff's patrol car but was certain it was following out of sight.

Instinctively I reached for my cell phone. Bad move.

"Hey, what the hell do you think you're doing?" Orlando grabbed my wrist.

"I was going to call my wife and tell her I'm going to be late."

"Your wife!" Orlando growled. "Bullshit, no phone calls! Do you hear me, no phone calls!"

That ended that. I managed a quick peek at the dashboard clock. Ten o'clock. The pit-pat of drizzling rain splattering against the windshield. We took a turn onto Veteran's Memorial Highway, Route 55. I leaned forward, enough to check the rearview mirror again. Although few cars were on the highway, the unmarked was following.

Bruno turned to me. "We're nearly there, cowboy," he whispered. "Hope you enjoyed the ride."

"Yeah, loads."

"What are you going to do with the merchandise?"

"It's none of your damn business."

"You really are something else, cowboy," Bruno smirked. "I'd like to do you right one day."

I had had enough. With the FBI right behind, I felt cocky. I reached over the seat and grabbed his shirt. "You son-of-a-bitch!"

"Hey?" Bruno angrily twisted free.

"Ease up, c'mon." Orlando ordered Bruno to keep quiet.

The truck took exit 29. I could barely make out the sign because of the rain, which had now become a downpour.

Another mile or two. Up ahead I could see lights and buildings. A strip mall.

*Civilization at last*, I thought. I caught a quick look in the rearview mirror. To my horror, I realized the backup wasn't there! Wilde had missed the exit. Hopefully, he would get back on track using the GPS.

Dejected, I sat back in the seat. "What's the name of this mall?" I asked, knowing that Richardson was listening.

"None of your fucking business," Orlando growled.

We passed a CVS pharmacy and a Subway sandwich shop. I was relieved to see late-night shoppers walking to their cars.

We drove through, rounded a bend, and approached a one-story building. This had to be a storage center. I knew it even before I saw the sign with the company's name, appropriately called Safe Storage. A flatbed truck was parked in front of one of three loading bays. The windows on the side of the building were secured with wire-mesh screens.

Stan backed the truck into the loading bay. Orlando's brother parked the car in front of cement steps that led to a metal door. He honked the horn twice. A light above the loading bay came on.

A short pasty-faced man with a huge stomach and several days' stubble opened the door. He was wearing denim overalls and a sweatshirt that barely covered his bulbous stomach.

Orlando got out and waved to him. I could hear him introduce himself: "Ken, it's Orlando."

"I remember you," the man smiled, wiped his right hand on his thigh before shaking hands. "Got a late-night delivery?"

"No, a pickup," Orlando said. "Let's go inside."

Minutes passed. I was relieved because I needed time. With not enough money to pay for the shipment, my only hope was the backup. They'd probably realized their error by now and were on the way.

Orlando opened the door and gestured for us to enter.

I got out and looked up the road, hoping to spot our backup or even hear police sirens. As soon as the backup arrived, I intended to serve the seizure order and conclude the investigation. I saw and heard nothing. Stan got out of the truck, and his eyes darted furtively from right to left. He obviously sensed our predicament.

We went inside and walked past rows of locked storage units. The larger ones were room-size, smaller ones locker-size. We followed Ken down a row. My insides were melting. *Where was the backup?*

"This is it, right here." Ken pointed to a locked room.

Orlando's brother bent over the combination lock and rotated it to the left and to the right, and then back again. The lock popped open.

Orlando turned to me. "Two hundred boxes are inside. Ken has a dolly for you to use."

I needed a reason to walk away from the deal. At any moment, Orlando would ask for the money—and the game would be over.

"Just a second," I said. "How do I know what's inside those boxes? I'm not paying for merchandise I haven't inspected."

I insisted on inspecting the merchandise, a code phrase my investigators use. It was an appropriate tactic: there were hundreds of boxes of apparel to inspect. Hopefully, I could stall long enough for our backup to arrive.

I opened a box, pulled out a sweater and inspected the familiar IG logo. I counted each item to make sure there were fifty to a box. I was running out of time. *Where was the backup?*

The Smith brothers quickly ran out of patience.

"Quit fooling around and give us our money," Orlando said angrily.

I managed to stall for another ten minutes. Finally, I said everything was cool.

Orlando told Ken to bring a dolly. When Ken returned, he told the others to help Stan load up the boxes. He turned to me and said, "Now let's settle up."

I told Orlando to come outside with me. I had one last trick to play.

When we were outside the building, I told Orlando I wanted to count out the money in another location, where there was light. Although the rain had subsided, there was enough of a drizzle coming down that my request didn't seem too unreasonable. Actually, I was hoping to lure him to a location where there were people.

"What the fuck! Give me the money now!"

"I want to count out the money away from this place, in case you try to rob me."

"Try to rob you? The merchandise is being loaded right now."

"Take me back to the mall," I demanded.

Orlando cursed, but finally acquiesced. I got in the car, and he drove us back to the mall. He kept insisting I count out the money, but I refused.

Orlando parked the Lexus in front of the Subway sandwich shop. My heart sank because there was no sign of the backup. I knew they were on the way, but even with the GPS, they would have to backtrack to Exit 29. I had to stall.

I needed to think of something fast. To buy time, I complained of a headache and told Orlando I was going into the CVS to get some aspirin.

"What the hell are you trying to pull?"

"Look, this will take a second."

"Why don't we count out the money in there?"

"No, I have a better place. Let me get some aspirin first."

Orlando warned me not to try anything. We exited the Lexus and walked to the CVS located next to the sandwich shop. He let me walk inside by myself and stood by the glass door and watched. What a break! Although Orlando could see me through the glass door—he could not hear what was said.

I walked to the counter. A young kid was handling the register.

"I'm a cop," I said in a low tone. The youth behind the register looked to be in his teens. He stared at me wide-eyed.

"I want you to dial 9-1-1 and tell the operator this is a Code 10-13. You got that?"

"Yes . . . yes, sir!" the kid said. "What's the problem?"

"Do as I say. I'm being watched."

I dropped a five on the counter and walked away without another word.

A Code 10-13 means emergency, officer needs assistance. Now I needed time before the police arrived. I walked outside and told Orlando I wanted to go to the motel across the street to count out the money.

"The motel? That's way the fuck over there."

We argued. Orlando told me to fork over the cash, but I refused and walked towards the motel.

He cursed, made a move to get into his car, cursed, and ran to catch up with me.

We walked into the motel lobby. I reached into the pocket of my jacket and pulled out the seizure order signed by the judge. I walked up to Orlando and slapped the document on his chest.

"You've been served! This is a seizure order!"

Orlando was stunned. "What? What?" he stammered.

"I'm an investigator. You've got about sixty seconds before the police arrive!"

As if by command, police sirens pierced the air.

Orlando looked at me in disbelief. He turned pale and fled through the door and out into the night.

Luckily, the kid at the register had called the police. This was the only time during a major investigation when I revealed I was an investigator without a backup.

With Orlando gone, I called Richardson. He was frantic. "Theo, where are you? We were so worried."

"Someone set us up!" I said.

"That's what we figured . . . Are you hurt? Where are you?"

"I'm fine. What happened, did you get lost?"

"Yes, you must have taken Exit 29. Wilde said he's sorry. He missed it in the dark."

"It's okay, it's happened to me."

"We waited outside for hours. We have night vision binoculars and knew no one had left. I thought about rushing in."

"Thanks for waiting."

"We're on the way."

I hung up and retrieved the seizure order Orlando had dropped and left the motel. Outside, the rain had stopped. The air was damp but refreshing and cool. I could see a police car parked by the pharmacy. Rotating lights, alternating sheens of blue and red, pierced the night. Uniformed policemen and a small crowd of onlookers huddled by the CVS. Orlando's Lexus was gone. He had snuck past the police.

I called Stan. To my great relief, he was unharmed. Orlando and the rest of his crew had piled into the Lexus and fled.

I waved my hands in the air as I walked. One of the policemen noticed me. The young kid shouted, "That's him!"

The police officer glared at me as I approached. "Did you call in this alarm?" he asked.

"Yes, I did. It was an emergency."

I identified myself as a private investigator to the two uniformed officers. They were from the Rye police force. I told them how I got separated from the seizure team. They were amazed when I mentioned I was working with the FBI and the Cumberland County Sheriff.

"The FBI?" An officer looked me over with a steely gaze, while his partner frowned.

I was spared having to explain because the CVPI roared down the street with the Sheriff patrol car trailing behind. The two vehicles parked in front of us. Richardson got out and headed for us, with the rest of the backup right behind.

"Ease up, I'm with the FBI." Richardson produced his badge and introduced himself and Special Agent Wilde. It seemed like the Rye officers were more impressed by the Cumberland County Deputy Sheriffs who had their shotguns at the ready.

"Someone radioed in a call for an officer in trouble," the cop said. He looked nervously at the two armed deputies.

"I understand," Richardson said. "This man is working with us."

Zeckindorff joined the others. The attorney looked relieved. He walked over and gave me a paternal hug. "B-a-a-by, we were worried."

Richardson explained how the buy-and-bust had gotten sidetracked.

"You should have contacted us," the Rye cop said. "We know this territory."

"You're right, officer," the ASAC said. "But there was no time. We got authorization for the seizure less than two days ago and had to execute it before the bad guys found out."

Richardson asked the Rye cops to accompany us to the storage facility. Before we left, I thanked the kid. When he asked who I was, I cut a joke and walked away.

# Chapter Twenty-Nine

STAN WAVED. HE WAS standing alongside Ken by the box truck. Even from a distance, I could see Ken's fleshy jowls shaking as the convoy of vehicles approached. His eyes bulged as the uniforms exited from their vehicles and surrounded him.

Richardson walked over. He looked at Ken. "Are you from Raiments?"

"Who—who me? I work here?" Ken was trembling.

"He's all right," I said.

Stan explained how Orlando had returned and told everyone it was a bust. His cronies jumped into the Lexus and drove away.

"Let's chase them," one of the Rye cops said. "I know the highways around here."

"No, it's more important to execute the seizure," Richardson said. "We'll head to Raiments and seize the business records."

©©

It was one o'clock in the morning when the four-vehicle convoy headed for Raiments. The moon was shining, and the highway was deserted. A vast silence engulfed the trees and nearby mountains.

The Rye patrol car was in the lead, with the other vehicles

trailing behind. I was riding with Zeckindorff in the CVPI. Although the mystery of the closed bank account and Caldwell's disappearance was starting to make sense, Richardson demanded an answer from Zeckindorff.

The usually brusque attorney was subdued. "Caldwell has some explaining to do."

"Damn right," Richardson said.

Wilde was silent and kept his eyes on the road. I realized why he had missed the exit. He had had to stay farther behind Orlando than usual because there were so few cars on the highway. With his vision hampered by the rain, he drove for several miles before realizing his mistake.

When we arrived, the empty parking lot was illuminated by the overhead light. No sign of either the Lexus or Orlando and his crew.

The lead car with the Rye police drove up to the entrance. The officers exited with guns drawn.

Richardson, however, had other ideas. He raced over before the officers could disperse. "I appreciate your help," he said, "but this is an FBI court-ordered seizure. Put your guns away. They're too many of us, and it's dark."

The two Rye officers exchanged glances. "No problem." They holstered their weapons. Richardson told them to guard the entrance. He told the two Cumberland County deputies to put away their shotguns and use flashlights to canvass the perimeter.

The ASAC tried the front door, but it was locked. "Let's see if we can find a way inside," he said. "If not, we'll have to break open a window."

Richardson ordered Wilde to check the right side of the building, while the two of us checked the left side.

Fortunately, we found a partially open window. Richardson helped me slide inside. I was near the fabric spreader. It loomed large and ominous. I walked slowly, one foot following the other in the dark. I cursed when I stubbed my foot on a wastepaper basket; it fell over with a clatter.

I found the door, unlocked it, and was greeted by Richardson who had returned to the front of the building

He peered past me into the dark interior. "Anyone inside?" he asked.

"I didn't see anyone," I said.

Wilde returned to the front to join us. The three of us entered the building. We scrounged in the darkness like blind men. Finally, I found a light switch.

We began opening doors and checking possible hiding places. Richardson and I went to the office where Stan and I had nearly been killed. No sign of Orlando or his men. The baseball bat he had tossed aside was lying on the floor.

I headed for the filing cabinets lined against the back wall. I opened a drawer and thumbed through the file folders.

"Are those business documents?" Richardson asked.

"Yes," I said.

With the building secured, Richardson went to the entrance to get Zeckindorff and Stan. Stan had retrieved folded cardboard boxes from the rear of the truck and was ready. Zeckindorff agreed to help and carried a bundle. They followed Richardson to the office. After Stan showed the attorney how to assemble a box, they began packing up the business files.

While they worked, I decided to check for phone messages. I plugged in the telephone that I had ripped out of the wall jack.

To my surprise, the first was from Bull Fogarty!

*"This is Bull Fogarty, head of the anti-piracy unit.*

*I'll be there in the morning after you get rid of those CREEPS. WATCH OUT!*

*Those guys are INVESTIGATORS.*

*Get rid of those motherfuckers fast."*

Everyone stopped to listen as I replayed the message.

"Who is this guy?" Richardson asked.

"Isn't this the asshole you bumped into?" Zeckindorff asked.

"The same," I said.

Richardson looked at Zeckindorff. "Who the hell is this?"

"Bull Fogarty is a private investigator," I said. "He used to be in charge at the Madison Detective Agency. Now it looks like he's in charge of the anti-piracy operation."

Richardson didn't understand until Zeckindorff told him about the newly formed anti-piracy unit.

I hit the play button again; sure enough, there was another message from Bull making an appointment to meet the Smith brothers in the morning. The messages had been taped the day before we arrived. The Smith brothers had to have had a follow-up phone call with Bull.

Richardson stroked his chin. "I don't give a shit who this guy is. We're seizing these records. All of them. Caldwell must be involved. He must have arranged everything with Bull."

I retrieved a hand truck, and everyone starting boxing the files. The filing cabinets were empty in minutes.

I took a break and listened to the taped phone messages again. I noticed how raspy Bull's voice sounded. All of a sudden I had a flash. *Bull is the anonymous caller making threats against me and my family.*

I took Stan aside, so the others wouldn't hear. "Stan, I know this is crazy, but I think the caller is Bull Fogarty."

I played the phone messages again. Stan shrugged, said he wasn't sure. I told him not to mention this and to take the telephone with him when we left.

At five in the morning, Richardson had the vehicles moved to the back of the building. The Rye police officers and Cumberland County deputies joined us inside. We huddled by the desk next to the punch cards and waited for Bull to arrive.

While we waited, I thought about Bull. I knew he was sliding downhill, but resorting to telephone threats? I found it difficult to believe he had sunk so low.

I didn't make the connection earlier because Bull's freefall had been so painful. Hard to believe he was so desperate. Yet, he knew personal details about me and had the technical background to scramble and record his voice.

I was thinking about Bull, when the door opened. I didn't recognize him. He'd put on weight and looked healthy. He looked imposing in a dark blue business suit and he was carrying a black briefcase.

"Morning, Bull," I said. "We've been waiting for you."

For perhaps one fleeting moment, he was surprised. His eyes narrowed as he assessed the situation. He appeared unfazed by the phalanx of law enforcement officers surrounding him.

"Waiting for me?" he replied flatly. "I have a business meeting. Where's Orlando Smith?"

"He's gone," I replied. "He's running a huge counterfeiting operation. We seized hundreds of boxes of counterfeit apparel with the IG brand name. This is Brian Zeckindorff. I believe you've heard of him. He's the attorney handling the seizure for IG International. These policemen are our backup—and over here is the FBI."

Bull hardly flinched.

I tossed a T-shirt, one of the ones seized earlier. He caught it with one hand and inspected it. A sly grin crossed his face. He began laughing, making a sound like a witch cackling.

He tossed it back. "Orlando may be counterfeiting other brand labels, but not this one."

"Who told you this?" Zeckindorff asked.

"Robert Caldwell sent me."

"You're lying!" I said.

"No, I'm not. Robert Caldwell was supposed to call you guys off before you executed this seizure. Give him a call, if you don't believe me."

"We've been trying to get hold of him," Zeckindorff said.

Richardson was bewildered. "Say, what in blazes is going on here? I thought this was a counterfeiting case?"

"It is," Zeckindorff said uneasily.

Bull snorted. "I hope you meatheads haven't executed a groundless *ex parte* seizure. If you have, the Smith brothers are gonna sue your asses off. Caldwell's trying to straighten things up with Saul Drake."

"We've got your voice on the answering machine," I said. "You told the Smith brothers to get rid of us."

"That's right! The Smith brothers were supposed to get rid of you."

Something had gone terribly wrong. Or perhaps Bull was trying to scam us. He now demanded that we turn over the IG inventory to him.

"No way," Richardson said. "These belong to the FBI, and we're taking the business records."

"Have it your way—" Bull looked at me in triumph. "You thought you were so high and mighty, Theo. This is a frivolous and unwarranted seizure. The Smith brothers are going to retaliate."

Bull left without another word. Richardson made a move to stop him, but I waved him off.

I should have left it like that, but as an afterthought, I chased after him. I walked out the door and caught up with him in the parking lot, as he was getting into his car.

"We've got your taped voice on the telephone answering machine," I said.

Bull turned to look at me. He smirked in contempt. "Yeah, so what? You've got nothing."

"No, Bull, the FBI and their experts are going to compare your voice to the voice from a message left at our office. The person who left that message is a sick individual using a voice scrambler."

I had hoped to shock Bull. But I was disappointed. He was either innocent or so cool under fire nothing could faze him.

"I—don't—know—what—you're—talking—about."

Bull said the words slowly, letting each word stand by itself in mid-air.

"Maybe you do, maybe you don't . . . I hope not for your sake. Because if you do, then you're the creep who has been terrorizing my family."

Bull's eyes narrowed with hatred. Without another word, he got into his car and drove away.

# Chapter Thirty

RICHARDSON THANKED THE RYE policemen and said he'd send a letter of commendation to their captain

"I hope it works out," an officer said and left with his fellow officer.

Everyone knew something was awry. The Cumberland County Sheriff Deputies shook hands with each of us in turn and asked Richardson to keep them updated.

After the officers had departed, Richardson turned his attention to Zeckindorff. "The government will want a full accounting from Caldwell."

"I understand," Zeckindorff said. "I'm going to call him later."

"Will he be there?" Richardson asked. "It's Saturday morning."

"I'll try anyway." The usually upbeat attorney looked fatigued.

"Some seizure. I'm not even sure if any of this is evidence." In addition to Asian Seas, files were discovered dealing with IG International. This added up to a nearly two boxes of evidence. Raiments financial and personnel record files amounted to five boxes. Richardson told Stan to store it in the trunk of the CVPI.

"How about the murders?" Zeckindorff asked.

"That's a big maybe. I'll reach out to Chris and tell him what happened here."

"What do you want us to do, Brian?" I asked.

"You made arrangements to have everything stored, didn't you?"

"Yes, I did."

"Store everything. I want you to meet me in Manhattan."

"Brian, I haven't taken a bath yet."

"You can't stink worse than Caldwell. Give me a call later, when you're ready to meet."

Zeckindorff left with the FBI.

©©

The investigation was over, as far as I was concerned. The legal eagles would scrabble over the legality of the *ex parte* seizures. What bothered me was why the Smith brothers continued to do business, especially after Bull had warned them. Greed had to be the answer. This was a deal for cash. When I waved the flash money, the Smith brothers believed I had thirty thousand.

We stopped for breakfast at a McDonald's, Stan's favorite. He looked bedraggled. His eyes were red, face pale.

"Tired, Stan?"

"It's been a long night."

"Let's get some food and hot coffee."

The coffee went down smooth. I was hungry after a long, terrible night.

"Are we going to store everything?" Stan asked. This amounted to thirty boxes of client files from Raiments and another two hundred boxes of IG apparel from the deal made with Orlando.

"We'll unload it at the warehouse in Union City. After that, we'll head into Manhattan. I want you to drop me off at 4 Times Square. Zeckindorff wants to see me."

"Oh, boy," he said. "What do you think Zeckindorff will do?"

"Fireworks are likely."

We traveled east on the New Jersey State Turnpike. A few miles from Manhattan, the truck slowed down and took the exit for Union City. While we unloaded the boxes, I called Stella at home and told her the outcome.

"You're lucky you didn't get killed," she said.

"I know. I'm heading into Manhattan with Stan to meet with

Zeckindorff. Stan's going to drop off the truck and head for the office. Can you meet him there?"

"I'm on the way," Stella said.

Stan drove the van into Manhattan and dropped me off. I walked into 4 Times Square and took the elevator. Even though it was Saturday, many attorneys and support staff were working.

Zeckindorff came to the reception to greet me. "Ba-a-a-by." He walked over and hugged me.

I followed him back to his office. Once I was seated, Zeckindorff said he'd spoken with Caldwell.

"Yeah? What did he say?"

"He claims he discovered the rapper has a handshake agreement with the Smith brothers."

"A handshake agreement? Is that a legal term?"

"That's the term Caldwell uses. I'm going to throw him out the window when I see him. He's in big trouble and needs help. He should have told me about this handshake agreement. Instead, he tried to fix things himself."

"And nearly got me killed."

"I'm truly sorry. I exploded when I heard Bull Fogarty's name. This asshole has jeopardized two of my investigations. I'm glad we got rid of him and refused to surrender the apparel."

"When did he become head of the anti-piracy unit?"

"Two days ago. Bull heard about Premier Equity Financial's start-up anti-piracy unit through a contact at National Wholesale. He applied for the job and was immediately hired."

"Great. What about the FBI?"

Zeckindorff pointed to the clock on his desk. His appointment was for eleven. "I'll tell you about it in the cab. Let's go, it's getting late."

Outside, he hailed a cab. During the ride, he told me deals were for cash, with a fifty-fifty cut on the profits.

"The handshake agreement was lucrative because IG International didn't receive any licensing income," Zeckindorff explained. "However, the Smith brothers crossed him up with Ahmad's help by substituting acrylic fiber for cashmere. The IG initially wanted to punish them, especially when he heard about the half-million dollar inventory at Asian Seas. That's why he approved the seizures."

"Weren't the Smith brothers involved in trademark counterfeiting?" I asked. "The sweaters were made of acrylic, not cashmere."

Zeckindorff shook his head. "Although the trademark is registered in Leon Owen's name, trademark counterfeiting is not involved. The rapper should have tried suing the Smith brothers for violation of their handshake agreement—but that's about it.

"The account with thirty grand was set up. Everything was going fine, until the IG confesses and tells Caldwell everything."

"Damn it! Then why didn't Caldwell call you and let you know what's going down?"

"Because Bull Fogarty was called in to handle this," Zeckindorff said. "Bull phoned the Smith brothers and said he would be impounding their inventory of IG apparel until this was cleared up. The bank account was closed. The Smith brothers were supposed to throw you guys out, so the seizure would never take place, and the *ex parte* seizure order, under seal as required by statute, would remain under seal indefinitely."

"But the Smith Brothers didn't throw us out," I pointed out.

"That's the funny thing about this whole investigation." Zeckindorff laughed and patted me on the back. "You executed the seizure anyway! Bull and Caldwell never counted on that. Never in a million years. Caldwell was totally blown away when Bull gave him the bad news. He called me right away."

"So now what?"

"For one thing, Caldwell has unwittingly perjured himself in filing those affidavits in support of the seizure. He has also authorized a frivolous seizure for which IG International will be liable. He has violated the attorney-client privilege. He could even be charged for obstructing the FBI's criminal investigation of Raiments."

"Wow, all that."

"And more."

"More?"

"He has to deal with me." Zeckindorff smiled wickedly. "I have a score to settle."

He said that on the ride to Newark, Richardson lashed out at him for shoddy legal work. "Luckily, Richardson didn't arrest anyone. Hopefully, the business files that were seized will link

Raiments to the five-hundred-thousand dollar inventory sitting in the sweatshop. Maybe a criminal case can be made."

We travelled to the Citicorp Center, rode the elevator to the corporate digs of IG International. We sat on the same leather couch and waited for Caldwell.

We waited for what seemed forever. Finally, Caldwell emerged, carrying a case folder. He looked calm, even tried to smile.

"Sorry to keep you guys waiting." He did not offer to shake hands. It was just as well. Zeckindorff glared at him condescendingly. I felt nothing but contempt.

We followed Caldwell to the conference room in silence. He motioned for us to be seated. I wound up in the seat at the head of the table, while Zeckindorff took a seat opposite him.

"I owe you guys a sincere apology," he said. "That's why I've invited you here."

He paused, perhaps expecting some encouragement from either Zeckindorff or myself. Neither of us said a thing.

"Yes, well . . . " He cleared his throat. "We have some slight legal problems to work through—"

Zeckindorff silenced him. "You're in a heap of trouble. Do you hear me? A heap of trouble."

His eyes turned red. For a moment, I thought he might start crying. He blamed everything on Leon Owen, who was constantly running into trouble.

"Much of my job is handling his paternity suits, gun and assault charges," he wailed. "Leon's latest is uploading his songs onto the Internet, so his fans can download them for free. Rappers like IG and Public Enemy are causing a stir with the record industry, which can't sue the copyright owners."

"I don't give a shit about any of this," Zeckindorff fired back. "You've lied to me and nearly got Theo here killed."

"Yes, you told me." Caldwell turned to me. "Brian said you pulled the scam of the century to get out of a tight spot."

I didn't reply. I had no sympathy for this pathetic cockroach with his custom-made suit and starched shirt.

"Leon had an under-the-table arrangement with the Smith brothers no one knew about, including me," Caldwell explained. "They split everything fifty-fifty, leaving IG International out."

"Why the hell didn't you tell us?" Zeckindorff thundered.

Caldwell sat back in his seat and pursed his lips. "This seizure was never supposed to take place. IG International could face legal action by Saul Drake and Raiments for executing unwarranted seizures. I've called you in to help fix this."

"Fix this!" Zeckindorff yelled. "You and IG International screwed up—not us."

"Easy, easy." Caldwell smiled. "Let's settle down. I have some documents for you to review and sign."

"What!" Zeckindorff roared.

Caldwell was nonplussed. He had drafted declarations in support of a motion to dismiss the seizure order, as well as a motion to drop the civil suit. After we signed the documents and filed them in court, Zeckindorff could negotiate with the Smith brothers and Saul Drake. He opened up the red weld folder and pulled out a stack of documents.

Zeckindorff was furious. He was so angry he might have thrown this corporate stooge out the window—but I beat him to it.

I lost my temper.

I reached over and grabbed Caldwell by the suit lapels and roared with a voice that would have made my acting teacher proud.

"YOU BASTARD! What the hell are you trying to pull?"

I probably would have done real damage to the guy, if Zeckindorff had not stopped me. He quickly escorted me into the hallway.

"Easy, Theo. This is a client."

"I can't believe the nerve of this guy—"

"I know, I know. Wait outside, let me handle this."

I found an empty chair and tried to relax, because I could have killed that jerk. In all my years as an investigator, I had never been set up by a client. Stan and I could have been severely beaten, even killed, and the asshole who was responsible was sitting in a conference room smug as tulips on a spring day.

A half hour went by, maybe more. I sat there nursing my anger. I could hear their muted voices from inside the conference room. Finally, Zeckindorff emerged. He was smiling. He walked up to me and patted me on the shoulder.

"Let's go," he said. "It's all taken care of."

I got up and followed Zeckindorff. "What about signing those documents?"

"We won't have to sign anything. Caldwell had some nerve drafting documents for us to sign. Some nerve! He figured he could end-run this nightmare by having the civil suit dropped. After that, he hoped to offer the Smith brothers a legitimate licensing agreement."

"Sounds like a plan."

"Except I'm not falling for any of it," Zeckindorff said flatly. "He screwed up—and we're walking out of here."

While we walked down the corridor, I apologized for losing my temper and grabbing Caldwell.

Zeckindorff smiled. "Fine, ba-a-aby. I admire your passion."

"What's going to happen to Caldwell?"

"It's a mess." He laughed. "That's why we're leaving. I want to pressure him into crawling on his knees for help. I'll turn this around for him—but on my terms. After I'm finished, I'll bill IG International a fortune in fees."

I thought we were heading for the elevator, until I realized he was headed in the opposite direction.

"Brian, where are we going?"

"You'll see."

I followed him. He seemed to know his way around.

We walked past cubicles for office staff. Most of the office doors were closed, but I spotted a young woman talking on the phone in one office; in another, a man was sitting at a desk typing into a personal computer.

He headed towards a large desk, where a young woman was seated. As we approached, he told me her name was Belinda. She was the IG's personal assistant. She was too gorgeous to be anything else. She had long curled hair down to her shoulders and large, luminescent eyes.

"Hel-l-l-l-lo, Belinda," he crooned.

She gave him a bored look in return. "You back again."

"*Fa'sho*, we're here to see the Ga-a-a-ngsta-a-a."

"He's busy right now."

"This can't wait." Zeckindorff walked past. I followed behind.

"Hey! You can't do that—"

She stood up and made a belated attempt to try and block us. She was wearing a micro mini-skirt and high heels that hampered quick movement. We were by her in a second.

He walked quickly to the door, knocked once, and entered. I followed right behind the attorney.

The office suite was sumptuous: plush carpet, wide-screen television, and life-size pictures of the rap superstar adorned the walls. The rapper was sitting behind a stately mahogany desk wearing headphones and scribbling onto a legal notepad.

"Ga-a-a-ngsta-a-a!" Zeckindorff wailed. "Number one with a bullet!"

He had positioned himself in the doorway, so that Belinda could not evict us.

"Leon, I'm sorry." Belinda peered over his shoulder.

The IG pulled off the headphones. He stroked his chin.

"Is a'right, baby. Come on in. I see you brung the heat."

The rapper motioned for us to be seated. There were four guest chairs positioned around the desk. Zeckindorff sat down in the middle, with me seated next to him.

"I wuz writing lyrics," the rapper said and placed the legal pad and pencil down on the desk. "What can I do you gents for?"

"We spoke to your man Caldwell," he said.

"Oh, him," the IG's voice soured. "Tha' *mo'fo* makes me shit. He can't scrap a lick, 'cause he got no dick."

"The Smith brothers have been raided."

The rapper's eyes opened wide at the news.

"*Boo-yaa!* Tha's what I like to hear. You guys got your swerve on." The IG was smiling like his latest song went platinum.

"*Ay yo*, ga-a-a-ngsta," Zeckindorff leaned forward and mugged and began sounding off on the IG's lyrics, tapping his fingers on the table.

The rapper laughed at his antics. "You guys is somethin' else."

"My man, Theo here, nearly got capped," he reached over and patted me on the shoulder. "Dem niggas at Raiments wuz bad. Dey beat up on Theo and 'nother investigator."

The rapper went silent.

"Sorry to hear 'bout dat." His eyes saddened. "Be startin' production on tha' video soon. I want you in it, dig."

"Fine," I said. I wanted to say something else, but the words escaped me.

"Your man Caldwell said you was dealin' with them chumps under the table."

"Yeah, well—" The rapper tried to laugh it off.

"You should have told me 'bout this shit."

The rapper took a deep breath. "Sorry 'bout dat. You know how it is, everybody's in it for the rock."

Zeckindorff scolded him. "The management at Premier Financial Equities are goin' to be fit when they find out 'bout you and the Smith brothers."

"Let 'em get twisted," the rapper spat. "Those white ass mavericks are jerkin' me, so I got a right to jerk dem. It's just like dat . . . Everybody's gettin' away with something."

I nearly cringed when I heard the rapper explain it that way. *Everybody's getting away with it.* I could make that refrain my middle name.

The irate rapper promised his "word would be bond" from now on, a street phrase from the Nation of Islam. A solemn promise to be forthright from now on.

Our meeting with the IG was finished. We each gave the rapper a pound handshake and left. Zeckindorff was all smiles. And rightly so. He stood to make a fortune in legal fees from IG International, and he had gotten the impossible out of the rapper—a promise to deal fair and square from now on. A promise like that, coming from a former street felon, was worth all the neon lighting up the theater district.

# Chapter Thirty-One

BEFORE HEADING TO THE office, I decided to get a soda and a slice of pizza. I was walking through Washington Square Park when a sixth sense kicked in.

*Danger, danger!*

What was it about the approaching stranger that was wrong?

The stranger wore a hoodie. His shoulders were hunched, and his head was bowed slightly so that the sides of the hood brushed against his face.

Of course, his face! The hood shielded it like a cowl. I remembered the dream Linda had. *A death-like figure in shrouds.*

This is it!

I saw the blade coming in time.

I managed to twist my torso—but was not quick enough. I felt the blade as it ripped through the shirt.

What happened next was automatic. Five years of weekend karate classes paid off as I executed a pitiful sidekick that somehow connected.

Now I saw him. There was no mistaking that scar on the side of his face. Bruno was not swaggering or even tough. Just surprised.

I ran like the blazes through the park and across the street to a restaurant and rushed inside.

I turned and looked behind to see if Bruno was following. He had disappeared. As I figured, he would not dare to follow me. He was a silent killer—and he had missed his mark. Probably the first time an intended victim had eluded him.

I sat down and inspected the shirt. It was a small tear, hardly noticeable. Delicately, I pulled back the fabric. There was hardly any blood, just a nasty scratch.

I looked around the restaurant. There was a couple seated at a table next to mine. She was a bleached blonde, laughing at her companion's joke, oblivious to my near assassination.

A waiter walked to the table and set down a menu. "What would you like?"

"A double whiskey."

"Goodness. We only serve beer."

"I'll take a Bud Light for now."

I walked to the lavatory and inspected the wound. I was lucky, a slender line below my left nipple extending downward for about two inches. There was hardly any blood. I wet a towel and wiped it clean, then washed my hands.

I pulled out my cell phone and called Stella.

"Stella, come quick. Bruno tried to kill me."

"Theo! My God!"

"I'm fine. I'm in the Santa Maria restaurant."

"That's around the block . . . Are you sure you're all right?"

"Yes, damn it! Use the van and bring me a fresh shirt. Bring Stan with you. I'll wait here."

I opened the lavatory door, made my way back. A beer was waiting. I took a swig, kept my eye on the window.

Within minutes, the van arrived. I dropped a ten on the table, walked outside. There was a cool, light breeze.

Stella rushed over. "Theo, thank God you're safe!"

I hugged her and got inside the van. Stan was the driver. I opened the door and sat in the front seat. Stella took a seat in back.

"What happened?" he asked.

I leaned forward and used my fingers to part the fabric to show them the wound. "It's a small cut, barely broke the surface."

"You're sure it was Bruno?" Stella asked.

"Positive. I got a look at his face when he lunged at me."

"Where is he now?" Stan asked.

"He disappeared. I knew he wouldn't follow me into the restaurant."

Stella handed me a familiar looking polo shirt. "Is this one of the seized counterfeits?" I asked.

"Sure is," she chuckled. "I'm glad you're safe."

"So am I."

Gently, I removed my shirt. Stella took a bandage from the first-aid kit and applied it. Finished, I slipped on the counterfeit shirt.

"Where do you want to go?" Stan asked.

"Nowhere," I said. "I called to let Stella know what was going down. I told her to bring the van because we'll be safe inside. I didn't know if Bruno was going to go after my staff. Thank God, you're safe."

I reached for my cell phone and dialed 9-1-1.

"What's your emergency?"

I paused, took a breath, and said, "Someone tried to kill me."

# Chapter Thirty-Two

WITHIN MINUTES, TWO PATROL cars showed up. After that, everything was a blur. I remember being driven to the stationhouse. Questions and more questions. Detective Harney and Lieutenant Ash arrived with even more questions.

All I could think about was my family. The clock was ticking, and the fatal hour had arrived. I had come within a heartbeat of never seeing Linda and Josh again. I called and told her there was some trouble and to eat dinner without me.

When I arrived, Linda and Josh were seated on the sofa in the living room. Josh was watching television.

She looked as lovely as I'll ever remember her. Brown hair tied back into a ponytail, gingham shirt and jeans. And a radiant smile, like the sun on a shiny day.

"Theo, thank god you're home." She stood up. Her open arms beckoned.

"I'm fine . . ." I walked over, held her tight.

She whispered quietly into my ear, so Josh wouldn't hear. "What happened? I was worried."

"It's nothing," I said in a low voice. "I'm home. Don't worry; it's taken care of."

"You mentioned the police."

I smiled and then kissed her cheek. "The police arrested the bad guy," I lied and turned my attention to JJ. "How are you, my little man?"

"Fine, Dad." Josh seemed to be disappointed. I turned to Linda, who gave me a wink and said he missed Aunt Mattie.

"Oh, you like being spoiled."

Josh smiled devilishly. "She bought me chocolate and a book."

I apologized for coming home empty-handed and asked what classes he had missed the other day.

"I missed homeroom and arithmetic," he said.

"What's for dinner tonight," I asked.

"I have left-over stew."

"Great. Why don't you heat it up? I'm hungry. I'll stay here with Josh. Maybe I can help with his homework."

"Homework? I finished it."

"Well, how about showing me some of your artwork?"

His art book was on the coffee table. He returned with it and sat down beside me.

"Josh, everything all right?" He looked worried, and I feared he knew what had happened yesterday.

"Is Mom sick?"

He looked forlorn, the way children sometimes do when trying to understand an adult situation. I put my arm around his shoulder. "She's going to be fine. She was tired and needed to get away for a day."

I ran my hand through his hair and hugged him. "Thanks for asking."

I walked into the kitchen. Linda was washing dishes, her back to me. Feeling playful, I let my hands slide around her waist. I kissed her ear and reminded her how good last night was.

"You're such a beast, my Caliban," she laughed. I made a rumbling sound and kissed her neck again. She laughed and pushed me away. "Be seated, loathsome beast . . . I'll get you a beer."

She went to the refrigerator and brought back a beer and a glass. She handed them to me and sat down.

"I was thinking about the other night." She sounded whimsical.

"It was good, wasn't it?" I smiled knowingly, as I filled the glass.

"Oh, be serious," she pouted. "I meant the caller. What's the

FBI going to do?"

"Whoever it is will be prosecuted and do jail time. Why do you ask?"

"After you called, I became concerned. He's a troubled kid."

"So that's it, you're worried about what the FBI will do?" I went to work on the beer. It tasted unexpectedly pleasant after a long day.

She nodded and reminded me she had worked with kids for many years. "Many of them get off the track," she said.

"I think the caller is Bull Fogarty," I said. "Do you remember him?"

For a moment she was speechless. "You know who the caller is? "

"I started out with him at the Madison Detective Agency."

"Now I remember. He was your boss! Why would he do this? What was he trying to accomplish?"

"Desperation," I answered. "He used to be good, one of the best, but he had a drinking problem. I never knew what haunted him but saw him slowly drink his life away. He was seemingly reborn with a new lease on life, but jealousy was his downfall."

"It's a shame." She sat down opposite me. "What will happen to him?"

"I'm not sure. If he's the caller, he won't call us again."

"I'm sorry about what I said in Riverdale," Linda said. "I couldn't leave you, at least not over something like this."

I took her hand in mine. "Thanks. Mattie told me you were acting like a mother when you said you didn't want to come back."

Pleasantly betrayed, Linda laughed. "Oh hush! Mattie never could keep a secret."

"Would you like to see *The Three Sisters*?" I asked, changing the subject.

"I'd love to. I haven't seen a production in years. Where's it playing?"

"Right here in Hoboken."

"At Stevens?"

"Opening night is next week," I said.

Stevens Institute of Technology was one of the top engineering schools in the country and had a fledgling drama club.

"I thought it would bring back the happy times, when we

were living together in the Village."

I told her about my acting gig. "Oh Theo!" she said.

"One of the clients is a rap superstar, and he wants me to appear in his latest video."

"I'm so happy for you."

"Maybe it's a start. Sometime down the road, maybe I can take on a partner and work part-time while pursuing acting. Would you like that?"

"I'd like that, especially if that's what you want in life."

We laughed and talked about our younger days, as I finished my beer. At one point, I remembered our discussion about Andy Warhol—and an interesting thought occurred.

"Do you remember the discussion we had about commercial art and trademarks?"

"So that's eating away at you."

"Yes, it's bothering me. Where does that leave me? I make a living tracking down counterfeits of that commercial art world. Don't I?"

"You don't get it," Linda said, exasperated. "Warhol was many things, but he was an artist. He saw art in a Campbell's Soup brand name and changed the way people look at things. That's what great artists do."

"What about machine-replicated art?"

"I don't agree—but that's my view of the world, not Warhol's. He's free to think and believe whatever he wants."

I grew silent. Then it all became clear, and I understood what had been eluding me.

*Artistic freedom!*

The truth was I used my acting skills in my profession and had more artistic freedom than I ever had on stage, and what I did was more important. There were risks and hardships, but these made me stronger and a better investigator. My wife and child had been threatened, but we would be better prepared next time. For now, life as a private investigator was what I wanted.

At one time, I thought time was running out for me—that I was destined to die violently like my brother, father, and all the males in the Jones family for generations. However, time is an abstraction with many meanings. My time was beginning, not ending.

I learned that there were other kinds of death—a spiritual death, a death of the spirit. This was a more terrible death than the corporeal. But there could also be a rebirth with a new lease on life.

I needed a moment alone.

© ©

Although it was late, I told her I wanted to go outside for a walk. I headed for a nearby park and sat on a bench.

I thought about Bull. Somewhere things had gone wrong for him; maybe he should have got out of the business. It was sad to think that Bull could have succeeded in stopping my career if I moved to another profession.

I was happy to be alive. I could have been killed in Washington Square Park and in many other places. I remembered when Linda told me our love was strong so long as we were both together. It was true. For one moment I had imagined what life would be like with one of us gone; the separation was unbearable. At least for now we would be a family. I sat in the park for a half-hour before heading home.

# Chapter Thirty-Three

I GOT THE NEWS from Richardson, who called me at the office on Monday.

"Bruno, Musa Ahmad, and the rest of them have been arrested." Richardson told me the police had little trouble tracking everyone down.

"That's great." I had questions, but Richardson told me to hold them until we met and asked if I was free.

"Are you kidding? I'll be there in an hour."

I was so relieved. I told Stella the good news and told her to tell the others as I headed for the door.

I remembered the telephone with the recorded message. I had promised Linda and the Bells that I would take up the anonymous telephone threats with the FBI. I figured the caller was Bull but needed to know for sure.

I had the telephone in a shopping bag beside my desk. I took it and a CD of the recorded death threat. I drove to Newark and took it with me into the building. The security guard gave me a curious look as he put the bag through the metal detector. I took the elevator to the twelfth floor. The receptionist buzzed me in.

Richardson walked over and hugged me. "Theo, thank God, you're all right."

"I'm fine . . ." I said.

"I heard about the knife attack from Chris," Richardson said. "He said you got nicked."

"Nicked?" I chuckled and told him how I nearly took a knife through the ribs.

He escorted me to his office. When we were seated, I told him about the assassination attempt and said it was luck and remembering what Jenny Ling had said about the killers wearing hoodies to disguise their features.

"What a coincidence," Richardson said. "You're lucky . . . and that goes a long way when working undercover. Bruno and the rest of them are in jail."

"That's where they belong," I said.

He nodded. "Thank God you weren't hurt. Bruno Glavocich is from Kosovo and entered the country about twenty years ago when he was a teenager."

"How come he's so good with a knife?" I asked.

"A knife is an accepted way of fighting in his native country," he said.

"What about the picture?"

"Jenny was unable to make a positive identification. We can charge Bruno for attempted murder, and we're working on charging everyone for the double murder."

I thought about mentioning Chen-Kuo, who could make a positive identification, but changed my mind. "Did a background check turn up anything?" I asked.

He said, "Bruno's clean; so is Ahmad."

He told me how he'd been back and forth on the telephone with Zeckindorff and the police. "Like I said, Bruno's arrest is going to pave the way for a criminal prosecution of Musa Ahmad and the Smith brothers for murder."

"What about the civil suits and seizures?" I asked.

He shrugged. "Those don't concern me. It's Caldwell's headache. If I'm correct, both Drake and the owners of Raiments can counter-sue. Unfortunately, the two felony counts for trademark counterfeiting won't wash. Brian told me about the handshake agreement the rapper had."

I had never expected such an outcome. The civil seizures were a wash, but not the arrest and criminal prosecution of

Bruno, Ahmad, and the Smith brothers.

"What about Musa Ahmad?" I asked. "Why wasn't he there? Also, how did Bruno know the agency's address?"

"Chris is looking into it. He believes Ahmad wasn't there because violence is what the Smith brothers handle. Ahmad has been arrested and may seek a plea bargain. As for your agency's address, that was probably supplied by Saul Drake. Chris is considering arresting him as an accomplice."

At this point, I told him about the threatening phone calls.

Richardson listened attentively. Although sympathetic, he was reluctant to get involved. "Have you tried the police? They would be better—"

"No good. The police rummaged through the Agency's files and questioned our clients for leads. I can't use the police."

"I don't see how the FBI can help, since we would follow the same procedure as the police."

"Take a look at this." I opened up the bag and showed him the CD and the telephone.

He refused to look at them. "I'm sorry, Theo. I can't get involved. Is it possible the calls were timed to disrupt your investigations?"

It was an interesting thought. The Drake's seizure would have been disrupted if Linda had called me an hour earlier.

"I'm working with a former NYPD security technician. He believes my house was being watched. I believe the caller is Bull Fogarty."

"Bull Fogarty? What makes you suspect him?"

"I started with Bull, who never forgave me for starting my own business. His career was in a freefall because of his drinking."

I told him what Frank had mentioned about filtering away the digital scrambling to produce an accurate voice print of the caller and comparing it with my taped phone calls.

"I've got Bull's recorded voice on this telephone," I said.

His eyebrows arched upwards knowingly. "Of course, the phone messages he left for the Smith brothers."

"That's right. I believe a comparison will identify Bull as the caller."

"Theo, this is interesting. I'm sorry the FBI can't handle this. Besides, if Bull Fogarty is the caller, you won't have to worry."

"I won't? How come?"

Richardson had learned from Caldwell that Bull had submitted his resignation and was already gone.

The relief I felt was like manna from heaven.

I talked for several hours about the arrest and criminal prosecution. I returned to my car and headed back to the office and told my staff the good news.

# Chapter Thirty-Four

LATER THAT WEEK, KIM and I took the subway to Flushing.

We exited and walked towards Jenny's apartment. The autumn breeze was refreshing. We walked past a Chinese bookstore and an herbal medicine shop. At one point, I asked Kim if she had ever thought of living here.

"Me? No way, I've never visited this neighborhood except on business."

"We're not here on business, remember?"

She smiled. "Yes, thanks to Joey Qin."

Qin, the guy who ran the dry cleaning store, had kept his promise and arranged for us to meet Lucy Zho at Jenny's apartment. He called me at the office. "I know about the arrest. The other workers have been contacted and told to surrender themselves to the police. After being interviewed, they'll be referred to the INS and issued a U-visa, which is for undocumented aliens who are victims of violent crimes."

"Thanks for the update, Joey. What about Lucy?"

"Yes, you wanted to meet her."

And a day later, Kimberley and I were on the subway to Flushing.

I knocked on the door. Jenny opened it a crack.

"*Ni hao.*" She greeted us happily. What a change. The slight waif had put on weight and looked rested.

"*Ni hao.*" Kimberly hugged her.

I hugged her in turn. "Thanks for inviting us."

To my surprise, the apartment was overflowing with brand label apparel and accessories. Boxes stacked upon boxes of Ray Ban sunglasses, Gucci shoes, Hermes scarves, and many other brands.

The Asian woman sitting on the sofa was stunning. Long black hair to her shoulders framed an oval face with dark eyes and perfect lips. When she stood up to greet us, the brand label accessories at her feet accentuated her regal bearing.

"You must be Lucy," I said.

She nodded. "Joey Qin said you and another woman wanted to meet me."

"*Ni hao.*" Kimberly walked over and gave her a gentle hug.

I moved aside three boxes of Jimmy Choo shoes so that I could sit on a recliner. Kimberly sat on the sofa next to Lucy. Jenny kicked off her flats and sat down on the rug.

"The Uncle's name was Tony Shaw," Lucy said. "We were lovers once."

She told us that she had come to the United States five years ago. Her English was good because it is a second language in Changle City in Fujian Province where she grew up. Many residents had left the mainland over the years by secretly traveling to nearby Taiwan, including many of her friends, who had illegally emigrated from Taiwan to the United States. Some used the snakeheads; but as relations with the United States improved, others travelled on visas and never left when their visa expired.

She was young and foolhardy and wanted to leave, but her parents wouldn't let her. She enrolled in college, but in her junior year she obtained a student visa without telling her parents and left for America.

When her money ran out, she worked in a massage parlor. It was disgusting, debasing work. She had hoped to do this kind of work until she had enough money to find something better. But she had no *guanxi*, no connections—until she met Tony Shaw, the Uncle. After she was arrested for prostitution and released,

Shaw gave her a job in Asian Seas.

"Tony was decent, at least that's what I thought," Lucy said. "He was greedy, cruel, and manipulative."

"She trapped, like me," Jenny said.

"So you two became friends," I said.

Lucy nodded. "I heard about Chen-Kuo and asked for his help."

"Yes, Chen-Kuo has helped me," Kimberly said. "I have worked in sweat shops."

"You must know what we were going through," Lucy said.

"I do."

"After Tony was killed, Joey Qin became my contact. I learned from Qin that five of the Asian Seas sweatshop workers were living in a motel and given jobs."

We discussed the upcoming murder trial in which both Jenny and Lucy would be testifying. Painfully, Jenny remembered how she was unable to connect Bruno's face with that of the murderer's.

"Try to remember terrible face," she said sadly. "Why kill? Why?"

"Greed. For money," Kim said.

"Why was Tony killed?" I asked.

"I don't know," Lucy said. "He dealt with many people who paid in cash under the table. The police think it was revenge because Raiments was going to lose a big order."

"That was Ahmad's downfall," I said. "He knew where I worked because a department store owner, a man named Saul Drake, gave him the location. Ahmad, Bruno, the Smith brothers, and others are going to spend many years in jail."

We talked about the murders. Finally, Jenny invited us into the kitchen. She made tea for us, and the discussion turned to happier topics.

"Is all this designer merchandise heading for China?" I asked.

Jenny smiled. "New business."

In broken English, she said she was hoping to obtain a license with the legitimate companies and sell to an exclusive clientele who wanted to buy the genuine product.

"That's wonderful." I was amazed at her resourcefulness.

"No more work for others," she said happily.

"Jenny, what about the snakeheads?" I asked.

"Snakeheads want money . . . willing to help me repay."

Ingenious, I thought to myself. She had used the underground organization to help establish her career. Instead of paying off her debt in years as a seamstress, she would be free.

Jenny slowly exhaled. "I thought my life ruined; I make new life." She apologized for acting abruptly when we mentioned Chen-Kuo by name.

"Sister, no need to apologize," Kimberley said and switched to Mandarin for her sake.

I sat back and sipped tea, while the three talked intimately like sisters and laughed.

I was inspired by Jenny's dream of freedom and happiness. Everyone should follow their dream. Jenny had hers, and I had mine.

# Acknowledgments

I'M GRATEFUL TO THE many people who helped me prepare the manuscript. I would like to thank real life private investigator David Woods, who gave me several interviews and opened up his case files. The manuscript was developed in several writing classes and reading groups. One was a class taught by noted mystery writer Grace F. Edwards at the Frederick Douglass Art Center in Manhattan; unfortunately the Center, which offered low-cost classes, is no more due to cuts in funding. I would also like to thank noted mystery writer Reed Farrel Coleman, who teaches at Hofstra University in Long Island. The manuscript was revised and developed in a writers group in the Hoboken Library in New Jersey where I live. I'd also like to thank my mother who is from China for her editing and assistance with the Chinese. I'd also like to thank writing coach Ceil Cleveland, formerly a reviewer with the Mystery Writers of America's Mentor Program, who graciously offered advice and support. Lastly, my friend Dave Bruce for reviewing the manuscript.

CPSIA information can be obtained at www.ICGtesting.com
Printed in the USA
LVOW10s0018051215

465433LV00002B/392/P